DARKEN

THE SIEGE SERIES

ANGELA FRISTOE

Little Prince Publishing
Nanaimo, Canada

Little Prince Publishing
Nanaimo, Canada

This book is an original publication of Little Prince Publishing.

This is a work of fiction. Names, characters, places, and incidents either are the product of the author's imagination or are used fictitiously, and any resemblance to actual persons, living or dead, business establishments, events, or locales is entirely coincidental.

ISBN **978-0-9949544-1-1**

For Calleigh,
my reason to keep going

PROLOGUE

December, 14 years ago

THE BOY STARED BACK at the man peering through the small window in the door. Seeing Dr. Sinclair meant it was his turn. His stomach clenched, mouth went dry. The trembling started in his hands, quickly spreading through his body.

The door slid open, and the boy pressed into the corner, curling his legs into his chest. Dr. Sinclair motioned for him to come, but the boy shook his head vigorously, wrapping skinny arms around his knees and tucking in his head until only the short buzz of dark-blond hair was visible.

"Three, don't make this difficult. Do you want me to call Aiden?"

The shaking stopped as pure terror enveloped the little body. "No."

"Then come along. Cooperate, and I may let you spend some time with the others."

It was a bribe the boy couldn't say no to. He would do

anything asked of him if it meant seeing the others. He stood, keeping his head down, eyes focused on his shuffling feet. When he reached the door, the doctor gripped his arm, leading him into the hall.

He wasn't sure how long it had been since he last saw them. A month, possibly more. He used to see them almost every day in the classroom. Then class stopped. He missed seeing them and Mr. Walker, their teacher. He was kind and always smiling. Sometimes he brought pictures of his wife and little girl to show them. Her name was Sky. Mr. Walker laughed when he told them. The boy didn't understand why her name was funny—he thought it must be nice having two names.

Up until a few months before, Ms. Tharp taught them. She hadn't hurt them like the doctor, but she wasn't like Mr. Walker.

The first day Mr. Walker came, he made a fuss about their names. He didn't believe they were only numbers.

The boy was Three. Mr. Walker called him Gavin; said it was a good name for a good boy. It made Three smile to hear it. Having a name made him feel like maybe he wouldn't always need to go through all the tests.

When Dr. Sinclair found out, he'd been angry, but that didn't stop Mr. Walker.

Gavin. The boy rolled the name through his mind, clinging to the hope it gave him. It didn't have much strength left. When your life was determined by the pain you suffer, a month with nothing is a lifetime.

They reached the end of the hall and turned the corner. Gavin glanced up at the window of One's door and caught a glimpse of his brother's face—Noah's face—before

Sinclair thrust him toward the lab.

Just inside the room, Gavin spotted Aiden, and instantly his entire body rebelled. His struggle did little good. Aiden was huge—well over six feet and bulging with muscles. Muscles he didn't mind using to get the boys to do what the doctor wanted.

A massive hand wrapped around the back of Gavin's neck, and he was dragged across to the table. Aiden let him go, and Gavin forced himself to get up on the table.

He lay back, staring at the apparatus overhead. It moved up and down with a light so bright it burned his eyes. It wasn't on now; that meant a new test. The lack of food all day should have given him warning, yet part of him held onto the minuscule piece of hope that it would be different.

Gavin knew how the process worked. He'd barely lived through it hundreds of times. The first day of testing the light would be off. Dr. Sinclair would order his assistants around, writing notes as they injected Gavin with needle after needle of drugs and samples. Then they'd wait with him strapped to the table. If he didn't react within the time they wanted, they gave him more. If he reacted sooner, they administered different things.

Through it all, they monitored and recorded everything. Once the doctor was satisfied, Gavin would go back to his room until the next day. Then they would start the poking, prodding, and cutting, checking whether whatever they injected him with had worked. That would continue until the doctor moved on to testing one of the others.

He swallowed and nearly choked from the dryness of

his mouth. A strap stretched across his chest, tightening until it strained his breathing, then his wrists, hips, and feet. Wires were taped to his chest and head.

The assistants worked in silence, never acknowledging Gavin as anything other than a test object. The only person to speak was Dr. Sinclair who barked orders.

Gavin watched as the doctor made his way over to the side of the table and looked down at him.

"This will be it, Three. Today will be the final test."

Gavin's blood turned to ice. His fear showed, and Sinclair laughed.

"Oh, don't worry. You'll live," he said and held up a syringe filled with a milky liquid. "Everything I've worked for is right here."

"Gideon?" a soft voice said from behind the doctor.

Lifting his head as far as he could, Gavin strained to see who dared speak in the lab, but other than a fleeting glimpse of brown hair, he couldn't see anything. No one other than the doctor and his assistants ever entered the lab.

"What are you doing here?" Dr. Sinclair kept working, wrapping a rubber tube around Gavin's arm and then twisting it for a view of the throbbing veins.

Whoever the woman was, she came over to Gavin's side where he finally got a look at her. He'd seen a female before; some of the lab assistants were women and Ms. Tharp, of course. That one was different. They usually wore blank expressions, but she gazed down at him with faint lines across her forehead deepening as her eyebrows drew together. It was how he imagined Mr. Walker's wife might look if something happened to Sky.

Would she help him if he asked? Would she make them stop the tests?

Gavin wanted to ask, but when his mouth opened, only a whimper came out. The consequences of arguing or fighting were too great. The lone time he fought back, Noah had suffered the consequences. The scar slashing across Noah's face was a reminder to Gavin of what would happen to the others if he dared again.

If Gavin were the one punished for his own actions, he would risk it. Even if it led to possible death, he would do it for the others.

Her next words made him glad he had remained silent.

"Have you considered my proposal to continue the experiments?" She leaned in and, using less than gentle fingers, widened Gavin's eyes one at a time before moving to one of the randomly beeping machines.

"There's no need to continue with this formula. You read the data from the other subjects. It's conclusive. The effects of this serum have been documented for weeks now." Sinclair placed the syringe on the metal tray beside him and focused on the woman. "We expect subject Six to display early symptoms within the next seventy-two to ninety-six hours. Five was done this morning. Three is the final one."

"You know I support your work, and the findings are ... extraordinary. The Board, however, is not prepared to simply end the study."

"What more do they want from me, Yolanda? Once this is done, they will have six subjects to proceed with to Level 2 training and modifications."

"I—*We* want to ensure maximum results are achieved."

She wandered across the room, and Gavin lost sight of her.

Sinclair huffed, gripped a sponge with a pair of tongs and wiped it across Gavin's inner elbow, leaving a rust-colored streak of liquid behind. "What do you suggest I do?"

The woman didn't respond as the needle pressed into Gavin's arm. The cool liquid spread through the boy's vein, traveling up his arm.

"Double the dose."

Sinclair jerked his head up, and Gavin flinched as the needle tugged painfully at his skin. "Are you mad? We have no idea what it could do to him."

"Him? *It*. You know better than to humanize the subjects."

"A slip of the tongue." Sinclair shook his head. "My concern has nothing to do with the subject being a human. It has to do with the risk of *losing* one of my subjects. In particular, subjects Three or Four. Having two subjects with identical genetic material created a unique circumstance enabling us to analyze the effects of varying formulas."

"Open your eyes, Gideon. You are not thinking like a scientist right now. Otherwise, you'd realize this is the next logical phase. Four received this treatment and displayed satisfactory results. Administering a large dosage to Three allows us to determine the ideal amount to maximize the effects."

Gavin listened to her heels click on the hard tile floor—yet another difference between her and the lab assistants. He felt her presence at the end of the table behind his head, so he tipped his chin up.

She smoothed her hands along the sides of his face, a gesture so deceptively gentle his muscles loosened enough that the prick of a second needle hardly registered.

* * *

S.I.E.G.E. Corporation
Shareholder Statement

Scientific Investigations and Experimentation through Genetic Engineering Corporation is excited to announce a five-million-dollar donation to the Sawyer school district to fund the development of their science programs. These programs will enhance learning opportunities and increase access to state-of-the-art technology, further preparing students for college and careers with the high demands of today's workplace.

The Board of Directors would like to extend their sympathy and apologies to the six young men who suffered at the hands of Dr. Sinclair during his work on the Posthuman Project. In addition to ensuring he is prosecuted to the fullest extent of the law, SIEGE Corporation is facilitating the adoption of the youths and establishing appropriate reparation.

We would like to also announce the appointment of Dr. Nielson as Chief Science Officer. Dr. Nielson comes to us with a stellar background in genetic engineering, having published her research findings in multiple professional journals. She will oversee the termination of the unauthorized Posthuman Project and spearhead a new study into possible links between fertilizers and the development of neurological disorders. A request for study volunteers will be posted on our website by the end of the year.

ONE

SHE WAS THE MOST beautiful woman Gavin Walker ever saw. Raven hair framed wide, brown eyes, and the sultry smile she wore spoke of a secret he longed to uncover. The photograph did little to hide the creamy, tan skin or the glow to her cheeks.

He'd loved Lela since senior year in high school. For him, there would never be another woman so perfect. This image was a reminder that he found his soulmate.

A soft hand brushed his back, and he tore his eyes from the perfection of the photo. He rolled over, flinging an arm over his eyes. A deep sigh coincided with the beep of his alarm.

He fumbled for his cell phone on the crowded nightstand, knocking over a bottle of water. At the absence of the sound as it hit the hardwood floor, he peeked over the side of the bed to find water seeping into a pile of clothing. He cursed. He'd have to throw them in the dryer before he left for work.

"Mmm, sugar, you don't have to go to work, do you? We could have a little more fun," Hailey purred, rubbing against him like a cat in heat.

Hooking up with her always seemed like a good idea until he woke with the hangover from Hell.

"Você não é nada para mim."

"I love it when you speak Spanish to me." Her fingers tickled through the scattering of hair on his chest.

Gripping her hand to stop its movements, he peered over his shoulder at her. With black mascara smudged under her eyes, she looked a mess.

"It's Portuguese." And if she understood what it actually meant, she wouldn't be so happy.

You are nothing.

He spoke the phrase to every woman he woke up next to. They reassured Lela and him that he recognized their place in his life. They meant nothing to him because they would never replace *her*.

He rolled out of bed and stretched his arms above his head, ignoring Hailey's wolf whistle. Her clothes lay scattered across the floor with his own. Grabbing anything vaguely feminine, he flung it at her.

"Get dressed. I gotta get going."

She huffed, and he wondered if he finally pissed her off enough she wouldn't be the easy lay he was used to. He enjoyed not having to work at getting a woman in the sack, and he refused to pussyfoot around them, either. He was devoted to his single life and had no plans to ever change that status.

"Let yourself out," he said, striding into the bathroom.

Hailey knew the drill. They first hooked up about six months before. A few nights a month, they played the same game at Porter's Pub, came back to his place, and fucked their brains out. In the morning, she left and all was good.

He pulled the door shut behind him, muffling whatever she said in response. The cramped space did little to ease the tension in his neck. If anything, the room seemed to close in on him, reminding him of the woman in his bedroom and of his mistake.

After turning on the shower, he stepped up to the vanity, giving the water time to heat. Avoiding his reflection, he rested his hands on the counter and hung his head. The pounding in his skull was nothing new. He dealt with hangover headaches every other day. Looking in the mirror would only make him sick with shame.

When steam filled the bathroom, he climbed into the shower, letting the scalding water wash away his disgust.

An hour later, showered and shaved, he felt passably human as he walked up to the entrance of Porter's Pub. He might actually make it through his first day working for his brothers.

The name of the pub, a tribute to their mother, Sarah, whose maiden name was Porter, was one of the few things Noah and Logan had left the same after buying the bar from their uncle two years ago. It had come a long way since then. They couldn't do much about the location on the wrong side of the tracks in Thompson Creek, but they'd fixed the place up and earned the reputation of not taking the same level of crap their uncle put up with.

"You look like shit." Noah folded his arms across his chest as he watched Gavin wander in. With dark circles around his eyes and the careful holding of his head, Gavin's problem was obvious. "You need to lay off the beer."

"Fuck you." The appropriate finger accompanied this. He got enough shit from their folks; he didn't need it from big brother, too.

Noah appeared less than impressed. "Well, don't be drinking on the job. I catch you boozing, you're gone."

Gavin's eyes glanced off the jagged scar slashed across Noah's check. Noah had stuck his neck out for him more times than he deserved.

What possessed him to take the daytime bartender job at the pub? He must have been drunk when he accepted. Noah had a major stick up his ass, and Gavin wasn't interested in being the one to pull it out.

"You listening?" his brother asked. "I catch you drinking, you're fired. Same as everyone else."

"Yeah, sure," Gavin said, gritting his teeth. The flip response worked like a trigger.

"Take it seriously or walk. Keeley asked for extra hours, and she's damn good behind the bar."

"Dude, it's good. I'm here on time, aren't I?" Gavin ran his fingers through his shaggy blond hair. Despite the lack of interest bartending held for him, he needed the job, or he'd be back living with his parents. Not the move any twenty-five-year-old guy wanted to make.

"You sure you're up to this?" Noah asked, his doubt more than evident. He wandered around to the other side of the bar and crossed his arms, leaning a hip against the counter.

"I'm fine," Gavin snapped. He didn't do touchy-feely crap, and his brothers were the last people he'd go to if he did want to discuss his feelings.

"You need to talk about it. Drag your sorry ass out of her grave."

His gut clenched at the pity in his brother's eyes.

"I don't need to talk about shit. If that's why you gave me this job, then shove it."

"All right, I won't push you about Lela." Noah glanced toward the kitchen door then back at Gavin. "Hailey said you're having night terrors."

"Hailey doesn't know crap." He'd miss the easy lay, but if she couldn't keep her trap shut, they were done. "And when the fuck did you talk to her?"

"You denying it?"

He didn't need any walks down memory lane, and that was exactly where his brothers went when they searched for explanations about how messed up they all were.

"I had a rough night. Done and over. I don't need you mothering me." He crossed his arms over his chest and met Noah's gaze head on. One blink and his brother would move in for the kill, but outlasting Noah in a staring contest never happened. Gavin blinked.

"I'll back off on Lela, but Sinclair is another matter. You know the night terrors are his calling card."

There was little Gavin could do to forget the lingering effects of Dr. Sinclair and his sick experiments. Over the last fourteen years, there were moments he almost forgot what he and his brothers went through during their time locked in the SIEGE labs. Nothing, though, ever erased the horrific memories seared into his brain. Reality eventually returned along with the realization he'd never be normal.

The night terrors were simply one way he was

reminded. While they all suffered each in their own ways, the terrors were his alone. Sporadically since his release from the labs, they hit him. At first, he brushed them off, but then he began to recognize them as a warning that Sinclair was nearby.

Sinclair and the SIEGE Corporation did so much shit to them, Gavin wouldn't be surprised if they'd implanted something in his brain to drive him crazy.

Gavin was aware of Noah's narrowed eyes following him as he moved across the room, but his brother didn't press.

"Fine, I'll leave it alone." Noah shook his head. "I'm heading out. I've got a meeting with the rep from the packing plant. We're hoping to sign on as a team sponsor for their baseball team."

"What, no training?"

"Cora's gonna set you up, show you where stuff is. She'll be here until the end of your shift. I should be back by then."

"Cora." The name sunk deep into Gavin's belly and he fought the urge to puke.

"She's been working here the past couple of months. Day shift and morning clean up on Sundays. She's in charge when Logan and I aren't on site," Noah said as he pulled off the towel slung over his shoulder.

"As in Coraline Evans?"

"Only Cora I know, and you can thank her for the job. She convinced me hiring you would be good for business. Something about your ugly mug bringing the ladies in a bit earlier, possibly convince them to stay a little longer."

It had been two years since Gavin last saw Coraline.

She'd been in the hospital covered in blood and bruises with a half-dozen broken ribs from the accident. She'd also been comatose, but she'd been alive. That was more than he could say about her passenger.

"This gonna be a problem?" Noah asked when Gavin didn't respond to the ribbing.

"No." Gavin knew Noah wanted more reassurance, but it was all he could manage.

"Good." Noah looked down at his watch, and then grabbed up a ball of black material from the end of the counter. He threw it at Gavin who shook it out. It was a black shirt with neon orange lettering across the back spelling out Porter's Pub. "Check in with me before your shift is done. I still need you to fill out some paperwork."

Gavin stared at the double doors long after they closed behind Noah. He heard Cora come in from the kitchen, aware that she waited for him to acknowledge her, but he wasn't ready.

Shit. If he'd known she worked here, he never would've taken the job. He could still bail. Living with his folks wouldn't be as torturous as seeing her every day.

"Gavin?"

He cranked his head from side to side, producing satisfying cracking noises from his neck. She wasn't going to disappear no matter how long he ignored her. He pivoted to glare at her.

She looked different. Still tiny, but she'd ditched the short hair that once gave her a pixie appearance. Curly strands of blond hair fluttered against her cheeks, making her softer, more angelic. She'd always been pretty, but now she was hot in a way that begged him to fuck her.

He mentally kicked his ass. It was Cora; one of Lela's closest friends.

"Why are you here, Coraline?"

"I work here." She gave a tight smile that vanished as he continued glaring.

"Why are you *here*?" he repeated.

"I needed a job, and your brothers were hiring."

"I suppose I should thank you for convincing Noah to give me the job."

"He would have given it to you anyway. One of the joys of nepotism, right?"

"I thought you were working at some fancy art museum," he said.

"Yeah, well, life doesn't always go the way you plan, right?"

Gavin understood better than anyone the truth of that life lesson. A muscle in his jaw ticked as he glared at her.

"I don't think I've ever seen you so scruffy." She gestured to her cheek.

"I guess that's what happens when you stop giving a shit about life."

"Gavin—"

He slashed a hand through the air, cutting off whatever she was about to say.

"Don't try to justify what happened, Cora. You're a pathetic drunk who should be rotting in prison for what you did. I'll never forget you're the reason Lela's dead."

There was an awkward silence, and with each second passing by, he saw the guilt and sorrow move across her face. For a moment, he regretted laying the blame solely on her.

Her face hardened, wiping away the effects of his spite-filled words. She flung a dishtowel at his head, smacking him right in the face, and he snatched it away, glaring daggers at her.

"You need to grab the kegs and a CO_2 canister from the store room. Then meet me in the kitchen and we'll go over your daily prep work." She spun on her heel and marched back through the swinging door to the staff area.

Watching Cora stomp away, Gavin almost forgot why he hated her and let himself enjoy the way her cutoff shorts danced along the edge of her ass. Her long blond ponytail swung in time with her hips. *When had cute little Cora turned into a walking wet dream?*

"You planning on doing any work today, stud, or are you gonna follow her in there and tap that ass?"

Gavin's head jerked around to glare at Keeley, a waitress and the bane of his brother Logan's existence or, at least, the guy's sex life.

"Work," he grunted. He tugged off his shirt and pulled on the one Noah gave him.

"Damn, Cora was right," she said. "You keep flashing that six pack of yours and the whole place will be flooded with the ladies all day. You're gonna be so good for my bank account."

He snorted, and she laughed at his unimpressed expression.

"Unless you plan on giving me a strip show and going full frontal, you may want to use the locker room."

She sauntered across the room leaving Gavin again wondering what the hell he'd gotten himself into. Between Keeley and Cora, he was destined to be in constant upheaval.

Shaking his head, he went to the staff locker room, waving to the cook, Mateo, as he passed through the kitchen.

Noah kept talking about dividing the change room to create two separate rooms, but that wouldn't happen until the club started raking in some serious cash. It hadn't been a problem until they'd hired the girls to work the floor. The complaints got loud enough that Logan put in folding dividers to split the space up.

The locker room was empty, and Gavin sank onto the short bench, rolling his shoulders. He'd only been on the clock ten minutes, and already he felt done.

How had he gotten so desperate he was slumming it bartending for his brothers?

There was nothing wrong with bartending, but at twenty-five with a Ph.D. in computer engineering, he always thought he'd be doing something more important with his life.

For a long time, he managed to do something good with the curse Sinclair made of his life, and then Lela died. He held himself together for a while, at least on the surface. As the months wore on, reality sucked away at the semblance of a life he'd built and making it to work day in and day out didn't seem important as he accepted Lela was never coming back.

The door swung open, and in walked Logan. Of his six siblings, he was closest to Logan or had been until the accident.

"He's alive," Logan announced with over-the-top drama. Gavin glared, but before he could respond, Logan held up a hand. "Please spare me the obligatory 'fuck you'."

"And miss out on the highlight of my day?"

"I take it you talked to Cora."

Gavin turned and opened the only locker without a lock. He threw in his shirt and slammed it shut.

"Fine," Logan said. "Why don't you tell me what the hell you're doing here?"

"I have a shift. Haven't you heard? I'm your newest employee."

Logan grunted. "You know that's not what I meant. You have a frigging Ph.D. and the mind of a genius. You should be using them for something other than mixing drinks. You should be working at some high-tech firm with Caleb."

"Says the guy who could make a killing in the octagon," Gavin said, ignoring the reference to his only biological brother.

"The difference is I might kill someone in a fight. You could be doing something good with what you've got." Logan leaned against the door frame, crossing his arms.

Neither of them wanted to discuss their unusual skills; why they scored off the IQ charts, why they thrived on three hours of sleep, or the heightened senses that for years left Noah struggling to function outside of the lab. Only Dean, their youngest brother, appeared to be normal.

Neither of them wanted to face the fact that these were the least of what made them anything but normal. There were monsters hidden within them, creatures that craved the darkness Sinclair brought with him.

"Dude? You still with me?" Logan snapped his fingers in front of Gavin's face.

"Screw off." Gavin batted his brother's hand away. "I'm not here for a heart to heart or a trip down memory lane."

"Great. Get your ass in gear. Your shift started ten minutes ago, and you're still in here sulking about Cora."

Gavin bit his tongue, barely containing the urge to lash out. He grabbed one of the bar aprons from the hook on the back of the door and stomped out to the storeroom.

As if he wasn't fucked up enough having to deal with Coraline, now they wanted him to think about Sinclair? What the fuck was he supposed to do about the guy anyways?

As lead science officer for SIEGE Corporation, Sinclair had run the Posthuman Project. To the public, the SIEGE-controlled project conducted government-sanctioned experiments on humans seeking to create bio-enhanced soldiers. Whether Sinclair's decision to use children as test subjects was also approved was debatable.

Then shit hit the fan, and the Posthuman Project imploded. The threat of exposing national security secrets kept Sinclair and the others from being prosecuted, and everyone from the top down denied knowing about Sinclair's use of Gavin and the five other boys as lab rats.

SIEGE Corporation funneled millions into damage control and reparations, even ensuring they were adopted into the same family. Yet normal life with the Walkers did nothing to repair the genetic mutations left by the experiments, and as much as Gavin wanted to brush off the nightmares haunting him, he knew better.

Putting Sinclair in the past wouldn't be possible until

the man was dead and to make that happen they had to find him first.

Sinclair was out there, and he was close.

TWO

CORA PUSHED THROUGH THE door hard enough it smashed against the interior wall before rushing back toward her. She slipped through the narrowing gap with a little sashay to the side. Mateo glanced at her when she drew in a shuddering breath.

"You okay, Cora?" Mateo paused in the midst of flipping a burger patty.

"Yeah," she managed to say around what almost became a sob. Lips pressed together, she turned from his curious eyes and placed her hands on the stainless steel counter, head hung.

Her mind echoed with Gavin's question. *What was she doing here?*

The question didn't surprise Cora. Noah and Logan asked the same thing when she came begging for a job, and in all honesty, she wasn't sure. She didn't belong in a place like this. This was not how she thought her life would turn out.

Growing up, she dreamed of living in Paris or Athens where she'd spend her days painting in the garden of her gorgeous estate. The older she got, the more realistic her dreams became, and working in the restoration department of a Denver museum was enough.

Up until six months ago, she'd been busy helping prep for a new exhibit. Now, she was waitressing in a slightly less than reputable bar in the middle of Montana surrounded by constant reminders of Gavin. Serving platters of nachos and beer wasn't just a step back, it was a complete fail in life.

Yet, she couldn't be sorry that she was there. She *needed* to be there.

Her brother accused her of having a martyr complex. Darren was convinced her willingness to take any and all punishments regardless of if she deserved them stemmed from years under their parents' thumbs. It was an explanation she couldn't help but give a slight bit of credence to.

She knew what coming to Thompson Creek and facing Gavin would be like. She saw it in his brown eyes, the way they drilled into her as if he saw every dark secret she hid. Along with that knowledge was the accusation. It's what had kept her from her best friend's funeral and ended her fragile friendship with Gavin. Logically, Cora understood he blamed her because he needed someone to blame, yet she also couldn't deny it.

If she hadn't flipped off the guy who nearly rammed them, he might not have flown into a rage. He might not have followed them and forced them off the bridge into the river.

When the shit hit the fan, she'd been too drunk to save Lela. If she hadn't downed that one last shot, Lela might still be alive.

Taking a long deep breath, she steadied her resolution. Gavin was right. Lela died because of her, but if he thought she'd bail on her job, he was in for a massive surprise.

No way could she tell him the real reason she took the job at the pub; he'd never believe her if she did. She wasn't even sure she believed it herself.

Gavin passed through the kitchen, and she let her eyes follow him. He took powerful strides with his long legs, and his shirt clung to his muscular chest. Gavin was no longer the boy she met back in high school.

Forcing herself to concentrate on what needed to be done, she loaded cutlery into a bin and placed a pile of napkins on top. She carried it out to Keeley, dropping the bin on the counter beside the till where the other woman stood counting the float.

"Someone piss in your porridge?" Keeley arched a brow.

"I think you mean cornflakes." The corner of Cora's lips turned up.

"Whatever." Keeley shrugged. "So, what's your problem?"

"Nothing."

"Uh huh, and does nothing stand over six feet tall with an ass begging you to test its thrusting power?"

"Oh, my God. No!" Cora swatted Keeley's arm, blood rushing to her cheeks as her friend laughed. "Now, can we talk about something other than Gavin?"

"Girl, I was talking about Logan, but now we know where your head is at. I'm not gonna need to put a leash on you to hold you back, am I? Though, I don't think that would help much; I get the impression the Walker boys are all into that kind of thing."

She started to protest but clamped her lips shut. Anything she said would only feed into Keeley's wickedly-dirty sense of humor.

A wise decision, since Gavin chose that moment to strut back into the bar, a soda canister and keg slung over each shoulder. She studied him as he placed the containers on the ground and started hooking them up. He was so different than when they first met ten years before.

Physically, he'd filled out, transforming from a tall, lanky teen to an Adonis. Lean muscles, a solid scruffy jaw and yes, nice ass, made it impossible to mistake him for anything but a man.

Yet the sorrow he carried in his eyes marked the greatest change as it dimmed the intensity that once drew her to him. He'd always thrown himself so completely into the aspects of his life he considered important. When Lela died, he crumbled.

"Cora."

She jumped at Logan's voice behind her and fumbled with the forks she held, hoping he hadn't noticed her watching Gavin.

"Hey, what's up?"

"Just checking in." Though he spoke to her, his gaze followed Keeley as she walked over to unlock the front door, then he shook his head and glanced at Cora.

"We're expecting a big group from TanTech at happy hour. I told Merrick we'd hold the two end tables."

"That's Keeley's section."

"Well, pass the message," he said even as Keeley made her way back to them. "I'll see you tonight."

He disappeared into the staff area, nodding curtly at the flirty smile Keeley gave him.

"Tonight?" Keeley looked at Cora. "Are you poaching?"

"No," Cora denied, rolling her eyes. "He's training me to do receiving and purchase orders."

"Well, good," she said and cracked a smile. "I'm meeting Sky for dinner, want to join us?"

Sky was the only Walker sister. Cora got along with her but they never really hung out, mainly due to the five-year age gap.

"Yeah, sure."

She finished the cutlery, pushing aside the bin, and then went back to the fridge to grab a bowl of lemons for drink garnish. Gavin was clearing the spray nozzle when she came back, carrying the bowl along with a cutting board and knife. She dropped the items on the workspace beside him and pulled a lemon from the bowl, tossing the fruit in the air for him to catch.

"Cut," she ordered.

"Can't Mateo do this?" Gavin called after her as she headed toward the staff area.

"He could." She glanced over her shoulder at him. "Except it's not *his* job to prep *your* bar. Start cutting. Celery and limes are coming next."

His eyes narrowed, and her chin lifted in challenge. Backing down would only fuel his belief he controlled things between them.

"Fine," he said. "My bar, my job. I'll get it."

Cora trailed him through the kitchen to the walk-in fridge and watched as he searched the shelves for celery. Eventually, he gave up and looked at her.

"Wrong fridge. This is for kitchen supplies only." She led him to the smaller walk-in fridge in the back across from the dry liquor storage.

"Wouldn't it make more sense to keep food in the kitchen?"

"Different budget, different inventory." She opened the heavy door.

Boxes of beer, wine, and clear liquor were stacked along the sides nearly to the ceiling, and she moved past them to pick up a small one full of garnish from the wire shelf at the back of the fridge. She twisted around to find Gavin only a foot away. He snagged the box from her and turned toward the exit. She followed behind and almost ran into him when he abruptly stopped.

"Where's the handle?" he asked.

"What handle?"

"For the door."

"It's the latch on the side. Just push." She poked his back to prod him along, but he didn't move forward. "Push it harder."

He twisted to glare at her. "I did. It's not opening."

To prove his point, he put the box on top of a shelf beside him and leaned his entire body against the door.

"Shit!" Cora squeezed past him, telling herself she didn't really feel the brush of his arm against her breast. She told herself she was only focused on the door and not on how the tight space left little room to do anything about the way her rear snuggled into his body.

Cora shoved at the door frantically, and when it didn't budge the entire room seemed to close in on her, sucking out the air as it shrunk. Her heart thudded loudly, and she pressed her back against the door, gasping for air.

"You're claustrophobic?" Gavin asked as she rubbed a hand over her chest.

"No." Or she hadn't been until a few months ago. Shutting her eyes, she calmed her breathing. *It would be fine. They were in the liquor fridge of a bar. Someone would be coming in here before they froze to death.* She opened her eyes again and found Gavin only inches away, watching her with a strange expression.

Her breath puffed out in a white cloud of condensation. She should have been cold, yet the heat radiating from him left her deliciously warm and wanting to move closer. Her tongue peeked out to slide over her lower lip.

Lusting after Gavin was nothing new. It started when she was sixteen, though now her thoughts were much more vivid. For years, she suffered the guilt of loving her best friend's boyfriend, yet that day, she couldn't bring herself to be the martyr anymore. Lela was gone, and Cora accepted it even if Gavin didn't.

She heaved a sigh, and the movement caused her nipples, tightened by the cold and desire, to scrape along his chest. With any other man, she would have retreated, but this was Gavin, and he intoxicated her.

Her hand lifted to rest on the side of his abs, and he stiffened under the contact. For a fraction of a second, she hesitated, then before she could have a second thought, his lips converged on hers.

Fire tore through her, a burning that started deep in her belly. Her lips parted, and his tongue thrust in, tempting hers into a delicious dance and filling her with the spicy flavor of him.

Finally. *Finally.*

What the hell was he doing?

The question came to Gavin as a soft moan escaped Cora. He ran his hands over her hips to cup her ass, and the question disappeared as his dick took over the thinking process.

Through her well-worn jeans, he stroked her lush curves, and his fingers dug into the flesh, squeezing, testing how much she was willing to take. Cora rose on her tip-toes, her hands winding around the back of his neck. The motion eliminated any space separating them. It was all he needed to know.

He gave a deep growl and pressed her up against the door. Her legs shifted open, and he slid between them. Even with layers of clothing they wore, he could feel the warmth of her pussy. His dick hardened, and he rocked against her.

She pulled her head back and nipped at his lip, catching it between her teeth and tugging until he groaned and took her mouth again.

Then she was ripped away, falling back into Keeley, who possessed the unfortunate luck of going to get a case of beer. The two of them stumbled backward until the wall opposite the fridge halted their fall.

Both women's eyes were huge. While Keeley's were in shock and humor as she realized what she'd interrupted, Cora's held mortification.

He quickly grabbed the box of garnish and, holding it low enough to hide the evidence of his encounter with Cora, went back out to the main room.

What the fuck had he been thinking?

He snatched up a celery stalk and slammed it onto the cutting board. With the butcher knife, he hacked at the stalk.

Making out with Cora topped his stupidest shit ever done list. *Cora, for Christ's sake.*

He grabbed another piece. *Whack!*

Fuck, she'd tasted good, sweet and smooth like a chocolate-dipped strawberry. And her ass. *Damn.*

Whack!

He stared down at the mangled vegetable in front of him. Cora was messing with his mind in ways he hadn't anticipated. He heaved a sigh. He didn't need any complications in his life, and that's what Cora was, a tiny, sexy, explosive ball of complications.

Throwing the mess he'd made into the garbage, he started over, making sure he actually focused on his work. It had been a couple years since he helped his brothers with the pub, but it wasn't so complicated he needed step-by-step instructions from Cora.

Not that he would have gone to her for anything. After what happened in the fridge, he planned to keep as much distance as possible between them. She seemed to have the same plan, because other than throwing drink orders and the occasional reminder at him, she avoided him the rest of the day.

Lunch hour and early afternoon were quiet at the bar, though Cora and Keeley's hands were full with food orders. He used the time to familiarize himself with his area, tidying up some of the chaos his brother Josh left in the wake of his evening shifts.

A bellowing laugh caught his attention, and he spotted the two women chatting with a group of men seated in the far corner. He recognized Noah's friend Merrick and figured it was the group from TanTech.

He couldn't hear the conversation, but even at his distance, he could easily see the difference in how the girls approached the customers.

Keeley waitressed like she did everything—she was loud and friendly with an untamable sauciness. Cora, on the other hand, managed to give off the sweet and innocent vibe like she was entirely unaware of the dirty thoughts no doubt running through those guys' heads.

The sweetness had always been Cora's defining characteristic and one of the reasons she and Lela had been best friends. Right up until she killed Lela. And if he'd had any doubt about how little innocence she possessed, their little episode earlier dispelled it.

The glass he held in his hand exploded from the pressure of his grip, raining shards onto the floor.

"Shit," he muttered and tossed what was left of the glass in the trash. He turned on the faucet in the small sink and placed his hand under the running water to remove any trace of glass, then grabbed the small broom from under the counter to sweep up the mess.

"What happened?" Logan asked, appearing on the other side of the bar.

"Nothing, just a broken glass," Gavin brushed the incident off.

"You need to get control."

"I'm fine."

"You look like shit, and you know damn well that leaves you open to—" Logan cut himself off as a customer approached. "Clean up the mess and get yourself in control."

Gavin turned away from his brother and wiped down the counter. With happy hour beginning, business picked up, humming with activity. By the end of his shift, customers lined the length of his counter.

Scanning the group of four ladies in front of him, he flashed his best cocky smile. The giggles he received in exchange were almost as satisfying as the tip he anticipated.

"What can I get you, ladies?"

"What's the best drink you make?" asked the tall redhead.

He contained his snort of contempt at the lame question. He wasn't a world-class bartender, but as long as you followed a recipe, it was hard to mess most drinks up. On the other hand, he wasn't about to break out a manual, either.

His eyes narrowed as he took in the polished appearance Red had attempted with her make-up and the fake-diamond tennis bracelet. Her desire to be seen as sophisticated was a bit too obvious, especially since she barely looked legal.

"Nothing beats my crantini."

"Perfect," she said.

"Crantinis all around?" He scanned the others as he snagged his martini shaker.

The other girls looked at each other and then back at him.

"Beer," they said in chorus and laughed as Red rolled her eyes.

He laughed. "My kind of ladies."

"Fine. I'll drink the vile stuff," Red said and held up a long manicured finger, pointing at her friends. "But one of you is responsible for getting me home."

He was pouring the last pint when he sensed someone behind him. From the smell of vanilla, he figured it was Cora.

"No overtime," she said.

He topped off the beer, letting the foam settle into the perfect head before sliding it across the counter to Red. After he added the order to their tab, he turned to Cora.

"I'm waiting on Josh," he explained.

"He's in the back, and that's where he'll stay if you don't go and get him."

"Thought I wasn't supposed to leave the bar unattended."

"That's why I stay here while you go get him."

Cora moved around him, invading his domain and started rearranging everything he'd organized. She picked up a rack of glasses and moved them into the far corner.

"Why don't *you* grab him?" He used his foot to maneuver the rack back to where he'd had it, enjoying the scowl the action brought to her face.

"Your brother's lazy, and he'll stall as long as possible if he knows you're out here."

He felt guilty he didn't defend Josh, but honestly, his younger brother *was* lazy. Not that Josh wasn't a hard worker, it was more like his easy-going attitude empowered him to ride the waves of others' hard work. Then again, what did Gavin know? Hell, Josh had held this job longer than Gavin ever held any.

"I can tell him you're waiting," she said when he didn't respond. "But chances are he'll let himself be distracted once I can't see him anymore."

"Fine. Stop messing with my space," he grumbled.

"Keep it tidy and I will. How you guys even function behind here amazes me." She shoved the rack of glasses back to where she'd moved it. "You keep the racks stacked here, so anyone back here doesn't trip over them."

She had a point, but having the glasses right next to him was easier. Rather than admit she was right, or to argue in vain, he trudged off to find his brother.

In the kitchen, he found Josh exactly where he expected—leaning against the wall, stuffing his face with peanuts.

"You're up," Gavin said.

Josh groaned, raking a hair over his short black hair. "Is Cora out there?"

"Yeah."

"Damn. She's gonna rake me over." Despite his words, he took another moment to swipe a handful of peanuts and stuff them in his pockets.

Keeley sauntered through the door and stopped to stare at Josh.

"What?" he asked her.

"Cora."

He groaned again but went out to his station. As he exited, she flicked her wrist and made a whipping noise.

When he gave her the finger behind his back, she laughed and repeated the noise.

"That girl has your brother trained like a lap dog. I swear he's got a thing for her." She must have caught Gavin's shocked expression, because she asked, "What? Didn't expect some brotherly competition?"

"Competition? For what?"

"Uh, the peanuts. *Cora*. Who else?"

"Not interested," he snapped. "And she's not someone I'd ever let my brother stoop to dating, either."

"Whoa," Keeley pulled back in surprise, shock contorting her normally beautiful features. "Chill. Cora's my friend, and I suggest if you have a problem with her you keep it to yourself, or we're gonna have a problem."

"No problem," he said through gritted teeth, grateful the natural noises of the kitchen kept Mateo from overhearing their exchange. The last thing he needed was complaints to Noah on his first day. Even though his brothers would fight to the death for him, there was no way they'd let him give Cora crap at work.

"Good." Keeley smiled as if he'd never even opened his mouth. "Now, we need to talk about your service technique."

"What's wrong with it?"

"You need to do less smiling, less flirting. We want the ladies to be at the tables, not the bar."

"Drinks are drinks, right?"

She reached up and patted his cheek. "Sweetie, they won't tip me if you're the one hooking them up with drinks. So, stuff the stud routine and send them my way."

"What do I get in exchange?"

"Standard fifteen percent cut. Unless I hear you talking smack about Cora again. Then it'll be my foot up your ass."

She blew him a kiss and sauntered off to the change room. It would have been funny, and maybe a bit sexy, except Cora stood directly behind the spot Keeley had just been. There was no way she missed Keeley's warning.

He waited for her to lash out, but she didn't. He untied the waist apron and tossed it in the laundry basket in the corner. Her eyes followed him, and his nerves got the better of him.

"Problem?" He let his eyes narrow.

Her lips thinned, though their natural fullness failed to give her the stern face he was sure she was going for.

"No," she said after a long pause then followed Keeley's path.

As much as he wanted to change, he wasn't going to risk being in a cramped space with Cora again.

THREE

THE MAN SITS IN his car, flexing his leather-clad fingers around the steering wheel, the only outward sign of his tension. He watches Gavin step out from the bar, the door drifting closed behind him.

In the rear-view mirror, the man's eyes hazel eyes flash with concentration. Cora tries to see more, but she is trapped within the man's gaze, seeing what he sees. And he is intent on his purpose.

Gavin rolls out of the parking lot in his Jeep. The man waits until the Jeep reaches the light a block down the road then follows, keeping a good distance between them all the way to the apartment complex. Then he watches again. This time, his fingers smooth along the barrel of his gun.

He raises it and finds Gavin in his sights.

Cora's eyes fluttered, reluctant to face the midmorning light streaming in through the blinds. She inhaled deeply, her stomach churning as she reached for the bottle of water on her nightstand and took a long sip.

Sleep had been an absent friend in the months since the accident. It started with nightmares about drowning; then a year ago, the visions started.

At first, she thought she was suffering some kind of hysteria, a kind of post-traumatic stress. She'd wake in the middle of the night, shaking with adrenaline, then be thrown into a vision of Gavin.

She brushed them off as semi-conscious dreams for the first few weeks. Sometimes, they bordered on fantasies, other times on nightmares. Then she discovered some of the things she saw actually happened.

Once she started thinking of them as visions rather than hallucinations, she searched for some sort of order. There wasn't any. She saw things from the past, others from the future. She accepted them for what they were—a glimpse into his life.

When the man first entered the visions, he'd seemed innocent enough. A stranger who caught a glimpse of Gavin at the store or outside of the bar. But as the visions came more frequent, his presence became something else; he became the sole set of eyes to view the events. That night's vision was nothing new.

Someone out there was trying to kill Gavin.

Telling him had been her first instinct until she realized how crazy it sounded. Up until a year ago, Cora never believed in psychic visions, but there was no other way to describe them. Yet, even though she believed in them didn't mean she expected anyone else to.

Moving back to Thompson Creek was the only way she could stop what would happen.

She dragged herself from bed and padded across the cold hardwood floor to her dresser. She jotted down a few notes about what she saw in a journal filled with other details. Not that she had much to go on. The location and time of the hit differed each time as if the man hadn't yet decided. As for identifying him ... Well, he was too nondescript. He looked like so many other older, white men. With hazel eyes. That was new. After work, she'd take the time to figure out how this vision fit in with the others.

Waitressing at Porter's Pub wasn't the most intellectually stimulating job, and it didn't utilize her degree in art history in the least, but it was fast paced even in the afternoon, and she loved the people she worked with.

Although by the end of Cora's shift that day, Keeley was driving her nuts.

"God, he's so yummy. I'd totally go for him if he weren't such a manwhore," Keeley said.

Cora glanced over at her friend who pretended to wipe down tables while drooling over Gavin. It was a habit Keeley picked up when Gavin started working at the club three weeks before.

She admitted he was yummy. His biceps stretched the sleeves of his shirt as he carried and she glimpsed the tattoo that snaked over his shoulder and across his back peeking out. He reached up to restock the bottles on the top display case, pulling his shirt up and revealing his abs and her body clenched at the memory of how hard they were.

"He's not a manwhore. He's just very ... social," she

said, defending him.

Keeley snorted, throwing her a disbelieving look. "Have you not seen him in action? Girl, he hooks up with a different piece of ass every week. Well, except Hailey. She's about the closest he's got to a girlfriend since ever."

"Not since ever."

Cora loaded the last of the dirty glasses on her tray and left Keeley to her drooling. Hearing about Gavin's sex life wasn't something she wanted to think about, yet it seemed to be the only topic Keeley wanted to discuss that afternoon. Which, considering Keeley's interest in Logan, was a little strange.

Avoiding Keeley, though, was next to impossible unless Cora quit mid-shift.

"So, have you known him for long?" Keeley asked when she appeared in the kitchen a few minutes later.

"Nine or ten years." Cora shrugged and tucked a wayward strand of hair behind her ear. "We went to the same high school until he graduated early."

"Please tell me you at least hooked up with him once in all that time. Other than your little petting session in the liquor room."

"He dated my best friend; besides, I don't think I'm his type." Cora ignored the reference to the liquor room.

Keeley gave a sad shake of her head, and Cora couldn't blame her. Compared to Keeley's life, her own was about as dull as ... Well, she couldn't even think of a good comparison for how dull it was.

"I think anything with boobs and an ass is his type," Keeley said.

Cora knew better. He had a type. *Lela*. With her huge

brown eyes and thick black hair, she'd been a beautiful mix of Portuguese and Armenian heritage.

"I thought you were still stalking Logan," Cora said, hoping to deflect Keeley's attention. She turned on the tap and scrubbed her hands with soap.

"Not stalking. I'm merely keeping an eye on the prize. One day's he's gonna crack, and I'll be there to swoop in and save him from the harpy he calls his girlfriend."

While she didn't say anything aloud, Cora figured Keeley stood a better chance with Gavin than Logan. Logan seemed to be looking for someone more grounded than Keeley. On the other hand, Gavin wasn't looking for any attachment, and Keeley fit his typical hook up perfectly—loud, assertive, and sexy.

"Obviously, stalking is on your mind." Keeley loaded a rack with clean glasses. "So I'll tell you now—you're bordering on it."

"W*hat?* Me? I'm not stalking anyone." Cora was horrified. *Had she been so obvious?* Not that she was stalking Gavin. *Okay, so maybe she kind of was,* but she had her reasons, and it had nothing to do with the erotic dreams she had of him every night.

"Girl, you keep telling yourself that and—Forget it, there's no way even you believe that."

"I'm not stalking Gavin. We've just run into each other a few times." She focused on the lemons she pulled from the fridge to avoid Keeley's knowing smile.

So it was more than a few, and she might have changed her shift schedule once or twice so she worked with him more often. *Okay, she did that four times.*

"It wouldn't be so bad if the guy didn't absolutely

41

despise you. He's got a hard-on for you, and I'm not talking about the one in his pants."

Cora rolled her eyes and laughed, but inside she died a little. Knowing it was one thing, having other people be so aware of it was another. She didn't need humiliation or pity piled atop her guilt.

"What did you do to him anyway?" Keeley immediately held up a hand. "Sorry, I'm being nosy, aren't I? You don't have to answer. Unless it's really juicy."

Cora took a deep breath and debated what to say. Keeley was her only close friend and deserved to know what she'd done.

"I'm the reason his fiancée is dead."

"You're shitting me." Keeley put down the glass she held and stared at Cora. "You can't even kill a fly, and you always make me take the spiders outside. How could you possibly have killed her?"

"We went out to celebrate our graduation. One last hurrah before becoming full-fledged adults with degrees and jobs and responsibilities." Cora almost smiled as she remembered how excited they'd been. "We were on our way home, and I was so smashed."

"Oh, Cora ..." Keeley said with such pity and disappointment, Cora cringed.

"Some guy almost rear-ended us, and I freaked out. Lela told me to calm down, but I gave him the finger. He followed us, and when we got to Thompson Creek Bridge, he rammed us and pushed us over the edge."

"Sounds like it was the other guy's fault."

"No." Tears welled in Cora's eyes. She wiped at them with her arm, then began slicing the lemons. "Her death was my fault."

"Girl, even if you drove drunk, the accident might not have happened if he hadn't gone into road rage mode."

"I wasn't driving."

"Even more reason for you not to be blamed."

"Lela survived the crash into the water, but her seat belt jammed, and I was too drunk to get her out in time. She drowned."

"And you think Gavin blames you?"

"I know he does."

"Then why the hell did you convince Noah to give him a job?"

"Because he needed it."

She didn't give Keeley a chance to grill her further. She scooped up the lemons, tossed them in a small bowl, and carried them out to the bar.

Gavin needed the job, and she needed to be close to him. She wasn't going to let anyone else die because of her.

From the corner of his eye, Gavin watched Cora move across the floor. The end of her ponytail swept the top of her low-cut jeans, drawing his eyes to her ass. His hands clenched in memory of how her lush curves felt as he'd squeezed them. His cock twitched, and he adjusted his stance to relieve the press of the zipper.

"Hey, sugar." Hailey slid onto the stool across from him. "You sticking around tonight?"

She batted her eyelashes. At least, he assumed they were eyelashes. With all the black gunk on and around them, he wondered if they were really spiders.

"I might," he answered as he mixed her usual

raspberry vodka on the rocks with a splash of cranberry juice.

He placed the drink in front of her, and she trailed her fingers along the back of his hand.

"Work is making you a dull boy. You need a beer and a good rub down."

Her offer was the same every time they hooked up, and until he started working at the pub, it worked. Now, well, after her mouthing off to Noah about his night terrors, Gavin wasn't interested.

Hell, if he was honest, his lack of interest in Hailey was because of Cora. She was everywhere. The first few months she'd been back in Thompson Creek, he never bumped into her. Now he constantly saw her. She hung out after her shift, turned up on the evenings he worked late, distracting him from other possible pursuits. She was seriously cramping his sex life.

He needed to get her and her ass out of his mind.

"All right," he said to Hailey and flashed his best cocky smile. "I could use a beer, but only if you're doing the rubbing."

The sudden smack on the back of his head sent him surging forward, and he caught himself on the edge of the counter before his face hit the hardwood surface. He twisted around and found Noah glaring at him.

"Watch your mouth, there're ladies around here," Noah ordered, crossing his arms in his "I'm the boss" stance.

"It's all right, Noah. I like it when he's a little naughty." Hailey giggled.

"I wasn't talking about you." Noah glared at her,

returning the middle finger she gave him. Noah's dislike for Hailey was no secret, and he took every opportunity to let her feel his contempt.

"Bite me," she sneered, snatching up her drink. She winked at Gavin. "Catch ya later, sugar."

She headed for a group of friends, and Gavin tried to find even a spark of lust. Objectively, she was sexy as hell, and sure, he appreciated the short shorts barely covering her ass cheeks, but he felt nothing.

"You still banging that bitch?" Noah asked.

Rather than answer, Gavin grunted and unhooked the empty keg, replacing it with a new one.

"Josh here yet?" he wiped his palms on his jeans.

"Logan is sending him out."

"I thought he only responded to Cora's orders."

"Yeah, well, we need to talk, and I'm not waiting until you're too shitfaced to give a fuck."

Noah stomped through the kitchen door, which swung back open as Josh sauntered through. He paused to talk with a pretty brunette.

Josh was a player, and Gavin had seen his brother flirt with a lot of girls, but not like that. He laid a hand low on her back, playing with the ends of her long, wavy hair. The touch was too personal for her to be just another woman. He would have stayed there if Noah hadn't stuck his head out the door to glare at him.

"What'ya do to piss him off?" Josh entered the bar area and began rearranging the glass racks.

"Breathe?" Gavin shrugged. "Ladies at the end have a tab, the bald guy hit his limit, and the short guy's been eying the girls' till."

He didn't stick around to see how Josh dealt with Shorty, though he knew his brother would handle that first. Noah and Logan wanted to talk, so they'd talk, then he could lose himself in a drink and Hailey.

In the back office, he found his twin, Caleb, with Noh and Logan pouring over a pile of documents spread across the desk. His shoulders stiffened as he identified the SIEGE logo stamped on the front of one folder.

Caleb had been digging. His job at TanTech Securities allowed him access to some of the most confidential operations in both the private and government sector, and while he didn't have clearance for the SIEGE files, he wouldn't let that stop him from snooping.

Gavin must have made a sound because both men stopped talking and looked up at him. The expressions they wore twisted his gut.

"We have a problem," Logan said.

"When don't we?" Gavin replied, reaching up to hook his hands on the door frame. It seemed like they never had a problem-free existence. At one time or another, one of their lives had been crumbling to some degree. "I thought we all agreed to stop hunting Sinclair."

"That was before Caleb found this on the security feed." Logan held out a stack of photos, but Gavin made no move to take them, so Logan held them up, forcing Gavin to look at the man who haunted them. "Sinclair was at the pub and your apartment building."

"Who's that?"

Gavin's arms dropped, and he spun around to glare at Cora, who stood almost directly behind him, peeking under his arm and into the office. She pushed past him, moving to take the surveillance image from Logan.

"Who is he?" she repeated, looking from the photograph to the brothers, fear tightening her face.

"Why?" Gavin stepped closer to her.

"I ... I thought I recognized him," she said, her eyes darting around the room. "But I'm probably wrong."

He could tell it was the truth, but not the whole truth. She was hiding something, and if it involved Sinclair, he wasn't going to let her get away without spilling the details.

"Anyways, I covered Keeley's break, so she's good till close," she said, dropping the photo on top of the desk. "See you guys tomorrow."

The four of them stared after her before turning back to each other. Gavin wasn't the only one she failed convinced.

"What was that about?" Logan asked.

"Fuck if I know." Noah shook his head. "I'll go talk to her."

The thought of Noah and Cora alone together in the change room rankled. Gavin shifted his body blocking his brother's path.

"I'll talk to her."

He went down to the locker room, knocking once to give her warning before opening the door. Only the very top of her head was visible above the screen in the corner, and it struck him how small she was.

She lifted onto tiptoes, and her eyes peeked over to peer at him. The fear lingered, though he could tell she tried to hide it.

"I'm almost done," she said, and her arms lifted to pull

on her shirt.

She walked around the divider, her blond curls hung loosely over her shoulders, brushing her breasts. Under his gaze, her nipples hardened into little nubs, pressing against the thin material of her shirt, and his mouth watered. *Fuck, he wanted to taste her*.

"Did you need something?" She tugged on a hoodie, snapping his brain back to what he needed to focus on.

"How do you know Sinclair?"

"I don't."

"Bullshit." He closed the distance between them, causing her to tip her head back in order to stare up at him. "I saw how you reacted to his picture, Cora. How do you know him?"

"I don't. I swear." She shook her head, sending her curls sweeping across her chest. "He just looked familiar."

There it was again, not a lie, but not exactly honest, either.

"If you're lying ..." He let the threat dangle between them.

"I'm not. Gavin, I promise you, I've never met the man." She held his gaze, and he believed her that time. "Who is he?"

"Nobody."

Her lips tilted in a half-smile. "I doubt that. Even if you hadn't freaked about me thinking I recognized him, Logan said the guy followed you."

He searched the soft angles of her face, so different than Lela's. Cora possessed a sweetness that would leave her forever looking younger than she was, a sweetness that begged him to share his secrets, to forgive her for what happened to Lela. Yet, he couldn't forgive.

His heart hardened, shutting out her false innocence.

"Sinclair is the only person in this world I despise more than you."

FOUR

COFFEE WAS A GIFT FROM God brewed in hell.

There was no other way Cora could explain the magical properties of such a nasty tasting concoction.

She walked into the coffee shop down the road from Porter's Pub and joined the mid-morning line. Inhaling deeply, she pondered the irony of how something that smelled so good could taste so vile. Yet as disgusting as she found it, she was a slave to its ability to wake her up and keep her that way. With the visions coming more frequently, she'd been getting even less sleep than usual and needed the boost.

The door chimed, and in idle curiosity, she peeked over her shoulder to see who else was subjecting themselves to their morning ritual. Her muscles tensed as Gavin took the spot behind her in line. Their eyes met, and she gave a tentative smile. When he continued to scowl, she faced forward, concentrating on the menu board.

Sinclair is the only person in this world I despise more than you.

Even a week later, his words haunted her. They hadn't

surprised her. After the accident, she gave herself up for him to blame. Yet, despite her brother's conviction it was because she was a martyr; she knew it was because she had been guilty. Maybe not of killing Lela, but somewhere deep inside her, Cora had wished Lela weren't in the picture.

The line moved quickly, and she placed her order for a double mocha latte before finding a seat at an empty bistro table in the corner while she waited. She used the time to check her email and was in the midst of typing a response to her brother when Gavin sat down across from her.

The cell phone lay forgotten in her hand as she stared at him in shock.

"Sinclair was the doctor in charge of the Posthuman Project," he said, gazing out the window.

Growing up, she heard the rumors about Gavin and his five brothers. She'd been a child—about seven when it happened—so the details weren't there, but there'd never been any question that the boys suffered as part of the SIEGE scandal.

"What I'm about to tell you doesn't go any further. My family has been through enough because of Sinclair." He turned to her, leaning across the table. "The only reason I'm even telling you is because you know him, and I think you deserve to be warned."

"I don't know him," she denied. "It's the truth, Gavin. He just looked familiar."

"I wish I could believe you," he said, his expression making it clear any belief was far off. "Did Lela ever tell you about what happened to my brothers and me before we moved here?"

"No, but there were rumors when you guys first arrived."

"We were born in the labs at SEIGE. Our mothers were volunteers; our fathers were sperm donors. Our sole purpose was to serve as test subjects in the development of experimental serums to facilitate the physical and psychological advancement of soldiers. We were restricted to the labs; our interactions with the outside world limited to the teacher."

He paused as the barista delivered their drinks. Cora took a sip of her latte, not wanting to say anything that might stop him from telling his story.

"What happened to us ... Sinclair tortured us under the guise of scientific discovery. We still don't know all of the long-term effects."

"Gavin," she said, reaching across the table to rest her hand over his. "You don't need to tell me this."

"I do because you need to understand what Sinclair is capable of. He's dangerous."

She nodded. In her visions, she saw Sinclair in action, his determination to kill Gavin. Everything inside of her screamed at her to tell Gavin about the visions, but she didn't. Despite the danger Gavin obviously realized Sinclair represented, it was still a long stretch to accept psychic visions.

"Okay," she said. "If I ever see him, I'll stay away."

There was an awkward pause while he must have been weighing the truth of her words. She didn't know what else to say to convince him, then realized nothing would. And honestly, she couldn't blame him because she wasn't being entirely upfront with him.

"Logan said Sinclair's been following you. Have you seen him?"

"No." He shrugged. "He knows better than to get close enough for me to spot him."

She thought about all the times Sinclair came within only a few yards of Gavin without detection.

"If he's been watching you, you should be more careful. He doesn't need to be close to hurt you."

"I got it covered." He sipped from his cup and nodded toward hers. "I didn't think you drank coffee."

"I do. I just wish I didn't have to." She gave a soft laugh. "I can't stand the stuff, but it keeps me going. Besides, this is a latte, so it's not as bad."

"Lela loved coming here," he said, his eyes scanning the coffee shop.

"I remember." She and Lela spent so much time there during college it became like a second home. "She'd bring her textbooks and sit for hours, studying and drinking her coffee."

"She had to. Her father wouldn't let her drink it at home."

"I think that's why she did it," Cora said. "It was her little rebellion against her parents."

"You're probably right. She could stand toe to toe with everyone else, but with her parents, she was too worried about their opinion."

Talking about Lela had always been painful—a mixture of grief and guilt. But at that moment, it felt natural. Like the both of them had reached a point where the mere mention of her name didn't tear a piece of their soul from them.

Cora wanted the moment to go on forever, yet as she started to say something else, the alarm on her cell phone went.

"I better get going. I'm working the afternoon shift."

"Me too. I'll walk with you."

Cora's heart jumped at his offer then she mentally told herself to calm down. It was only a walk down the street. A walk that was done in silence.

As the day wore on, the olive branch she hoped his offer was withered into a switch that lashed at her back with the cutting glances he kept throwing her way.

By the end of her shift, she decided that she'd imagined the friendly exchange.

"After you've finished scanning everything, file the packing slips here," Noah said as he pulled out the drawer of the filing cabinet. "We clear them out after tax season."

"Doesn't the computer keep track of everything?" Cora gestured to his laptop.

"It does, but as much confidence as Caleb and Gavin have in technology, I don't trust it."

He sank into the chair behind his desk, and she sat across from him, groaning as her feet pulsed from their new position. Five straight shifts left her drained. That day, she did seven hours on the floor before spending the last hour learning the receiving system.

"I'm exhausted," she said as Noah chuckled. "What happened to the six-hour shifts?"

"Business has picked up since Dixon's pub closed." He sifted through some papers before tossing them back on the desk. "We're hoping to hire at least two more girls for the floor and possibly another bartender. The options are pretty slim, though."

"Maybe you shouldn't limit it to women," she suggested.

He held up his hands to stave off any further argument. "Hey, I have no problem with guys working the floor, but I know our clientele."

"Sexist?"

"Men who like to look at pretty ladies."

"Sexist."

"Business is business, and even though my brothers manage to bring in some of the ladies, it's not enough for me to forget who's paying the bills."

"That's only because you refuse to consider Keeley's proposal."

Noah snorted. "There's no way Gavin and Josh are going to work shirtless."

"I'm sure Josh would be up for it."

"Yeah, well, don't give him any ideas. So, you still interested in learning the business side of this?" he asked.

"Of course."

Her head nodded, but she couldn't help thinking of the job she left in Denver. It had been an entry-level position, but it had been a start—a path to becoming head curator of a museum or gallery. At least assistant managing Porter's Pub would give her managerial experience.

"You ever going to tell me why you're really here?" Noah stared at her, a dark eyebrow lifted in warning that he wasn't likely to buy any lie she gave him.

"I decided I wanted to experience working in a bar." Her response earned a snort of disbelief from Noah.

"There's no way in hell little Coraline Evans, world traveler, and art connoisseur *actually* wants to learn how to manage a bar in Thompson Creek."

Her lips tipped up. "So it's not what I'd planned to do with my life, but it's where I need to be."

"Anything to do with my brother?" He sighed when she didn't say anything. "Cora ..."

"Don't say it."

"Someone needs to say it. Gavin is lost. He's buried in that grave with Lela, and if you give him the chance, he will hurt you." Noah held up his hand when she made a weak sound of protest. "Back in high school and college, it was pretty obvious you had a crush on him."

Her face burst into flames. She always thought she'd done a good job of hiding her feelings. But if Noah—someone she rarely interacted with back then—figured it out, who else had?

"Lela was my best friend. I would never have ..."

"I know. You were a good friend to Lela."

She could tell he was thinking of how Lela died. But long before she let Lela drown, trapped in the car, she had envied her friend and used her as an opportunity to see Gavin. Deep down, she always knew that if Lela and Gavin hadn't been together, she wouldn't have made such an effort to keep in touch with her friend, but her unhealthy need to torture herself pushed her to desperately hold onto a childhood friend who provided a connection with Gavin.

In the end, Lela was more of a means to an end.

"You're wrong," she said, the bitter taste of guilt turning her stomach sour. Before Noah could argue or offer her meaningless platitudes, she stood. "I better get going. I'm meeting a friend for drinks."

Her escape from the conversation with Noah seemed like the best plan until she walked into the change room and found a shirtless Gavin. He was digging in his locker, his back to her.

The tribal tattoo spiraling over his shoulder and down one side of his back did only partially concealed the scars crisscrossing his back, forcing her to face the reality of what he must have gone through as a child. That morning, he'd said they'd been tortured, but something inside her hadn't let her consider that it what that truly meant.

The door clicked shut behind her, and Gavin glanced over his shoulder at her. She nodded her head curtly and opened her locker. From the corner of her eye, she watched him pull on a clean shirt.

Life had not been fair to him.

"I would have traded places with her," she said, her words nothing more than a whisper.

"I know."

"You hate me for what happened."

He rubbed a hand across his face. She pulled out her coat and shut the locker, staring down at her trembling hands.

"Maybe," he finally responded. "And I want to because hating you would be so much easier than this."

Only steps away from him, the sound of his deep breaths flowed around her, and then she sensed him moving behind her.

He stopped within a breath of her, not touching her, but close enough for the heat of his body to warm her and send a rush of tingles through her, tightening her nerves in anticipation. His hand came up to press against the locker door in front of her, and he leaned in, his lips skimming her ear.

"Cora," he said.

His rough voice tugged her back, and she sank into him, the hard ridges of his body keeping her from melting. His other hand slid across her ribs and settled low on her belly. The pressure of his hand held her in place as his hips pushed forward, rubbing his erection between the cheeks of her ass.

She arched her back, nestling her head into the crook of his neck. Her hands grasped his forearms. His teeth nipped at her ear, and a low moan escaped her.

Then something hit the wall outside the room. They both froze, processing the sound. Cora squeezed her eyes shut as she committed the moment to memory. Even though she expected it, when he tore himself away from her, she gasped at the loss of contact.

She turned around to look up at him, trying to figure out what he was thinking. But he was impossible to read, his face hardened into an emotionless mask.

Grabbing her purse and coat, she walked to the door where she paused, grasping the handle with a tight grip.

"It's okay to hate me."

In the silence following her words, she pulled open the door and left.

Her apartment was only a few blocks away, but the walk felt like an eternity. Every step of the way, she kept thinking about Noah's prediction about Gavin hurting her. She knew it would happen eventually, but she didn't know how deep it would go.

A car honked, stopping her in her tracks and she realized she'd nearly walked into traffic and past her place. The ground floor of her building housed commercial properties with a bookstore, antique shop, and a couple of clothing stores. Her apartment was on the second floor along with three other units. The front entrance, a battered old door between the bookstore and antique shop, consisted of a small foyer for their mailboxes and the stairwell.

She reached her apartment and tossed her bag and jacket on the couch. The sparsely-furnished space was a far cry from the cozy rental she'd had in Denver. She spent almost over a year turning that apartment into a home, accumulating little knick knacks and making it hers. When she returned to Thompson Creek, she left almost everything behind, bringing only her clothes and what little she could cram into her Toyota Matrix.

She could have rented a moving truck, but she opted to save her money. The job market in town was scarce, and she ended up dipping into her savings before she was hired on at the bar.

A life in Thompson Creek had never been in her plans. During college, she lived at home to save money. After ... Well, she had more than enough reason to leave.

She'd enjoyed Denver, but coming back home only made her realize how much she missed small town life. When she ran into Eve, an old high school friend, at the grocery store, she been hesitant to meet at the bar. But the more she thought about it, rehashing high school might not be so terrible.

After her shower, she pulled on her favorite skinny jeans and a white, chain strap, halter top. The top had a hi-low cut, so the front skimmed the top of her low-cut jeans, giving an occasional peek of her tummy.

She pulled out her phone to text Eve, letting the other woman know she'd meet her at the pub. Taking her car didn't make much sense when she lived so close by; besides, driving meant not drinking and she was in the mood for something stronger than soda.

She entered the bar, finding it busy for mid-week, but nothing Keeley and the other two girls couldn't handle. Noah and his girlfriend, Alicia, sat at a table by the window with Merrick and another woman she didn't know. She gave a small wave and then headed to the bar. She considered Noah a friend as well as her boss, but Alicia never seemed that friendly. While Merrick seemed like a good guy, other than knowing he owned TanTech and that he'd recently divorced, she knew little else about him.

She finished her scan of the room and found Gavin precisely where she expected him to be—at the pool table, cue in one hand, beer in the other, and Hailey hanging from his arm.

Instant irritation swept through her. It was hard not to hate Hailey. She was loud, mouthy, and catty. Oh, sure they were similar qualities to those of Keeley, but with a few massive differences. Hailey was a bitch, and she had Gavin.

"Cora, my love." Josh appeared behind the bar. "Whatcha doing here? I thought you were off?"

"I am." She glanced down at her clothes. "Do I look like

I'm working?"

Josh laughed and wisely didn't answer.

"What can I get you?"

"Something fruity."

"Fruity and fun, huh?" Josh winked, and she might have bought into his flirting if she wasn't aware of the thing he had for a girl in his philosophy class. "You hanging solo?"

"No, waiting on an old friend from high school."

He filled a tall cocktail glass with ice, added the shots of light, dark, and spiced rum, then poured in orange and pineapple juice and a dash of grenadine. He placed a cherry on top and slid the glass over to her.

"One Bahama Mama. Just watch out; these fruity things are deadly."

"I have in fact had a drink before." She smiled at his warning—it was the same one he gave her every time she asked for a fruity drink and he gave her a Bahama Mama.

She took her drink and found an empty table where she could watch the door for Eve. The fact that it also gave her a clear view of Gavin was a nice side benefit. Well, nice wasn't exactly how she would describe watching Hailey draping herself all over him. She took a long sip from her drink.

A few minutes later, Eve appeared in the entrance. Cora half-rose from her chair and waved to catch Eve's attention. They hugged briefly before sitting just as Keeley came over. Eve ordered a beer while Cora asked for another Bahama Mama. Somehow, she'd nearly drained her glass while waiting those few minutes for Eve.

"Sorry I'm late. I had to run my little brother, Jamie, to

his dad's place." Eve pushed the loose strands of light brown hair behind her ears.

They chatted until Keeley came back with their drinks.

Eve took a long drag from her bottle then licked a drop from her lip.

"That's so good," she said.

"I take it you haven't been out in a while?" Cora said with a chuckle.

"Not since I took in Jamie. I love the little guy, but paying for a sitter—heck, *finding* a sitter—makes it hard. I lucked out that his dad was able to take him tonight."

"How long has he been with you?"

"Since our mom split a couple years ago."

Cora nodded. She remembered how Eve had always kept quiet about her family, though most people were aware that her mom was an addict. Secrets in a small town like Thompson Creek never lasted long. Even if you didn't know someone personally, chances were you heard of them and their life story.

The Walker family, or at least the boys, were a rare exception. The most anyone had ever known were sensationalized rumors.

"We were down in Boulder, but Jamie's dad is here and offered to help out taking care of him." Eve tipped her beer bottle to the side, letting it roll along the rim. "He's mentioned going for custody, but frankly, the guy can hardly handle overnight visits."

"Any word from your mom?"

"Not since Christmas. Enough about me. Last I heard you were living in Denver running some museum. What the hell are you doing back here?" Eve asked her.

"I wish I ran it. I only did inventory, but things didn't work out," she hedged. "I loved my job, but I left Thompson Creek for all the wrong reasons."

Eve nodded. "You left after Lela died."

"It ... It was hard to be here and face what I did."

"What happened to Lela was not your fault."

If only guilt could be vanquished by those simple words. *Not your fault.* Cora chugged the last bit of her first drink and started on her second.

The sudden touch of hands on her shoulders caused her to jump in her seat. A glance up revealed Josh's smiling face.

"Cora, my love, you didn't tell me you were meeting *the* Evie Fray," he said.

"Evie?" Cora's eyebrows lifted, and she looked to Eve, who shrugged.

"Evie Fray, breaker of my heart. Rejected my most sincere invitation to attend the Valentine's dance during my freshman year. Why did you so callously reject me?"

Eve laughed. "Possibly because you called me Evie?"

Cora relaxed back in her seat as she dragged her thoughts from Lela and Gavin and into the present. That was what she needed. No more moping. For the night, she was going to forget about martyrdom.

FIVE

HE SENSED CORA'S PRESENCE before he saw her, though describing the sensation was impossible. It was more of a mental perception than a physical one, yet his mind's ability to pick up on subtle details and changes to the environment was one he never doubted.

She was at the bar, talking with Josh. Apparently, his brother was turning on the charm because Cora smiled and gave a soft laugh. Gavin's lips compressed as he realized how rare a sound that soft wispy laugh was.

Her head tipped to the side, and her long blond curls swayed from side to side. He could almost smell the gentle vanilla scent of it that hovered in his memory. The soft tangle of those curls brushing along his jaw had stayed with him in the hours since he'd been pressed against her.

He still didn't know what the hell had possessed him to touch her. He couldn't say what he'd been thinking, probably because he *hadn't* been. He wanted to hate her. Hell, she *told* him to hate her. But he didn't.

What happened to Lela—

A stinging slap on his ass jarred him from his thoughts. Hailey cackled loudly as she rested her chin on his shoulder. He barely kept himself from coughing at the overpowering odor of her floral perfume.

"You're up, sugar," she said and slid her hands around to his chest, letting them sink low.

Not one for public displays, he grabbed them before they could reach their goal. He stepped to the side and placed his beer on the ledge running the length of the wall before grabbing his pool cue from where it rested against his stool.

Lining up his shot, he called it then sunk the ball. He repeated the process, one after another, until only the eight ball remained. Playing pool always relaxed him. It was a game that came naturally to him. Well, not naturally so much as it was skill courtesy of the side effects from Sinclair's experiments. When Gavin studied the table, he could almost see the angle lines floating there like a grid spread across the table.

After he made the final shot, he scooped the balls from the pockets and rolled them to the end of the table. He was racking them again when he noticed Hailey standing with her arms crossed over her chest. The stance pushed her breasts up enough they threatened to burst free.

"You hoping to distract me?" he asked.

"Just wondering if you're here to play, or if you're here to play pool?"

He almost asked what she meant, but while he could be oblivious sometimes, he wasn't stupid. He flashed a cocky half-smile and gestured to the perfect triangle of balls.

"Your break."

He watched Hailey bend over, pushing her ass in the air and giving a little wiggle. The glance she gave over her shoulder told him it was a less than subtle attempt at seduction. Like all her other attempts to grab his interest lately, it failed, yet he winked to reassure her, and she turned back to the game.

Hailey didn't have the same level of skill as he did on the table, but she was damn good, so he wasn't surprised when she cleared nearly all her balls before he had a shot. He hit the three ball in first, and the cue ball glanced off the eight, sinking it and ending the game.

Not used to losing, Hailey gave a little pout. She took her time racking the balls, and as she lined up her next shot, his attention wandered.

Cora sat with a woman he vaguely recognized. He tried to place her, but nothing clicked. They must have been deep in conversation, because when Josh appeared at their table, neither of them looked up. At least not until Josh placed his hands on Cora's shoulders and slid them down her arms.

Gavin's grip on the cue stick tightened as Cora tossed her head back and laughed up at Josh. Before he even realized what he was doing, he was walking over there.

"What are you doing?" he asked Josh, who now sat with the two women.

His brother stared up at him confusion, wrinkling his brow. "I'm having a drink. What are you doing?"

"Aren't you working?"

"Finished my shift ten minutes ago, so I thought I'd

hang with my favorite girl."

Gavin's eyes narrowed, and he glared at his brother, his fists itching. Josh might look a little on the scrawny side, but he possessed the same iron-fisted strength Gavin did. It wasn't often Gavin had an opportunity to fight, and Josh was always game to exchange blows, but Gavin knew his anger would give him an edge that could cost him his control. That knowledge was enough to convince him to step back.

Josh peered around Gavin. "There a reason you're playing boss?"

"Nah, just making sure you're not making an ass of yourself," he said with a smirk.

"I think you covered that for him," Cora's friend said, and Gavin turned his gaze to study her.

Up close, he got the sense again that he should recognize her, but still couldn't figure it out. She was on the plain side with her mousy brown hair, although her big hazel eyes were pretty.

"You remember Eve?" Cora motioned to her friend. "She went to high school with us."

"Ah, I thought I recognized you."

"That's okay, I don't think we ever had any classes together."

Unless she was a couple years older than Cora, they wouldn't have. He and Caleb only attended the high school for a year before they were on their way to college. The time they did spend there had been in advanced classes with the seniors despite being three years younger.

Cora giggled, and the three of them turned to stare at her.

"I just got it," Cora said, clearly experiencing the effects of her drinks.

"Got what?" Josh asked.

"Eve called Gavin an ass." She laughed again and took a sip of her drink.

Gavin frowned. "What are you drinking?"

"Bahama Mama Mama." She lifted her drink to toast him, and it waved dangerously close to his face.

"You know those are triple shots, right?"

She gave Josh a mock-angry look. "You didn't tell me that."

"Hey, I warned you they were deadly."

She nodded. "You're right. You did. Now if you boys would please leave. I am here to catch up with Eve, and we don't want to be distracted by your gorgeous faces."

"All right, we're going," Josh said. He stood up and slapped Gavin on the back. "I've got a hot date, and you've got a pissed off bitch."

Gavin twisted around to see Hailey shooting daggers at him with her eyes from across the floor.

"Shit." He stomped off, ignoring the sound of laughs and a sweet, slightly-drunken giggle behind him.

He gave Hailey a shrug. "Sorry. Needed to ask Josh something."

Judging by her narrow-eyed glare, she didn't buy it, but he wasn't about to explain the real reason he'd gone over there. He wasn't even sure he could explain it.

"If you have something better to do ..." she said, her words trailing off.

"No. I'm here." He drained his beer then ran a hand over his mouth. "I'm gonna grab another, do you want one?"

He didn't wait for her answer. Hailey was always up for another drink. When he got back with the beers, all was forgotten, and she challenged him to another game.

For the next hour, he tried to focus on Hailey and the pool table. Not the easiest task. Despite her short shorts, Hailey held no interest for him, and pool didn't take much concentration.

Making it even harder was the fact that Josh's date must have fallen through and he was back at Cora's table—she obviously found him more amusing than possible. Even then, she was leaning into his brother, and it took everything in Gavin to not storm over there and drag Josh away from her.

A cue stick slammed into his chest, and he looked down at Hailey. Somehow, he'd missed seeing her standing right in front of him. If he thought she'd been pissed earlier, it was nothing compared to the expression she wore then.

"Do I look freakin' stupid?" she asked. Guessing it was a rhetorical question, he kept his mouth shut. "I don't do games."

"What?"

"Look, Gavin, I like what we've got. It's fun. No strings. But I'm not sticking around if you're spreading it around."

"What does that mean?" He had no clue what she was talking about.

"It means I'm not gonna play second to Cora, and I'm sure as hell not gonna stand here and be ignored." She tossed her hair over her shoulder and straightened her back. "Give me a call when you're done with your little waitress."

Denial was on the tip of his tongue, but he held it in, recognizing it for the lie it was. He wanted Cora. As fucked up as it was to want the woman responsible for destroying his life, he wanted her with a fierceness he'd never felt before.

Hailey snorted at his lack of response and snagged her coat from the hook on the wall. His eyes followed her path to the exit before returning to Cora.

He remembered when he first met her back in high school. She'd been so little, especially standing next to Lela. In so many ways, the two of them had been opposites.

Lela had been tall and slender, with an outgoing and headstrong personality that drew him to her the instant they met. She never sat back and waited for someone to speak for her. Cora, on the other hand, had been a tiny blond mouse, blending into the background so much he sometimes never even noticed her presence.

Staring at her now, he wanted to still see Cora as that young girl. He didn't want to think of her as the person responsible for Lela's death, and he sure as hell didn't want to see her as a sexy woman whose husky moans left his body aching.

"See you finally managed to shake loose from Hailey," Noah said as he approached the end of the table.

Gavin grunted and reached out to roll the last few balls into pockets, clearing the surface.

Noah propped his shoulder along the wall, crossing his arms. Already a big guy, the pose made him appear even bulkier. It would be normal if he actually needed to work out, but thanks to the Posthuman Project, working out wasn't something any of them needed to do.

"You want to talk about it?"

"Fuck no. Hailey's fine."

"I'm not talking about Hailey. I'm talking about Cora and this silent battle the two of you are in. I understand you've got your issues with her, but you can't keep raking her over for what happened." He waited for Gavin to say something, but when he was met with silence, he turned on his heel and went back to Alicia.

Gavin scraped a hand over his face, letting out a sigh of defeat. If only it were that simple. If it was only a matter of blame, he could handle it, maybe one day even get over it. Noah was right; Gavin was in a battle, and it was one he couldn't win. No matter what he did about Cora, things were gonna get fucked up.

He grabbed his beer and walked over to where she sat with Eve and Josh. When he sat beside her, the three of them briefly glanced at him, and he gave them a terse smile. Eve and Cora went back to talking while Josh was busy giving Gavin a knowing smirk.

Gavin sat there, listening to the two women share memories of high school. Some of the things they talked about were familiar, stories he'd heard from Lela only with a different perspective.

"Do you remember the time Terrance Melton toilet papered the teacher's lounge?" Eve asked.

"No." Cora shook her head and squinted as if searching for the memory. "When was that?"

"Eleventh grade. Wait, it might have been when you were in—" Eve's words were cut off by the chiming of a text message alert. She checked her message, her lips tightening as she read it. "I've gotta go. Jamie's dad got called into work and needs me to pick Jamie up."

"That sucks," Cora said, scrunching up her face.

Gavin couldn't help the slight chuckle that escaped him. Sober Cora never scrunched her nose, and this new beyond tipsy Cora was cute.

"Yeah, that sucks, Evie." Josh gave an exaggerated pout.

Eva gave Cora a hug then slugged Josh on the arm. "Keep calling me Evie, and I'll hit you harder than that."

"All right, no more Evie." He held up his hands. "Promise."

"Sure," she said with mock-belief and grabbed her jacket.

"You're not driving, are you?" Gavin studied her, trying to determine how intoxicated she was.

"I'm fine. I've been nursing my first." She dropped a bill on the table. "I'll give you a call next week, Cora, and we can figure out a day to go for lunch."

She left behind an uncomfortable silence, broken only when Gavin kicked Josh under the table.

"Hey!" Josh leaned down to rub his shin, glaring at Gavin. A brief staring contest ensued until his eyes widened in understanding. "I need to check with Noah about the schedule. I'll catch you guys later."

Cora finished her drink and twirled the cocktail straw around the empty glass. Her entire demeanor change once she was alone with Gavin. Her giggles were gone, and she avoided his gaze.

"Cora—"

"We shouldn't talk," she said.

"About what?"

"About Anything. Lela, Hailey, you ... me." She squeezed her eyes shut and shook her head, sending her curls fluttering across her face. "Talking between us doesn't work."

Her eyes opened, settling on him, and the sorrow he found in their blue depths made his chest ache.

"Then what does work?"

"Nothing."

"Both of us know that's not true," he said, wondering if she could deny how right it had felt to be pressed against each other, feeding the embers of lust to a degree he'd never experienced before.

"We definitely shouldn't talk about *that*." She threw the straw onto the table.

Six weeks before, he would have agreed. Now, though ... He knew how she tasted, how snugly she fit into him. As much as he wanted to go back, he couldn't.

"Maybe that's *all* we need to talk about."

Her struggle played across her face in the tightening and relaxing of her lips, the way her cheeks warmed to a soft pink.

"You both good for another?" Keeley stopped at the edge of the table. He hated the escape she provided Cora.

"I'm done," Cora replied and handed Keeley the cash to cover her tab.

"Put her stuff on my tab," Gavin said. He didn't worry about paying, a bonus of being a brother to the owners. He was certain Logan kept track so one day he could collect for some huge ass favor.

Cora looked about to refuse, but changed her mind and gave Keeley a grin. "Then consider it all a tip."

Keeley rolled her eyes and said, "That only works if I don't know what you're getting paid, girl."

She pulled out a ten and passed the rest back to Cora. Then she turned to Gavin, leaning in and poking him in the chest with a sparkly, blue manicured finger.

"I'm trusting you."

He didn't ask what she meant. He didn't need to.

"How are you getting home?" he asked Cora when Keeley had gone.

She kicked up her feet. "These boots were made for walking."

"Alone at this time of night?"

"Phff. It's Thompson Creek."

He thought of the pictures of Sinclair Caleb found on the surveillance cameras. She wasn't the one Sinclair was after, but her connection to him and his brothers made her a possible target.

"I'll walk you home." He stood, looking down at her gaping face.

"What? Why?"

"Because it's dark and you're drunk."

"I'm not drunk. I only had ... three Bamamamamas."

"Yeah, three triples. More than enough. Let's go."

Out came the cute little pout. "Fine, but not because you said so."

She rose and walked to the door, leaving him to pick up the purse she'd forgotten and follow her outside. When he caught up with her, she stopped and spun around to face him.

"You're really bossy. You can't tell me what we need to talk about."

"I merely suggested that maybe we need to talk about what happened today."

"No. We don't need to talk about it. That'll only make me think about it." She started walking again, only to turn around a few feet away. She stomped toward him. "You made me go the wrong way."

He held up his hands. "I don't even know where you live."

"I know. You don't know anything about me." She took her purse from him.

"Not true," he said, walking beside her. "I know lots of things about you."

"Okay. Give me the top five Cora facts."

"Top Cora facts? Is that what you have for me? Top Gavin facts?"

"Five. You pretend you're a loner, but you really like being with people. Four. You're super smart, and if you weren't so determined to waste away, you'd be working at TanTech with Caleb. Three. Your brothers are your best friends, even when you complain about them. Two. You look at me and see everything that went wrong with your life."

She picked up her pace, and he was surprised at how quickly her short legs ate up the distance.

"You forgot one," he said.

"One. You don't know anything about me, or the person I am, or what I've done."

He grasped her hand, slowing her until she stopped and glared up at him with defiance that did little to conceal the hurt she attempted to hide beneath it.

"I know you better than you think." He pressed a finger to her lips when she would have protested. "Five. You are an amazing artist, but don't have the confidence to pursue it. Four. Your move to Denver was less about the job than about running away.

He tugged her closer and dipped his head down to whisper in her ear. "Three. You love the feel of my breath on your skin."

She shivered in response and his tongue peeked out to moisten the sensitive spot below her ear.

"Two. You want me."

He covered her lips with his, and she let his tongue slip inside. The flavor of the Bahama Mamas had lingered, blending with the sweet taste that was Cora. It also served to remind him that she'd had way too much to drink. He broke the contact of their mouths and rested his forehead against hers.

"One. You would do anything for your friends."

Her hands, which at some point had snuck between them and curled into his shirt, now shoved him away.

"That just proves how you *don't* know me," she said. She wobbled a moment before steadying herself and crossed the street. They passed the bookstore, and she opened a door in serious need of a new paint job. "This is my place."

"So which one are you denying?"

"I'm not denying any of them." She went into the small foyer and glanced back at him. "I would have done anything for Lela. I'd never have done anything to hurt her."

"I know."

"Yet, you think I killed her," she accused.

He stepped up and gripped the sides of the door frame. "I think you made a stupid mistake. Driving drunk—"

She pushed his chest again, cutting him off.

"Well ... *screw you,*" she yelled. "I wasn't driving."

Her words were a fist to his chest, slamming the air from his lungs.

SIX

CORA TRUDGED UP THE narrow staircase, ensuring she kept a firm grasp on the railing as the steps seemed to waver under her feet. When she got to the top, she glanced back down to see Gavin standing frozen in the entryway to the building.

The dim light in the foyer lit up his blond-streaked hair but cast long shadows across his face, concealing his features. She wasn't certain she wanted to see him. She wanted to sleep until she was strong enough to forget the sensation of his lips on hers.

"Good night, Gavin," she said and entered her apartment, quietly closing the door behind her.

She made her way across the living room area and flopped onto the couch, exhaustion finally hitting her. What had possessed her to go out? She should have vegged out in front of the TV and caught up on *Criminal Minds* episodes. Now, she was going to suffer the hangover from hell.

Lifting a leg high into the air, she ran her hand along the smooth black leather. She adored those boots. They made her three inches taller and were sexy as hell. She pulled down the zipper and undertook the task of wiggling her foot out. She'd managed to get the left one off when there was a knock on the door. Maybe she would ignore it. Then again, she couldn't remember locking the door. With one boot still on, she hobbled toward the door.

Gavin didn't wait for her. He'd flung the door open, stepped inside, and slammed it shut before she even made it halfway across the room. A scowl wrinkled her face as she tried forming some sort of reprimand about knocking, but he did knock, and she couldn't come up with anything else.

"What the fuck do you mean, you weren't driving?" His voice was deceptively soft. She recognized the anger and confusion in his hard eyes. "I came to you. I asked you to explain what happened. You told me you were driving."

"No. *You* said I was. Forget it. Don't listen to me. I'm drunk," she said and stumbled back to the couch.

Why didn't she listen to Josh when he told her the drinks were deadly? Her mind and mouth refused to cooperate and work together. She never intended to tell Gavin about the accident, but she been unable to hold it back any longer.

"That's a bullshit excuse." He jutted a finger in her direction, and her eyes crossed as she attempted to follow the waving digit. "You were driving that night. Lela wouldn't drive drunk."

"But I would?"

That shut him up. She wondered if he realized that if everything he claimed to know about her was true, how could he explain her doing something like that?

Cora tipped her head back and stared at the ceiling tiles tinted yellow with age. They were old and tired. Just like her continued determination to play the villain in Gavin's mind. She didn't want to be blamed for something she hadn't done. She'd made plenty of mistakes that night, but driving drunk wasn't one of them.

"We were so happy. Four years at college and we were finally done," Cora said, her lips curling into a smile as the bittersweet memory took over. "We spent the whole evening dancing and drinking. Or I did. Lela knew I hated driving at night, so she only had a couple because she planned to drive back. She wanted you to come so you could drive."

"I would have gone, but she told me it was a girls' night."

"Because I didn't have a date, and she didn't want me to feel left out" Cora's head rolled along the back of the couch. "Did you know she couldn't dance?"

"I knew," he answered.

"Of course, you did. Dancing was the only thing she couldn't do perfectly."

"There were others," he said. "She just didn't let it stop her from doing them."

"Maybe, but that night, she learned to line dance. I taught her the Electric Slide. She said she was going to take you dancing and surprise you."

She paused and gazed at Gavin. Her stomach heaved, and she really regretted that third drink. Two she could have handled, but the more she drank, the more she talked. This conversation was the prime example. It was a conversation she'd never planned on, but keeping the words trapped inside of her became impossible.

"What happened, Cora?" His voice cracked on her name.

"Right before we hit the bridge, some idiot almost rear-ended us. I got so mad. Lela told me to calm down. She was going to let him pass, but I rolled down my window and gave him the finger." She squeezed her trembling hands into fists. "He rammed us, and Lela lost control."

Gavin's fingers plowed through his hair, clenching the ends tightly before he took a deep breath. His mouth gaped as if he couldn't form all of the questions racing through him.

"Why didn't you tell me? Why did you let me believe you'd been driving? That you caused the accident?"

"Because it wouldn't change anything. I'm still the reason Lela died. The guy hit us because of me. The car filled with water so quickly because I opened my window. Lela drowned because I was too drunk to get her out."

He didn't say anything, and she took the silence for agreement. It was hard to argue with those facts.

"I couldn't even get myself out," she said.

"What do you mean? They found you on the bank of the river."

"Someone driving by spotted the car in the water. He pulled me out, but by the time he got to Lela, it was already too late."

He straightened and moved forward so swiftly; Cora held up a hand, worried she would lose her balance and somehow he would fall on her. Or was it him lose his balance? Either way, he was moving too fast.

He went to his knees before her and gripped her

shoulders. Her eyes widened, trying to adjust to the new close-up view of his face.

"What do you mean, someone?" He shook her gently, and her head spun at the way his face danced before her eyes.

"Someone. A person."

"Who?"

"I don't know. I passed out after."

Passed out. The words didn't accurately describe falling into a two-week coma. If she'd been sober, she might have described it differently, but even the police referred to it as passing out.

"Did you tell the police about any of this? The guy who rammed you? The person who stopped to help?"

"They said I suffered head trauma. That I might not be remembering right. There was nothing they could do even if I were right."

"Why didn't you tell me? I would have believed you."

"Like you believed I'd drive drunk?"

His lips tightened, and he let go of her shoulders. An overwhelming sense of sadness filled her. *How could she blame him for believing the worst of her?* She'd let him. She never once challenged him on any detail about the accident.

Lifting a hand, she cupped his face in her palm, in part to connect with him, and partly to stop the back and forth movements his head made.

"It doesn't matter. She's gone, and you hate me."

She stood and walked to her bedroom, using the wall to stop her from falling over. There was something seriously wrong with the floor; it slanted to one side. She fell backward on the bed, her legs hanging over the edge. She saw Gavin standing in the doorway, watching her.

"I don't hate you, Cora."

She wanted to believe him so badly. When he held her in his arms, everything disappeared. Everything except the feel of his hard body and the taste of him. There was no anger or shame, only passion. Yet, those fleeting moments did little to dispel the truth.

"Lela wouldn't want me to," he said.

"She used to talk about you all the time. She loved you. Really loved you." A massive yawn escaped her, and she let her drooping eyelids to close. "I hated listening to her talk about you. I didn't want to hear. I just wanted to pretend."

"You should have told me," he said.

She snorted but didn't bother opening her eyes. "It's easier this way."

"What's easier?"

"Protecting you."

Cora talked in her sleep. Nothing coherent, simply a soft mumbling mix of words and phrases that made no sense. Whatever her dreams held, it wasn't peace.

Gavin pressed his back to the wall and slid down to sit on the floor, attempting to process everything she told him. *How much of it was truth, and how much was the ramblings of a woman who'd had too much?*

Her story made sense. It fit with the Cora he knew. So why the hell didn't she ever told him he was wrong?

God when he thought of all the horrible things he'd said to her; the things he'd thought— He felt sick.

She tried to roll over, but her dangling legs hindered

her. He gave a slight smile as he took in the one remaining boot she obviously forgot to remove. He rose and walked to the bedside. After unzipping the boot, he slid it off and tossed it to the corner of the room out of the way.

Staring down at her, he contemplated what to do next. It was obvious he wouldn't get any more answers from her.

He tugged her up until her head rested on the pillow. He considered putting the covers over her, but that would require him somehow moving her off them first. She was light enough he could easily lift her without waking her, but he decided that bordered on being a creepy invasion of her personal space. Strange thought, considering less than an hour before he had his tongue in her mouth and his hands on her ass. But she was out of it, and that was a line he didn't cross.

He went into the living area and scanned the small space. Her place wasn't what he'd expected. He'd expected fluffy, colorful furniture, pictures of her family, and a homey atmosphere. This place with its bare walls and simple furnishings lacked the warmth he always associated with her. He found a crocheted quilt folded up on the floor at the end of the couch and picked it up.

After he laid the quilt over Cora, he went to the small kitchenette and poured a glass of water. He gulped the water and rinsed out the glass, leaving it in the sink to dry. With a heavy sigh, he braced his hands on the counter and let his head drop.

He needed a beer or whiskey. Fuck, he'd take anything to block out the echoes of every nasty word he'd said to Cora. Locking the door behind him, he headed back down to the street toward the pub. With every step, he played back the pieces of Cora's story.

It made sense Lela would be driving that night. The idea of her getting in the car with a drunk driver, or of Cora making the choice to drive drunk, had always been a detail that never meshed with what he knew about either woman.

It was all the new details that didn't fit. *Who was the other driver? The stranger who stopped to help? Why the hell hadn't the police done any follow-up?*

Fury snapped at Gavin's control, propelling his body toward survival mode. His muscles contracted and then snapped back, expanding and straining his skin. His eyes darted around, pinpointing minute details, and he inhaled deeply as he instinctively assessed the area for danger.

Yet natural instinct had nothing to do with it. His body's response to a perceived enemy and the accompanying rage were all by design. The Posthuman Project had made them the perfect soldiers. They blended in with the general population, appearing normal, then transformed into a monster when the enemy neared. Their muscles enlarged, magnifying the superior strength they already possessed. The more uncontrolled they became, the more pronounced the physical changes were.

He slammed his fist into the brick wall of the building he'd stopped beside. The brick crumbled around his knuckles, and he pulled back to shake off the dust. The force of the impact would have broken the bones of a normal human, yet the mild stinging Gavin experienced was merely an annoyance and did little to relieve his frustration. Yet, it gave him a moment's pause to pull himself back from the brink.

He dragged in another slow breath and let his senses reassure him of the absence of danger. He reined in the anger prodding at him and focused his thoughts back on Cora.

She claimed she reported everything to the police, but he read the reports months before, and there'd been nothing in there about another car or anyone rendering aide. Even if they doubted every word she said, there should have been some mention of her version in the file.

A block from the bar, he pulled out his cell and dialed Noah's number.

"Did you know?" Gavin asked when his brother answered.

"Gavin? I can't hear you. Let me go outside." There was a pause as Noah exited the bar. "What's up?"

"Did you know?"

"About what?"

"Did you know Cora wasn't driving the night of the accident?"

Gavin heard Noah sighing on the other end of the line, and he wanted to reach through and rip his brother's heart out.

"How long have you known?" He gritted his teeth as adrenaline tensed his muscles. The urge to succumb to the monster festered within him.

"Since she came out of the coma. I listened to her give her statement."

"Why the fuck didn't you tell me?"

"Would it have mattered? And don't just say yes. Think about it. You were so angry at the world afterward. You wanted someone to blame. You *needed* to blame someone. Some faceless stranger wasn't going to cut it. You wanted to see the guilt. So, Cora let that be her."

"What I fucking needed was the truth."

"You weren't ready for the truth."

"That wasn't your call," Gavin snapped. "How the fuck are we going to find this guy now?"

"Find who, Gavin? Cora couldn't even give a description of the vehicle let alone the driver. There's not any evidence to even start looking."

"What about the person who stopped to help? They might have seen something."

"You don't think we looked? It's a dead end."

"We? Who else knew about this?"

"The family and Merrick." Not surprising; their family didn't keep secrets from each other.

Gavin rounded the side of the bar and came face to face with Noah, who stood just outside the entrance of Porter's. He hung up and shoved the phone into his back pocket.

"We looked into it," Noah said. "Merrick pulled every piece of surveillance footage he could get his hands on to see if someone followed them. Dad and I questioned every possible lead, but it was weeks too late."

"We could have gone to the media, offered a reward. Something." The ache of helplessness settled inside his chest.

"The cops advised us against that."

Gavin stared at his brother, shocked. He couldn't believe they'd roll over for the cops without some good reason.

"You let Lela's killer get away with this because the cops told you to back off?"

"There wasn't anything else we could do."

Believing his brother would have been so much easier if Noah would have looked at him. Instead, Noah gazed off to the side.

"That's bullshit. You're hiding something."

Noah ran a hand down his face, rubbing his short beard and then craned his head to the side until there was a crack from his neck.

"Sinclair. He was the guy Cora saw on the river bank. We think he or one of his lackeys also forced them off the road."

Gavin's stomach clenched, and he almost hurled right there in the street. Instead, his fist swung out and landed a solid punch on Noah's jaw.

Noah's head snapped back, and he stumbled a few steps to the side. When he steadied himself, he lifted a hand and touched the spot where Gavin had made contact.

"Two minutes ago it was a dead end. No evidence. Too late. And now it's Sinclair? How the fuck did you decided to keep this from me?"

"This wasn't my call," Noah said. "It was too late for the cops to find anything. Merrick and Caleb, on the other hand, weren't bound by the need for warrants. It took a couple months for them to find anything."

"That doesn't explain why I wasn't told."

"You needed time to heal. To get past losing Lela."

Gavin clenched his fists, every ounce of his being wanted to pummel Noah or anyone in his way.

"Who decided?"

"Gavin ..."

"Who?"

"Mom."

He spun around and strode through the parking lot to his Jeep, ignoring Noah's calls.

Of course, Mom made the call. She was the boss. From the moment the five of them walked into that house, the pecking order was established. Everyone shared their opinion, they even got a vote, but Sarah Walker had the final say.

This time, though, she'd been wrong.

The overwhelming desire to go to the house and confront her pulsed through him, yet he realized it would be pointless. He drove around aimlessly, making it almost to Billings before turning around. He pulled off the main highway onto the back road to town. He slowed to a crawl before eventually coming to a stop at the entrance to Thompson Creek Bridge.

He got out of the car and walked out to the middle of the bridge. With his forearms resting on the wooden barrier, he peered over the side at the water below. At that time of year, the creek was shallow from the hot temperatures, only a few feet of muddy water concealed the rocky bottom, nothing like in the spring when rainwater and mountain runoff caused it to surge to a couple meters deep.

His head dropped into his heads and his shoulders jerked.

Where did he go from here?

SEVEN

THE MORNING SUNLIGHT STREAMED through the thin curtains and Cora reached across the counter to drop the blinds. It might have been almost nine in the morning, and she might have been up for over an hour, but with her raging hangover, it was way too early to be so bright.

She took a sip from her glass of orange juice, then poured the rest down the sink as the acidic liquid settled uneasily in her stomach. Definitely not what she needed.

Glancing around her apartment, she contemplated what she would do with the day. Working full time and then spending her spare time at the pub watching over Gavin left her with a pretty sad personal life.

Every vision she'd had with Sinclair showed him making his move in the evening, so there was no need to torture herself all day. She needed to do something other than stew.

Her gaze fell on the long forgotten sketchbook wedged into the top shelf of her bookcase. She wandered over, tugged it free and leafed through the pages of her work.

They were a documentation of her artistic growth since

her brother first gave her the book for Christmas eight years before. There were the standard still lifes and portraits, but her favorites were the fantasy-based sketches she'd done of mythical beasts.

The sketches trailed off during her time in college and finally stopped after Lela's death. She loved art, but day-to-day life took over, and she'd been busy with her job at the museum.

She closed the sketch book and tossed it onto the coffee table. Going to the bedroom closet, she searched through boxes for her art pencils, but couldn't find them. She'd need to go to the art supply store in Billings for a new set.

She grabbed her cell and dialed her brother's number.

"What's up?" Darren asked when he picked up.

"Hello to you, too."

"Forgive me, Coraline, dearest sister of mine. How is your health?"

"I'm fine, thanks for asking."

"Oh, you know me. Your health and well-being are my top priority."

"Yeah, sure." She did know him, and that meant he was focused on his work, and she was lucky he even bothered picking up. She went to the front closet, and wedging the phone between her ear and shoulder, slipped on her sneakers. "How are things going?"

"I'm doing good. Went up to Mom and Dad's place last week. Mom said you were busy and haven't been up to see them in a while."

"I've been working. Besides, I don't trust my car to make it up the mountain."

Their parents lived in Thompson Creek until Cora finished school, but shortly after she moved to Denver, they bought a new place in the mountains. She'd gone for a visit once, and her car had barely made the trip—no way she would risk it again. It was a convenient excuse that she was more than ready to use.

"So? What's up?" her brother asked.

"I'm heading into Billings and hoped we might be able to meet up for lunch."

"I'd love to, but I've already got plans. How about next week?"

"I'm working," she said. "I could maybe do Thursday?"

"Yeah, sure. Give me a call on Wednesday to remind me, K?"

They chatted for a few more minutes before hanging up. Cora finished tying her shoes then grabbed her keys and purse. It wasn't until she got into her car that she began debating whether it was even worth the drive.

She could probably find a set of pencils online and save the gas money. Not that Billings was far away, but it was a trip she didn't like to make. Going to Billings meant going past the Thompson Creek Bridge unless she took the longer route, but the idea of sitting in her apartment all day reliving her conversation with Gavin was just too much. She needed to clear her head, and she couldn't do that in her apartment.

What she didn't expect was to find Gavin's car at the entrance to the bridge. She pulled up behind and parked, scanning the bridge. For a moment, panic set in when she didn't see him, and she wondered if she should be searching the water, but as Cora got out of her car, she saw him sitting on the hood of his Jeep.

"Gavin?" She walked quickly around to the front of the car. "Are you okay?"

He didn't say anything, simply sitting there staring straight ahead. He wore the same clothes he'd been wearing the night before. The stubble along his jaw and his red-rimmed eyes confirmed he hadn't even been home. *Had he been here all night?*

"Gavin?" She laid her hand on his arm, and he jerked in response as if just noticing her presence.

"Hey. What are you doing out here?"

"I'm going into Billings for the day. Have you been here all night?"

He glanced around possibly realizing night had long since passed. "Yeah, I guess. I just ... I needed to think, and this place ..."

"Come on," she said, taking his hand in hers. "I'll drive you home."

"No, no. I'm okay."

"Gavin, there's no way you're okay to drive. You haven't slept all night."

"I'm not ready to go yet," he said. "I'll call one of my brothers to come pick me up in a while."

He looked so lost. She wanted to say something—*anything*—to comfort him, but there wasn't anything to make it right. *If she hadn't*—Cora pressed her lips together. She couldn't think like that, not anymore. Gavin deserved the truth, and telling him what actually happened was something she should have done a long time ago. But she wasn't alone; his family had known what happened, and they made the choice not to tell his as well.

"All right," she said. "But you need to promise you'll call someone."

"I promise."

She gave his arm a gentle squeeze then went back to the car. She sat there a moment before eventually driving off. A few miles down the road, she pulled over and took out her cell phone.

"Hello?" Noah answered.

"Hey, it's Cora."

"Everything okay?"

"Yeah. Well, not really. Gavin ..."

"Yeah, I talked to him last night. Did he go back to your place?"

"No." Cora sighed. "He's at the bridge. I think he's been there all night. I offered him a ride, but he won't go."

"I'll come and get him."

After hanging up, Cora turned the vehicle around and drove to the top of a small hill that crested before the bridge. She could make out Gavin still perched atop his Jeep. She waited until she saw Noah's car drive up, and then satisfied Gavin was safe, she made her way to Billings.

The entire drive, she kept thinking about Gavin struggling to make sense of what he'd learned. She fought against the urge to go back and see him. There was nothing she could do now. If anything, she'd done too much already.

She reached the edge of Billings and tried to get her bearings. She'd only been into the city once since moving back. It wasn't difficult to do. Compared to Denver,

Billings was a small town. When she first returned to Thompson Creek, she'd anticipated missing the bustle of the big city. She'd grown accustomed to all the conveniences that came along with the metropolitan area. Now, after a few months in Thompson Creek, Billings was more than big enough.

Using an app on her phone, she found the new art supply store nestled in-between two jewelry shops downtown. A string of bells hanging from the door jingled lightly as she entered. She inhaled deeply, loving the odor of paint and other raw materials. Some people might have found it overwhelming, but for Cora, she loved the flood of memories it brought back.

She took her time wandering around, her mind racing as she visualized all the pieces she could work on. The temptation to grab a basket and completely fill it with paints, brushes, and charcoal and graphite pencils was almost too strong to resist.

As much as she wanted to dive back into her art, she knew her wallet couldn't afford it. Rather than torturing herself anymore, she went over to the graphite pencils and looked for her favorite brand.

After a brief chat with the store clerk about the benefits of various sketchbook paper, she made her purchase and headed to the mall for lunch.

An hour later, she sat in the food court eating her lunch. The greasy cheese pizza wasn't the best thing for her diet, but with such limited choices she figured she may as well enjoy what she was going to eat.

Her eyes flitted around the tables as she sipped at her drink then choked when she spotted Hailey. She groaned as the other woman noticed her and moved toward her.

For the past few months, she and Hailey had obeyed an unspoken agreement not to interact with each other at all costs. Unspoken because they didn't speak to each other. Cora considered her options; she could bail on her lunch but then she be hungry on the drive home, or she could wait and see how bitchy Hailey wanted to be.

"Mind if I sit?" Hailey placed her tray on the table and pulled out the chair across from Cora. "Thanks."

Cora arched a brow and continued eating. Maybe if she ignored her, the other woman would simply disappear. That, however, would require luck, and lately, it didn't seem like Cora had any of that.

"This place is so sad," Hailey said as she unwrapped her soft taco and proceeded to pour hot sauce on it before rolling it back up. "Every time I come here, it reminds me why I do most of my shopping online."

"Mmhmm." Cora ripped off a piece of her crust and dipped it into the small container of jalapeno ranch sauce.

"You don't like me, do you?"

Cora looked at the other woman. "I don't know you enough to not like you."

Hailey made a disbelieving noise. "God, don't you ever get tired of being so prissy?"

"Any reason in particular that you're sitting here?" Cora glared at Hailey.

"I thought we should talk," Hailey said. "I mean, we both got the hots for the same guy. Maybe we need to decide who gets him when."

"What are you talking about?" Cora's cheeks flooded with heat. It was a stupid question to ask. She knew what

Haley was talking about, or rather *who* she was talking about.

"Please." Hailey rolled her eyes and not for the first time. Cora wondered how she could see through so much mascara. "I've seen you watching him. He may not have noticed yet but trust me everyone else has."

"Gavin and I ..."

"Are friends?" She leaned over the table. "Yeah, I think we both know that friendship isn't what you and Gavin have. Try again."

Cora pursed her lips and let her eyes wander the food court. This was not the conversation she wanted to have with Hailey. And definitely not right then. With all the crap that went down the night before with Gavin ...

"He's a good guy," Hailey said. "But he's got some serious issues. If you let him, he'll hurt you."

"I've known him for a long time," Cora said.

"That has nothing to do with it. We both know that he's still dealing with what happened to Lela."

Cora snorted. "So what? You're warning me away from him because you think I might get hurt? Or because you want him for yourself?"

"See? That's the difference between you and me. I know exactly where I stand with Gavin. We have a good time, we hook up, and that's it. You want something more."

"And you don't?"

Hailey laughed. "If he was offering, yeah sure, I'd take more, but that's not what he's offering. To either of us."

The pity reflected in Hailey's eyes had Cora squirming in her chair. She did want more, and if she was honest, she was jealous of what little Hailey had with him.

"I'm giving you fair warning that as long as he's offering something, I'm willing to take it," Hailey said. "Now, if the two of you start hooking up, I'm out."

Cora studied Hailey. She'd always taken her at face value, never thinking about the person underneath the heavy makeup and bleached hair.

"Do you love him?" Cora asked.

"No, but that doesn't matter. He's sexy as hell and a good guy." One side of her mouth tipped up into a smile. "Don't tell me, you're one of those girls who thinks you only sleep with someone when you're in love? Oh my *God*. Are you a virgin?"

"No!"

"You are in love with him, though."

Hailey waited for her answer, but Cora wasn't prepared to admit or deny it.

"Fine, enjoy living in denial," Hailey said. "But be careful. He could hurt you, but I think you could hurt him just as badly, and if that happens, I won't play so nice."

With that, Hailey gathered her food back on her tray, picked it up, and found a new seat on the other side of the food court.

Cora finished the last few bites of her pizza and then tossed the garbage on her tray and dumped it into a nearby bin. She browsed at a few stores, picking up a couple new tops for work, and then headed back to her car.

On the way back home, Cora replayed the conversation she'd had with Hailey. She'd always considered Hailey to be a bitch, and then ... Well, maybe she still was, but somewhere in that conversation, Hailey had shown she wasn't the horrible person Cora expected.

As she turned off the highway to the rural road leading to Thompson Creek, she noticed the car behind her followed. In the rear-view mirror, she tried to see if she recognized the vehicle. Thompson Creek was well over six thousand, and if you included people in the unincorporated areas, it was closer to twenty so she couldn't claim to know everyone, but some cars stuck out in a rural area.

The car was generic enough, but something about it left her feeling uneasy. Something about it felt *off*.

The closer she got to home, the more frequent she checked her mirror. The car was still there, closer and her sense that something was off intensified. She considered pulling over, but if the person in the car intended to hurt her, that would only make her a sitting duck.

Behind her, the car closed the distance between them. She sped up, and so did the other vehicle. She went over the hill, and the bridge came into view. Her hands clenched the steering wheel as her stomach churned. Her foot pressed down on the gas, accelerating her toward the bridge.

She glanced again into the mirror. The driver behind her was so close she could make out his features. He was young, possibly in his mid-twenties, with dark hair and sunglasses. She'd never seen him before.

As she crossed over onto the bridge, it happened. He rammed into the back of her car. She lurched forward, jerking the steering wheel in response. Instinctively, her foot pressed down the accelerator, and she flew across the bridge, fear tearing through her.

He hit her again as she crossed the end of the bridge and the impact sent her careening into the ditch. The front of the car slammed into a tree, crumpling the hood. A loud bang filled the air, and something exploded, hitting her in the face.

Dazed, she straightened in her seat, coughing as some kind of dust or powder floated around her. Her door opened, and she tried to see who was there, but the dust and something dripping in her eyes blurred her vision. Whoever it was grabbed her arm in a painful grasp. She tried pulling away, but her seat belt kept her from moving. There was a sharp prick on her upper arm and then the hold was gone.

She turned off the car and then fumbled with the buckle until her seat belt popped free. She wiped her eyes, and her hand came away covered with blood. Gingerly scooting out of the car, she glanced around for the other vehicle, but whoever hit her was long gone.

Turning her attention to her car, a groan escaped her as she took in the crumpled hood. It was totaled, and she was a good ten miles from town. She was going to need a tow, and more than likely a ride to the hospital.

EIGHT

ADRENALINE IS A FUNNY thing. When the accident happened, it pumped through Cora's veins giving her the strength to get out of the car, to call 911, and to make it to the bridge where she sat on beside the railing. But as it faded, she'd been left utterly drained, unable to even lift her arm and flag down the ambulance as it approached. Three hours later, adrenaline had been replaced by the constant ache in her head.

"Did you manage to find anyone to come pick you up?" the nurse inquired.

Cora started to shake her head then thought better of it. "No, not yet."

She'd been trying her brother for the past thirty minutes, but it repeatedly went to voicemail. She left one message, keeping it light so he didn't freak out. He might not come across as the most caring brother in the world, but he'd picked up Mom's habit of panicking at the first hint of even a cold. The thought of calling her parents was even less appealing than having her brother come and hover over her.

"I'm going to try a friend," she said and smiled at the nurse.

Giving up on her brother, she dialed Keeley's number. It rang twice before Keeley picked up.

"Hey! Where are you?" Keeley yelled to be heard over the music playing in the bar. "I thought you were coming for drinks this afternoon?"

"I'm in Billings, at the hospital."

"*What*? Let me go in the back so I can hear you." The music faded as Keeley left the main floor of the bar. "What happened?"

"I was in an accident on my way home. I'm a bit banged up, but mainly bumps and bruises. My car's totaled, though. I was hoping Darren would be able to give me a ride home, but he's not answering. Would you be able to pick me up?"

Keeley cussed under her breath. "I can't. I've already had a couple beers. Let me check around and see if maybe Noah or Logan could come."

"Thanks."

In the background, Cora heard Keeley talking to someone. Whoever it was must've agreed to come get her because when Keeley came back on the line, she told Cora they'd be there in half an hour and take her to Keeley's apartment for the night.

When the nurse eventually came by again, Cora told her someone was on the way. A wheelchair was brought into the exam room, and despite her assurances that she was fine to walk, the nurse forced her into the chair, wheeling her down to the pick-up door.

Covering her eyes against the harsh glare of the

overhead lights, Cora waited inside the automatic door. Twenty minutes later, a vehicle pulled to a stop out front, and she lowered her hand. Her stomach took a flying leap upward before plunging down as she recognized Gavin's Jeep. She was going to kill Keeley for not telling her he was the one coming.

He climbed out of the Jeep and came around as she leveraged herself out of the wheelchair and through the door.

"Are you okay?" He leaned down to inspect her face. "Keeley said it was a car accident. What happened?"

"I ran off the road and hit a tree. I'm okay, just a little sore."

"Then why were you in a wheelchair?"

"Hospital policy. They wheel you in, they wheel you out." She moved toward the vehicle, and he pulled open the door for her, placing his hand on her elbow to help her up.

He climbed back in behind the wheel and turned to look at her. His eyes studied her, and she shifted self-consciously. She was a mess. Thanks to the bump her head took against the window, her entire face had been covered with blood when she got to the hospital. Even though she'd managed to wash most of it away, she was pretty sure it was still caked into her hair. It was definitely all over her shirt.

"So, what's with the bandage?" he gestured to her forehead.

Her hand lifted to trace her fingers over the edge of the large white bandage along her hairline. "Eight stitches and a headache."

"Is that the official diagnosis or your attempt to downplay it?"

"Yes, a headache. Happy?"

"Hardly. You could have a concussion. Didn't they want to keep you overnight?"

She carefully shook her head. "Nope. I need to keep an eye out for any kind of signs of a concussion, but otherwise, I'm good."

He looked skeptical and took the pamphlet she held up with the list of symptoms to watch out for. He scanned the list. "Half these things you can't even monitor yourself."

"Which is why you're dropping me off at Keeley's," she replied. "I'm spending the night there."

Looking partially pacified, he pulled away from the hospital and drove toward Thompson Creek. As the city streetlights disappeared into the distance, Cora sighed and leaned her still aching head against the headrest. Luckily, the pain meds the doctor had prescribed were kicking in and the pounding wasn't so bad.

"You going to tell me what happened?" he asked.

Cora hesitated. She didn't want to hide the truth from him again, but what happened that afternoon ... It was so similar to what happened with Lela, she just didn't know if it would even be believable. The cop who took her statement hadn't believed her. She wasn't even sure she believed it herself.

She glanced at Gavin's profile. For two years, she'd protected him from the endless wondering and questions of someone out there who would never be brought to justice, but by not telling him the truth, she only delayed his healing. Yet, when she found him that morning on the bridge, he'd been lost, trying to process everything all over again. Two years before, hearing the truth might have given him something to focus on, something to keep him moving—healing.

Hiding the details of her afternoon would only compound the problems she'd created.

"Someone ran me off the road," she said after a long pause.

The Jeep jerked to the side, and she grabbed the panic bar above the window, wincing at the twinge of pain that shot through her head. They slowed as Gavin pulled onto the shoulder. He put the vehicle in park and twisted in his seat to face her. His mouth moved, but nothing came out as if he was trying to figure out what to say but his mind was running too quickly to form a complete sentence.

"I went into Billings to do some shopping and have lunch." She decided against telling him about meeting Hailey. "On my way home, I noticed someone following behind me when I pulled onto the back road."

"So you saw the vehicle? If it was following you, why didn't you call someone?"

"At first, I thought they were simply going the same way. It's not like they had a sign on their hood saying criminal or asshole. They were just a boring sedan going the same direction."

"Okay, so you pulled off the highway, then what?" he asked impatiently.

"Right before the bridge, he tapped my bumper." Eyes squinting, she tried to recall the details. "My foot went down on the gas pedal, and I managed to get across the bridge. On the other side, the guy hit me again, and I lost control. I went into the ditch and slammed into a tree."

"You told the cops all of this, right?"

The question stung, but she couldn't really blame him for asking.

"I told them. Whether they believe me, well ... According to the officer who took my statement, it's all a bit too coincidental. Same bridge, same method."

"That's bullshit."

He slammed his palm against the steering wheel then flung open his door. He disappeared behind the vehicle, and she adjusted the mirror so she could she see him. He'd rested his forearms on the back window and pressed his forehead to the glass. Intense concentration lined his face as he squeezed his eyes shut.

She watched as he craned his head to the side, revealing the tensely corded muscles along his neck that seemed to pulse with each breath he took. He rolled his shoulders, and as he straightened up, she fixed the mirror and stared straight ahead.

"Is that it?" he asked as he got back in the Jeep.

His eyes drilled into her, and she realized she needed to tell him everything, no matter how strange it was.

"I banged my head pretty hard, but I remember my door being opened. I don't know if he was trying to pull me out or what, but he grabbed my arm and held it for a moment and then he was gone."

"Why would he do that?"

"I don't know, but ..." She rubbed her upper arm then rolled up her sleeve. A dot in the center of a small bruise confirmed her growing suspicion. "Oh God, I think he stuck me with a needle. Why would he do that? Should I go back to the hospital? Get them to do blood work?"

He rubbed his hand across his mouth and sighed.

"No, they can't do anything for you."

Her eyes widened. "What does that mean?"

"It means I know who did this."

"Who?"

"The same person who killed Lela." He stared back at her. "Sinclair."

"Sinclair? Why would he be trying to kill me?" she asked, confused.

"That probably wasn't his objective."

"Then what was he doing?"

"I guess that's the question. That, and what did he do to you the last time?"

Every instinct Gavin possessed screamed for him to immediately begin hunting Sinclair. The cop was right; it wasn't a coincidence. It was Sinclair. *But why the fuck would he target Cora?*

When Noah told him about Sinclair being involved in Lela's death, a suffocating weight had settled on his chest. The idea that her death was linked to SIEGE left him sick to his stomach because he knew Sinclair targeted her to get to him.

Going after Cora, though? It didn't make sense.

Her blue eyes watched him as he drove, and he wondered what she was thinking. He wished he could answer her questions, but most of them were the same as his own. For the moment, though, the questions of *why* didn't matter. The only thing they had to determine was when Sinclair would strike again.

"This isn't the way to Keeley's place," she said.

"I'm not taking you to Keeley's." He pulled into his parking spot in front of his apartment building.

"Why?"

He didn't answer her immediately. Instead, he got out and went around to the passenger side to open her door.

"Sinclair's targeted you," he said. "We don't know what he's gonna do or when he's gonna do it. Do you really want to take the chance that he'll make his move when you're at Keeley's? Get her hurt in the crossfire?"

"No, but—"

"You can stay here tonight, and we'll worry about tomorrow in the morning."

It wasn't until he was unlocking his front door that he realized that while this plan was the best alternative, it also meant that Cora was going to be in his apartment with him. Alone. His hand hesitated on the doorknob.

"What's wrong?" she asked.

Gavin cleared his throat. "Nothing. Just thinking."

He pushed open the door and flipped on the light before punching his code into the security alarm keypad. A quick glance around had him regretting that he hadn't taken the time to tidy up when Noah brought him home. Unlike the bare feel of her apartment, his was obviously inhabited. Dishes hadn't been done for a few days, and he had a habit of undressing in the living room.

"Come on in," he said and held the door open for her. "It's a bit of a mess, but ..."

A breathy laugh fluttered from her lips. "Would you be mad if I told you didn't expect anything less?"

A smile cracked his face as he locked the door behind them.

"How's your headache?" he asked.

"It's gone." Her fingers probed the bandage. "Do you mind if I clean up?"

"Yeah, sure. The bathroom's the door on the right."

At the door, she paused and glanced back at him. "Do you have a shirt I could use?"

"A shirt?" His forehead wrinkled, and she plucked at the front of her T-shirt, pointing out the bloodstains. "*Oh.* Yeah, let me grab one."

He brushed past her to go to his room and pulled a shirt from the closet. When he handed her the shirt, she took it and raised a brow looking from the shirt back to him.

"This explains a lot," she said. She held the shirt up in front of her, and he realized why she'd given him such a strange look. He snorted at the gag gift his brother had given him for his last birthday.

If you think my gun's big, you should see what I'm packing.

"You can thank Josh for that."

She clutched the material against her chest, and the movement drew his eyes to her breasts. The hallway seemed to shrink, the space between them reduced to a breath. The temptation to reach out and touch her left his hands clenched into fists at his sides.

Cora had just been through a traumatic car accident; she was covered in blood for God's sake. She didn't need him going all horny on her.

"Towels are under the sink." He reached around her and flicked on the bathroom light.

In the kitchen, he grabbed a beer out of the fridge and

cracked it open. From the bathroom came the sound of the shower running, bringing with it the image of Cora standing naked under the spray, water sliding down her chest only to catch on her nipples. His cock hardened, pressing uncomfortably against his zipper.

He was in hell.

Chugging his beer, he tried to put the image out of his mind. As he tossed the empty can in the garbage, his cell phone buzzed, and he pulled it from his pocket. Keeley's name was illuminated on the screen.

"What's up?" he asked.

"Where are you guys?"

"Change of plans. Cora's going to crash at my place."

There was a brief, stunned silence before Keeley ripped into him.

"What the hell do you mean she's crashing there? Boy, I know there's some kind of thing between the two of you—"

"There's not a thing between us," he denied.

"Yeah, whatever. She's just been an accident. She doesn't need you pawing at her."

"I'm not planning on touching her at all. There was something strange about the whole incident, and I figured it would be safer if she stayed here."

"What you mean strange?"

"It's probably nothing. I'll tell her you called. See you tomorrow." He disconnected the call before she asked any more questions. The shower was still running, so he figured he had time to call Caleb.

"Hmmm, hello?" the woman answered in a sultry bedroom voice.

"Is Caleb there?"

"Caleb? Is this joke?" she said with a giggle. "Come back to bed."

He and his twin were used to being mistaken for each other both in person and on the phone, but he had to say having his brother's hook up invite him back to bed was a first.

"This is his brother, Gavin."

"Oh, sorry." More giggles. "Hold on a moment."

He listened to the rustling of sheets as she left the bed to search for Caleb. A few minutes later, his brother was on the line.

"Took you long enough to call me back," Caleb said. "I left like three friggin' messages. Did you even listen to them?"

He'd listened to them, but they were identical to the ones he had from Noah, Logan, their parents. Hell, the only one who didn't call was Dean, and that was probably only because he was in college halfway across the country.

As much he appreciated their concern, he had no interest in hashing over it seven different times.

"We have a problem," he said, ignoring Caleb's question. "Sinclair."

"That's not new. Sinclair's been a pain in the ass ever since he was released from custody."

"He almost killed Cora tonight."

"With the fuck do you mean, almost killed her?"

"As in ran her off the road right by the bridge almost killed her. She's with me right now, but—"

There was a noise behind him, and he looked over his shoulder to find Cora standing awkwardly at the end of the couch wearing that horrible T-shirt that reached almost to her knees and her jeans. He started to tell her to have a seat when he realized a pile of laundry was scattered across the couch.

"Gavin? You still there?"

"Hey, let me give you a call back."

He hung up on Caleb and rushed forward to gather the clothes in his arms. He carried them to his bedroom, tossing them into the dirty laundry hamper even though he suspected they were clean.

"Sorry about that," he said.

"Who was that?" She sat down, curling her legs underneath her until it looked like she wore only the t-shirt.

"Caleb. I was going to ask him to check on a few things." He went back to the kitchen area and grabbed a couple beers then traded one for a bottle of water. "Keeley called wondering where you were."

"What did you tell her?"

"That you were over here."

Cora groaned and dropped her head into her hand.

"Was that the wrong thing to tell her?" He placed the water in front of her on the coffee table and pulled over his computer chair to sit.

"No," she said and sighed. "It's fine. I still think this is a bit extreme. I get not involving Keeley, but I could have gone home."

"The whole point of you staying with someone was so they could look for the symptoms of a concussion. Second, if Sinclair is targeting you, then you definitely shouldn't be alone."

She took a sip of her water then traced a pattern through the condensation clinging to the bottle. When she placed it back on the table, she stood and paced the narrow space between the couch and the coffee table before walking over to the window.

"I don't think this is a good idea," she said.

"Staying here? Why?"

She didn't answer right away. Instead, she peeked through the blinds out onto the street below. Finally, she turned and leaned against the window and stared at him. With her hands holding onto the sill behind her, the T-shirt pulled taut across her breasts and beneath the thin material, he made out the tightened peaks of her nipples.

"Things happen when we're alone," she said.

Things. Their tongues locked in a battle of wills, his dick pressed snug against her pussy. His cock twitched as he mentally told it to keep down.

He stood and slowly moved toward her until only a few inches separated them. He cupped her face with his hands, tipping her head back until he could look into her eyes.

"Cora—"

Whatever he was about to say was cut off by a knock at the door.

NINE

CORA GAZED UP AT Gavin. His dark brown eyes pulled her in, and she wanted to lose herself in their depths.

The knocking came again, but neither of them moved, reluctant to break the spell between them. It was only at the sound of the key in the lock that Gavin went on alert, moving quickly toward the opening door.

In only a few long strides, he reached the door, pressing his hand against the wood to prevent it from opening any further.

"Hey!" Caleb's voice came from the other side of the door. "You going to let us in?"

Gavin lowered his hand and backed up to let Caleb, followed by Noah and Logan, into the apartment.

The four brothers focused their eyes on Cora, and she crossed her arms over her chest self-consciously. Noah stepped forward, taking in the white bandage and bruise on her forehead.

"How are you doing? Did the doctor give you anything?" Turning on his "in charge" mode, Noah grasped her elbow and guided her over to the couch. "You should be sitting."

"I'm all right. It's worse than it looks," she reassured him, but she followed his advice and sat.

"She has a concussion and eight stitches." Gavin cut through the small space between Noah and Cora to sit beside her.

Cora gave him a sideways glance. "It's a headache, not a concussion. I just need a good night's rest."

Noah's eyes narrowed on Gavin. "Have you been watching her for symptoms?"

"Do I look like an idiot? Of course, I have."

"Guys! Enough." Caleb slashed his hands through the air, looking back and forth between his two brothers. "As far as I know, neither of you are Cora's father or her boyfriend. So back off."

Cora wasn't sure if she should be blushing or laughing. The thought of Gavin worrying about her like a boyfriend sent a thrill through her, but she appreciated Caleb's straightforward, cut-the-crap attitude.

Seeing Caleb always threw Cora for a moment. Despite his more clean-cut appearance, he and Gavin were nearly identical. For a hot minute back in high school when she first met the two of them, she thought she might have a crush on him, then she'd found herself falling for Gavin.

She knew a lot of people got Gavin and Caleb confused just by looking at them, but Cora had never had a problem figuring out who was who.

Caleb was always alert, ready to make his move. He didn't mess around or let anything distract him from his goal. It was a trait he carried on the outside. Formal posture, hands hanging loosely by his side, eyes that perused the room, evaluating each detail to determine its value to obtaining his goal.

Gavin, on the other hand, looked like he couldn't care less about what was going on. Oh, he knew every little thing that was happening; it wasn't in his nature to not be observant, but he didn't show it. He always appeared relaxed, as if he hadn't a care in the world.

"Maybe we should all stop giving Cora a hard time," Logan said. "Although, it would help if we all knew what the hell was going on. Gavin?"

"I'll let Cora tell you what she told me." Gavin rested his hand on her knee, and she jumped at the contact.

She knew he believed it all had to do with Sinclair. And yeah, there was a small part of her that considered he might be right, but it was a small part and not enough to make her think that everything was more than some bizarre coincidence.

He nodded his head encouragingly, and she looked from one brother to the next then back to Gavin. If she was right about it all being a coincidence, they might be able to convince Gavin.

For the next ten minutes, she recounted the events from the time she left Thompson Creek to when Gavin picked her up at the hospital. It wouldn't have taken long, except Caleb continually interrupted to ask for details that seemed of little consequence.

"When I told Gavin all of this, he thought it had something to do with this Sinclair guy," she said, finishing her tale. "And that's why he had me come here instead of going to Keeley's."

"You did the right thing," Noah told Gavin. "We don't

need Keeley involved in this. Though, if Sinclair is willing to target Cora, he may already be watching her as well."

Cora's eyes widened. That was not the response she expected. *Where were the reassurances that this was just some random act of violence? Some idiot hopped up on drugs thinking it would be funny to see if her little car would make it through the accident unscathed?*

"This is crazy." She shook her head. "How can any of you be sure? The picture you had of that guy Sinclair, he didn't look anything like the guy driving today."

"No, but that doesn't mean Sinclair didn't hire him," Noah said.

"What do you know about Sinclair, Cora?" Logan asked, crossing his arms over his chest and leaning against the kitchen counter.

"I told her the basics," said Gavin. "She doesn't need to know everything."

"I disagree." Logan arched a brow. "She needs to know what we're up against."

"I'm with Logan on this," Noah agreed.

Gavin looked to Caleb, and she realized they weren't just talking. They were voting on whether or not to tell her about Sinclair.

Caleb didn't say anything for a long time. He and Gavin simply stared at each other, and Cora wondered if they were communicating with twin telepathy. At that point, after her vision and the accidents, she wouldn't have been surprised.

"She needs to know," he finally said.

Gavin surged off of the couch. "This is bullshit."

"None of us want to dig it all up again." Caleb hooked

his thumbs through his belt loops. "But you're not thinking about it logically, Gavin. If Sinclair did this, she has the right to know. She's going to *need* to know."

"I'm not fucking doing this." Gavin stopped toward his bedroom, smashing his fist into the hallway wall as he went.

"Well, that went well," Logan said. "Who's going to do the honors?"

Apparently, it was a rhetorical question because Logan and Caleb both immediately looked to Noah.

"Sinclair was in charge of the Posthuman Project," he said. "The project's goal was to develop a genetically modified virus that could enhance the effectiveness of soldiers in combat. When the project began human trials, protocol required that he work only with adult volunteers. According to SIEGE, Sinclair went rogue. To ensure the host DNA would allow for a successful bond and future modifications, Sinclair determined his best chances were to inject the initial virus prenatally. Once we were born, our lives became a series of experiments followed by observation."

"We were lucky to survive; not all of the subjects did. On the outside, there's little evidence of what he did to us," Logan said. "But on the inside—our DNA, our brains—we'd never be mistaken for normal."

"What do you mean?" she asked.

"The mutated DNA from the virus was used to kill off certain enzymes, create others, and manipulate our genes to do things they weren't meant to do. Run faster, longer. Heal at an accelerated rate. Synthesize and construct information from patterns and details the average human can't even recognize."

Cora nodded; that was basically what Gavin had told her.

"Okay, I get that Sinclair is dangerous, that he's some kind of crazy mad scientist, but what I don't understand is why you think he'd be after me."

Noah looked to Caleb. "Care to share your theory?"

"Of course," Caleb said and turned his attention to Cora. "We already know Sinclair was responsible for the first accident. We always assumed the purpose had been to kill Lela to hurt Gavin, perhaps as an attempt to see if he could push him over the edge. The fact that he had you pulled from the water never made any sense."

"Not that we're complaining," Logan interjected. "We're grateful he saved you."

"What would make you think he was responsible for what happened today?"

"Because I don't believe in coincidence," Caleb said. "What I do believe is that Sinclair had you run off the road and injected you with something that is going to modify your DNA. The question becomes not if he did it, but what effect will it have on you?"

Unease settled in Cora, and a shiver ran down her back. Logan said not everyone survived Sinclair's experiments.

"Effects meaning whether it kills me or not?"

Caleb shrugged. "That would be the most obvious, of course, but there are other possibilities."

So much for thinking of Caleb as a friendlier, more tactful version of Gavin. He'd definitely changed since high school.

"If you've finished scaring the crap out of her, you guys can take off and let her rest," Gavin said from his bedroom doorway.

"Are you suggesting it would've been better to leave her clueless?" Caleb asked.

Gavin's lips pulled tight. "No, but I think it could've waited until the morning."

"Gavin's right." Noah rose from the recliner. "Cora needs to rest."

Logan pushed away from the kitchen counter. "I'll talk to Keeley and Janice about covering your shifts this week. We can see how you're feeling on Friday."

"You guys," Cora pleaded, "Seriously, the doctor said it was a headache, no concussion. I'll be fine by tomorrow."

Despite her protests, both Logan and Noah were adamant about her taking the week off. After a few minutes of trying to argue, she gave up and shooed them out of the apartment.

From her spot on the couch, she watched as Gavin went through the process of locking up behind them and setting the alarm. With his brothers gone, the tension he'd carried in his clenched fists vanished until he was the laid-back Gavin Cora knew. Yet, their sudden absence had the reverse effect on Cora.

All she could think of was the fact they were alone again. She suspected she'd need to make a decision. *Was she willing to accept what Gavin offered? Could she be like Hailey and accept that sex was all she would ever get from him?*

"You can have the bedroom. I'll take the couch," he said. "Just let me grab my stuff."

"I don't mind sleeping out here. Really. This thing is like a foot too short for you."

The look he gave her told her there was no way that was happening.

"My mom would kill me if she found out I let you sleep on the couch." He disappeared into his room only to reappear a few moments later with a pillow and blanket. "I'm serious, Cora. Besides, I want to watch the game I recorded, and I can't do that if you're trying to sleep."

"It's barely seven," she said.

"Yeah, but you've been through a lot, and I saw you yawning a few minutes ago."

She relented and picked up her water bottle before heading down to the bedroom. She could sense Gavin's eyes following her, and as she turned to close the bedroom door, she met his gaze, hesitating at what she saw reflected back.

"Goodnight," he said and glanced away.

"Goodnight," she replied.

She closed the door and surveyed the room. Considering the state of the living room when she arrived, she guessed that he'd been in there cleaning while she spoke to his brothers.

She took off her jeans and folded them before placing them on top of the dresser. She gazed at the king-sized bed dominating the room. A dark blue comforter was pulled over it and a pile of matching decorative pillows, probably a gift from his mom, had been thrown haphazardly on top.

Her skin tingled at the thought of sleeping in his bed. *How many times had she dreamed of this?* Probably dozens just in the last few months. Except, in those dreams, she wasn't exactly sleeping. Or alone. With a sigh of disappointment and acceptance, she switched off the light and climbed in, tugging the covers up to her chin.

Despite her denials about being tired, she was asleep within minutes, falling into the distorted reality of her dreams. Her subconscious pulled forth a replay of the accident only, this time, it was Gavin in the car behind her and then reaching into grab her. As her dream-self tried to fight him off, her arms became tentacles reaching out to wrap themselves around him, squeezing until he fell to the ground.

Her eyes fluttered open and scanned the room as they adjusted to the darkness. Some sort of noise had woken her up, but she wasn't sure what it had been. She listened carefully, and it came again. A gentle tap on the door.

"Gavin?" she called out.

The door creaked open, and his head and naked shoulder peeked through the narrow opening.

"I was just checking on you," he explained. "The pamphlet said to check every few hours."

"What time is it?"

"Almost midnight," he said. "How's your head? Any dizziness or extreme tiredness?"

"It feels better, or at least, I don't have a headache anymore. The stitches are a bit uncomfortable."

"I'll let you go back to sleep," he said and left.

Cora stared at the door long after it had closed. On the other side, she could hear the soft sounds of him moving around. She waited until the sounds stopped and she assumed he'd lain down before her eyes closed. Yet, the silence was louder than his movements, because it was filled with her thoughts of him lying there with no shirt on.

She rolled onto her back, desperate to think of anything other than Gavin and his sexy chest. Yet, lying on her back allowed the cool autumn air to gently brush along her puckered nipples. She took a sip of her water, but as she went to place it back on the nightstand, she misjudged the distance, and the uncapped bottle fell onto the bed.

"Shit!" she cried out.

She scrambled away from the growing wet spot but found herself trapped by the quilt. The door flew open, and the lights flicked on.

"What's wrong?" Gavin asked.

"Help me! The water spilled, and" —she tugged at the blanket—"I can't get" —another tug— "out."

He laughed, and she tossed him a sour look. Before she could regret her reaction, he grasped the end of the quilt and yanked it, dragging her along with it a good foot down the bed. Unfortunately, her wet shirt was trapped beneath her back, and while she rolled down, it rolled up.

The blanket fell to the ground as they stared at each other. His eyes flicked down to her panties, making her aware of how exposed she was. He averted his eyes, and she pulled the shirt down as she scooted off the wet sheet. She yanked off the sheet, using it to absorb the dampness from the mattress.

"What happened?" he asked as he went to the closet and pulled out a fresh sheet.

"I missed the nightstand and dropped the water bottle

on the bed." She took the end of the sheet he handed to her and tucked the elastic corners around the mattress while he did the same on the other side.

The sheet in place, they both reached for the quilt, pulling back, and they realized the other was also doing the same thing. Cora gave a nervous laugh and picked up the blanket to toss it over the bed.

When she was done, she turned to find him staring at her. Everything inside her stilled, hanging on to the edge of passion she could see his expression.

"I should ..." His voice trailed off as he gestured toward the living room.

"Stay," she said, moving closer to him.

"Cora, you were in a major accident. You banged your head." He shook his head.

"I know what I'm doing. I know what I want."

And she did. For so long she'd wanted Gavin. Now, she had her chance. Maybe it wasn't forever. Maybe it wasn't love. But it was something, and she wanted it.

She pressed her hand to his chest and slid it up to curl around the back of his neck. Rising up on her tiptoes, she pressed her lips to his.

For a moment, only the presence of her hand kept him there then he took control. His hands grasped her hips and pulled her against him before skimming along her ribs and up into her hair, tangling in her wild curls. A soft moan escaped her and her back arched. His lips opened for her tongue, and she explored his mouth, loving the way his tongue danced with hers.

He stepped in closer, moving them until the back of her knees hit the bed, and they sank onto the mattress.

The pressure of him atop her caused her legs to part, and he settled between them. The rough material of his jeans scraped along her thighs as his hips rocked his hard cock along her folds and her thin panties grew damp with her excitement.

Cora's teeth playfully caught his lower lip, nipping at him until he crushed his mouth along hers. She pushed against his chest, and he lifted up on his knees, breaking the contact of their lips. She grabbed the bottom of his shirt, pushing it up, then he took over and pulled the shirt over his head. Her fingers traced the rippling muscles of his abs, but her fun was short-lived as he nudged her hands out of the way so he could pull off the oversized shirt she wore.

With the barrier between them removed, he gazed down at her with an intensity that threatened to overwhelm her. She wondered what he saw. *Did he see the slight stretch marks along the side of her breasts? The less than flat surface of her belly?*

"Fuck, you're beautiful," he whispered, and any thought of insecurities vanished with the seductive timbre of his voice.

He cupped her breasts, gently squeezing them before capturing her nipples between his thumbs and forefingers. She felt the light pinch all the way to her core, and her body clenched in response.

Desperate to feel him drive into her, she reached out and let her fingers play with the spattering of hair that disappeared beneath his jeans before opening the snap of his jeans and carefully lowering the zipper over his hard flesh. She cupped the bulge she found and firmly stroked her hand along his length.

"I want you inside me." Her voice was a wispy rasp.

"Fuck."

He moved off the bed, and she lifted onto her elbows to watch him remove his pants and briefs. His penis stood up at an angle, and her mouth watered at the sight of the thick bulbous head. He placed a knee on the bed so he could lean over and hook his fingers into her panties. She waited for him to take them off, but he hesitated.

"Are you sure?" he asked.

In answer, she lifted her hips, and he slid the fabric down her legs.

Free of any barriers, she lifted her knees for him to kneel between. He leaned over her and placed his forearms on either side of her shoulders to support his weight. She placed her feet on the back of his legs. The position let his cock nestle within her folds, and her hips pivoted, letting her clitoris rub against him. She wrapped her arms around him and lightly scraped her nails over the muscles of his back.

His head dipped, and he captured a nipple with his lips. She drew in a sharp breath as he sucked on it then let it pop free. His ragged breath across the moist nub sent shivers through her. He moved to the other breast, sucking and nipping until she withered beneath him.

Gavin shifted his weight to one arm and reached down with the other until his fingers found the curls shielding her entrance. He parted her and slid two fingers into her hot pussy. Curling them upward, he slowly moved them in and out while his thumb skimmed across her sensitive clit.

Her fingernails dug into his back, and he lifted his head to look at her.

"Enough," she panted. "I want you inside me."

His slipped his fingers out of her and replaced them with the head of his penis. Her back arched, angling her hips to encourage him deeper inside. He pressed in until he was fully engulfed in her snug channel.

Her moan was met by his answering groan, and his hips surged back and forth then he suddenly pulled back, leaving her pussy aching with emptiness.

"Condom," he said.

She thought of telling him it was okay. She didn't want anything between them. She wanted to feel the hot spill of his seed fill her. Yet, she also knew he'd been sexually active during the last few months.

Gavin reached over to the nightstand and pulled a condom from the drawer. She took it from him and ripped it open then handed it back to him. As fun as it would be to play around with him, it would be much faster if he put it on himself.

It took only a moment for him to roll the condom on, then he sank back in, and passion consumed her. His hard thrust left her breathless as his pubic bone ground against her clitoris. She met each thrust eagerly, tension building in her and tightening her muscles.

He reared up and his hands gripped her legs behind her knees, pulling her legs apart farther to deepen his thrust and expose her clit. She reached down to press a finger to the sensitive nub, circling it until the tension inside her exploded.

"Come for me, baby," he groaned. Her muscles

quivering around him, he froze deep within her. She relaxed as the last tremors of her orgasm faded, and he started moving again until he tensed above her. He growled harshly as his back arched and his fingers bit into her legs.

Collapsing on top of her, he caught his breath then pulled out and rolled to the side. Cora lay there with her eyes closed, completely exhausted, and listened to the sound of him moving around. There was a click of the light switch being flicked to off, water running in the bathroom, then the shuffling of his feet as he returned.

The bed dipped under his weight, and she curled into his side, exhaustion and satisfaction sending her into a deep dreamless sleep.

TEN

THE MORNING AFTER WAS Cora's least favorite part of sex. With the temporary boyfriends she had in college, and the couple one-nighters since morning always meant the same thing to her. *Guilt*.

She felt no shame in relieving the cravings of her body, although she was certain that's where her mother would hope the guilt came from. Instead, it was the knowledge that while they had sex, she was thinking of Gavin, and when she got out of bed in the morning, all she could think of was how she'd used them.

Maybe it was silly to worry about such things, but she did. How could she not? Especially that particular morning. Because while she didn't feel guilt, she knew Gavin did.

When she first awoke, she lay on her side with him spooning her from behind. The heavy weight of sleep kept his arm resting on her hip. She faced the starkness of his room; it was no more a home than her own apartment was. The messiness made it appear lived in, but nothing about the room gave a sense of home.

A wave of dizziness swept over her, and she closed her blurring eyes, waiting until the vision that woke her took over.

He is watching again. He sits on the park bench, his gaze following Gavin as he makes his way from the coffee shop to his Jeep.

Cora trembles with the titillation pulsing through him, the thrill he experiences being so close to his unsuspecting prey. His fingers tighten around the cold handle of his pistol, yet he makes no move to draw the weapon.

He isn't ready yet. But soon.

The image of Gavin climbing into his vehicle faded as Cora returned to the present. The morning sun peeked through the partially-open blinds, and a faint beep from outside the bedroom was followed by the sound of the coffee maker percolating.

The shift in Gavin's body was subtle at first, just a slow tensing of muscles before he withdrew from the intimacy of their embrace.

Cora stayed curled up, pretending to sleep as he moved away from her. The bed shifted as he went, and something on the nightstand fell to the carpeted floor. Slowly, she rolled over to watch him pick it up. He faced away from her, but she could see what he held—the engagement photo of him and Lela.

She glanced away, her chest tightening. She must have made a sound because he twisted around and gave her a gentle kiss on the forehead.

"I love you," she said, staring into his eyes.

He didn't want to hear it, but she couldn't hold it in

any longer. She was done hiding things from him.

"Cora ..."

"I have for a long time." She cupped his jaw in her hand, loving the rough stubble pricked her skin. "I never intended for you to be hurt. You need to heal and blaming me let you move forward."

"I needed the truth," he said gruffly.

"I know that now. That's why I am telling you this. I love you."

He covered her hand with his and pressed his mouth into her palm. His eyes closed and she felt his lips moving. Then his fingers linked through hers and raised her hand above her head.

He lowered his head until his lips hovered only a breath away from hers. The anticipation of the kiss sent shivers along her skin. His tongue peeked out, tracing her lower lip, but when she opened in invitation, he pulled back to look down at her.

"Você não é nada para mim," he said with a sad smile.

You are nothing.

Everything within Cora froze as those simple words shattered her heart, its jagged pieces stabbing her. That he would say such a thing to her after she laid her soul bare to him, that he would smile while saying it, left her speechless.

Can a heart break and still beat?

She shouldn't have been surprised. She had known this was how it was for him. She realized he didn't love her. To Gavin, she was just another Hailey—a warm body to temporarily ease the needs body and then put aside.

Yet, she made this choice with her eyes wide open. She

asked him to stay, told him she knew what she wanted. And she had; she thought she might never have another opportunity to be with him.

She accepted it then. In the harsh, guilt-ridden light of the morning, was she willing to take what he offered? Did she really want to be on the other side of that morning after guilt?

She wasn't sure she could accept it, but with his hard body caressing hers, she didn't have the willpower to refuse.

He brushed a strand of hair from her cheek, and she could almost pretend the words he'd spoken meant something completely different. The hot press of his mouth nearly convinced her that he loved her, too.

Gavin's tongue swept along the seam of her lips until they opened under the pressure. The heat of his breath melded with hers as their tongues danced. She tangled her fingers into his hair, trying to hold him to her.

Wrapping an arm around her, he rolled them as they lay facing each other. His hands trailed down her spine to her lower back then around to grip the fullness of her ass. At the slight bite of his fingers, her pussy clenched, aching for him to fill her.

One of his hands slipped between them to palm her breast then slid down to the hardened nub of her clit. A hoarse cry erupted from her as his fingertip flicked the erect flesh before teasing it with a firm circling. Her hips lifted uncontrollably, desperate to find relief.

He shifted her onto her back and moved over her. She wrapped her legs around him, and her pelvis tilted back and forth as she rubbed herself against him. She pressed her fingernails into the hard flesh of his ass, straining to pull him closer.

"Now. I want you now," she moaned as she tore her lips from his.

She reached down to grip his penis, stroking him firmly. His hips jerked, and she relished the power she had.

"Oh God, baby. You're killing me," he said and surged forward again. He took her hand away and kissed her palm before reaching over for a condom.

He positioned himself against her opening then drove himself in. A gasp escaped her at the rasping of her tender flesh.

Gavin stared down at Cora. Her eyes were hooded, and between her gently parted lips, he saw the tip of her pink tongue. She was absolutely absorbed in the feel of him moving inside her.

He sensed the tension building in her by the way her heels dug into the back of his thighs and the subtle twitches of her warm passage around his cock. He paused the movement of his hips, and her eyelids fluttered.

The blue of her eyes seemed to sparkle, and in them, he saw the truth of the words she had spoken. She loved him. He didn't deserve her love. He didn't want it. He just wanted a body to take away the ache that had existed inside him every day since Lela died.

Love was not part of this. Sex. That's what he wanted. It's all he gave. He wanted to lose himself as she had in the physical, to close his eyes and pretend she was someone else.

Dipping his head, he buried his face in her hair, his

hips instinctively taking up their thrusting motion. Yet, he couldn't escape the fact she was not Lela. The lush hair against his cheek had a natural wave rather than a silky straightness, blond rather than black, and there was no comforting, gentle scent of strawberry shampoo. Instead, fresh mint filled his senses, and he froze.

He couldn't do it.

He needed to be able to pretend, and with Cora, he couldn't.

Withdrawing from her, he rolled onto his back and stared up at the ceiling. Cora didn't say anything, and that made him feel worse. Performance anxiety wasn't something he ever experienced, though he wasn't even sure this qualified. His body was raring to go, his arousal nearing painful. It was his mind that rebelled, refusing to let him sink into his memories because Cora's presence couldn't be denied.

For the past few months, she'd been gradually sinking into him, and every time he touched her, tasted her, she only dug in deeper until the space Lela occupied in his thoughts began to erode.

He hadn't asked for this. He hadn't asked Cora to take up that space. That wasn't what he wanted from her.

He squeezed his eyes shut as his vision blurred. Cora brushed her hand against his face, and when he would have looked at her, she laid a finger over his lips.

"Don't say anything. Just close your eyes," she said.

She leaned over and kissed his eyelids, his cheeks, the curve of his stubble-covered jaw. Arranging herself atop of him, she began a slow rocking rhythm. Heat built quickly, and he gripped her waist, taking control. He increased the pace and angled himself to deepen their joining.

A tingling crept down his spine, and he drove faster and harder into her until he pulled her hips down and ground into them as he exploded within her. When his release finished, he continued his rhythm, his hands reaching up to cup her full breasts, rolling the nipples between his thumb and forefinger.

Cora tossed her head back and gave a shaky cry, her entire body trembling with ecstasy. When the tremors subsided, she collapsed across his chest, relaxing into the arms he wrapped around her.

He swept her hair over to the side and let his teeth skim along the sensitive skin where her shoulder and neck met. His hold on her loosened, and she rolled off him.

His eyebrows drew down at her abrupt withdrawal, and he watched as she went to the bathroom, firmly closing the door behind her. There was the faint sound of water running as she turned on the shower.

He tried to recall the guys she dated in the time he'd known her, and could only picture a couple—both safe and boring types from college. That was the kind of guy she should be with, one who wanted to settle down and give her babies. *So, what the hell was she doing with him?*

Settling down and having babies didn't figure into his life plan anymore. Loving her would never happen. He couldn't even say he'd still be attracted to her in a month.

There was every chance that when she came out, she'd be expecting him to tell her he loved her. Then he'd have to deal with her tears and her broken heart. Maybe there'd be anger. He hoped it was anger because the thought of her crying twisted his gut. She knew when she invited him to stay what the game was. Cora, of all people, understood that his heart was buried with Lela.

"Você não é nada para mim. You are nothing," he whispered.

He closed his eyes and pulled up the memory of when Lela and he had first made love. It had been the week after prom. Lela had wanted to do it after the dance, but he hated the idea of being cliché. Everyone was doing it then, and he didn't want their first time together to be lumped in with all of the bullshit his buddies would be spewing the next day. He could still feel the brush of her hand along his, still taste the chocolate cheesecake she'd eaten for dessert on her lips.

At the click of the bathroom door, his eyes opened, and in the brief moment before he looked at Cora, he decided how he would handle her. But when he finally met her gaze, she seemed oddly composed. And dressed. He sat up, the sheet falling to his waist.

"I need to get home," Cora said. "My brother probably told my parents about the accident, and knowing my mom, she's already halfway to town."

"Sinclair is out there. It's not safe," he protested. Even to his ears, it sounded weak, though he wasn't sure why he even bothered to say anything other than *okay*.

That was the way he liked it. No messy clinging, no need for him to come up with excuses to get her to leave.

"As far as I can tell, your brothers have no plans for capturing him today or this week, or anytime soon. I can't hide here indefinitely." She gave him a tense smile. "Besides, my mom really will be in town soon, and I doubt you want her coming here and asking details about last night."

"Yeah, maybe not the best idea."

"Well, I'll see you on Friday then."

"Cora," he said with a sigh.

"Don't." She sat on the end of the bed with her back to him and pulled on her socks. "Don't make this into anything other than what it is."

"And what's that?" he asked. He could've kicked himself. *What the hell kind question was that?* He knew what it was. He definitely didn't want to hear her tell him it was anything different.

She stood and gazed down at him. What he saw reflected in her eyes withered his stomach.

"Sex."

It was the simple, straightforward answer he wanted to hear. So why didn't he feel relieved? Even after she left, he was unable to shake the feeling that he should've asked her to stay.

ELEVEN

"YOU'RE LATE."

"Nice to see you too, Mom," Gavin said as he entered his parents' house.

"Don't be going all sassy on me. You know good and well that I told you six sharp." Despite her snappish response, she pulled him in for a hug and a quick kiss on the cheek. Then she pulled back to give him another stern look.

"Mom, it's a quarter after."

"As I said, late." She lifted her nose in the air. With any other woman he might have taken it seriously, but not only did Sarah Walker enjoy teasing her kids, she was also habitually late for everything.

"I'd feel bad about it if I hadn't seen you getting out of the car as I drove up."

She gave him a playful scowl then marched toward the kitchen. Gavin followed while trying to keep from chuckling. With his mom, teasing was usually a one-way street. She had no problem dishing it out, but she didn't take it from anyone.

"How is the job hunt going?" she asked with a pitiful attempt to be nonchalant.

"I have a job."

"Bartending is not a career." She held up a finger to stop him from interrupting. "Noah and Logan own Porter's Pub, and Josh is working his way through college. It's not the same thing as you giving up your position at the firm in Billings. Have you talked to Caleb or Merrick about getting on with TanTech?"

"Mom, stop. I'm working, and I enjoy bartending."

Her mouth contorted as she struggled to hold back what was most likely some other protest about his lack of ambition.

"I just want to make sure you're thinking about your options. I don't want you to miss out on something because you can't be bothered to look." She folded a tea cloth into a tidy square then placed it in the drawer beside the oven.

He could have admitted that he was considering his options. He enjoyed working at the bar, but it lacked much in the way of intellectual stimulation there. He missed the challenge of developing high-level security programs and the stress of knowing the safety of millions of dollars' worth of inventory and information depended on his ability to out-think criminals.

But a job with TanTech or any other security firm would require a clear head, and he couldn't do that. Especially now that Sinclair wasn't only back in the picture, but a threat to Cora and his family.

"You look tired," she observed. "Have you been getting enough rest?"

"Yes." *No.*

"Stick your tongue out," Sarah ordered.

"Why?"

"Because lies turn your tongue purple."

He rolled his eyes. "I'm a little old to believe in stories like that."

"Only a liar would refuse."

Reaching into the fridge, he grabbed a beer. He cracked the can open and took a long, slow sip before setting it on the counter and looking at his mother.

The past two nights with only a few hours sleep were having their effect. The first night, the lack of sleep had been welcome, as he spent much of it inside Cora. The night after, though, had been hell. Every time he closed his eyes, he saw the empty, expressionless face Cora wore as she walked out the door.

She put on a good show that morning, almost getting him to believe she was satisfied with it just being sex, but as she'd opened the door, he told her he'd call. She turned back to him, and he saw it—the absolutely devastating acceptance that the person you wanted, who you loved with everything in your being, was forever beyond your grasp.

He hadn't called, but she knew he wouldn't. What she didn't know was how many times in the past fifty-two hours he'd picked up the phone and started to.

"I don't see the apple pie you promised, so are you going to tell me why I'm really here?" he asked, watching as she poured herself a glass of water.

"Do I really need to tell you?"

She didn't. The collection of cars in the driveway and

out front were enough.

"So, why the secrecy?"

"Because I know you," she said, "And of all my boys, you like to avoid your problems the most."

God, he hated when she was right.

In the fourteen years since Sarah and Mark Walker took the six of them in, they'd only had a handful of family meetings. He had no doubt the one planned for that day was going to be all about Cora, and there was no fucking way he'd have come if he'd known.

He wasn't ready to talk about her. Hell, he could hardly *think* about her without his guts twisting into a knot. Yet, for the past two days, that's all he could do. He'd be having a normal conversation with someone and then BAM—he'd be picturing Cora straddling him, her breasts bouncing in time with her hips.

He coughed and then took a sip of beer as he pushed the image back.

"Everyone's waiting for you in the den," Sarah said. "So get moving."

His lips tightened as he held in a sharp retort. Pissing off his mom would only guarantee her not siding with him. He stomped his way through the kitchen and down the stairs to the den.

Other than the dining room, the den was the only place in the house large enough to seat all nine of them. Although with Dean away at college, there were only eight so they could have squished into the living room.

His dad, Mark, sat in his recliner flipping through channels on the TV. Josh was spread out on the small sofa, his legs hanging over the end. On the large couch across from him were Sky and Caleb. Noah, ever the barman, was behind the wet bar mixing a drink while Logan tried to give him directions.

Sarah prodded Gavin forward by jabbing a finger into the middle of his back. As he walked into the den, he couldn't help but cringe as everyone turned to stare at him.

On the surface, his family looked normal, though obviously not blood-related. Other than Gavin and Caleb, the six brothers looked nothing alike, and even less like Mark, Sarah, and Sky. Still, within the realm of normal looking for a blended family.

It was when they got together for a family meeting that they became a pack of wolves hunting their prey. He'd been one of those wolves before, but that day he was the prey.

"Gavin, I'm so sorry." Sky pushed off the couch and rushed toward him, wrapping him in a tight squeeze. "I voted to tell you. I told them hiding this was just going to make things worse."

"I know you did, squirt." He returned her squeeze then grasped a strand of her hair, giving it a quick tug.

That's the thing about Sky. She was all about honesty, almost to the point of being extremely frustrating. He couldn't remember how many times he'd gotten in trouble because of her big, honest mouth ratting him out. That penance for oversharing the truth was a habit she picked up from Mark. While she was the spitting image of their mom, tall and athletic, with a mop of curly brown hair, personality wise she was the female version of their dad.

He was actually surprised she'd managed to hide this,

although, Sky did her best secret sharing in private, and he didn't spend a lot of alone time with his sister.

"Sky, let's not dwell on that," his mother said, pointedly. "Let's all sit down and figure out what's happening now."

His sister went back to her spot next to Caleb, and Sarah lightly smacked Josh's sock-covered feet.

"Give your brother room to sit," she told him.

While Josh was more than willing to follow Sarah's directions, swinging his legs over the front end of the couch so he was sitting properly, Gavin continued his mission of small defiance and joined Logan at the bar.

Sarah sighed and gritted her teeth as she took a seat between Sky and Caleb.

"Okay, let's go over this from the beginning," she said. "Caleb, you start."

"Wait," Sky interrupted. "What about Cora?"

"What about her?" Immediately, Gavin went on alert.

"Isn't she going to be here?" Her eyes darted from Gavin to Sarah and then back.

"Why would she be here? This is a family meeting." The muscle in his jaw twitched. "She's not part of this family."

Sky's eyes widened, and her mouth gaped like a fish. "How can you say that? We've known her for almost ten years. She was Lela's best friend. She's been protecting you for two years."

Gavin's fists clenched as his stomach churned with something akin to guilt. It was a sensation he didn't like.

"When your mother and I decided to take you boys in," his father said, "We made you family."

"She has her own family." The noose tightened a notch around Gavin's neck as he took in the expressions on his family's faces.

"Gavin," Mark sighed, his disappointment clear. "We've always been willing to accept others into our family. Especially those hurt by Sinclair."

Tense silence filled the room, and the weight of his family's disappointment pressed down on him. They were right, but even though everything they said was true, it didn't make Cora family. She wasn't.

"This isn't a conversation we need to have now," Sarah said. "Let's get the details and then we can decide what we need to do with Cora. Caleb?"

Caleb launched into the details of the investigation he and Merrick did after the first car accident. They'd found images of Sinclair outside the nightclub where Lela and Cora had been, then there'd been the damaged rental car, the altered statement Cora made to the police, and the official report determining the accident resulted from driver error.

The most damning evidence of Sinclair's involvement, though, was video surveillance of him going into Cora's room at the hospital the day after the accident.

"What was he doing?" Gavin asked.

"We don't know." Noah twisted off the cap to a beer. "At first, we wondered if maybe he was taunting you, knowing we'd find it if we started looking. Then we found footage of him going back again. We thought maybe he was doing something to her."

"You didn't think that was important enough to tell me? I get why you didn't tell me about him taunting me, but how the fuck do you not tell me about Sinclair using Cora as a test subject?"

"Watch your mouth," Mark snapped, and Gavin pressed his lips together.

Logan twisted on this stool and rested his elbows behind him on the bar top. "By the time we found out, it'd been a few months. If he did anything, Cora would've shown side effects."

"Can we get on with this?" Josh ran a hand through his shaggy brown hair. "I've got a date at eight."

"Josh, this is more important," Sky said.

"Why? Because it's Sinclair? Or because it's Cora and you've got some crazy idea she's in love with Gavin, and you want him to marry her?"

At that moment, Gavin was pretty sure everyone was glad Cora wasn't there.

"Sky's right, Josh," Noah said. "Sinclair targeting Lela and Cora means he's not done with us. Any of us or our friends could be next."

"We shouldn't have let him get away with it before," Gavin said.

"There's no point in dwelling on what's done and over," Sarah interjected. "Gavin, tell us about what happened on Sunday."

Going through the whole process of retelling the accident seemed redundant. Noah and Logan heard it straight from Cora, and from the way the others nodded and made little noises of agreement, it was obvious they'd already heard. But arguing would only delay the process.

"Where's Cora now?" Sky asked when he finished.

He shrugged. "She only stayed the one night then she

went home. She mentioned something about her mom coming down to visit."

His sister just stared at him, and the knowing he saw in her eyes had him shifting uncomfortably on a stool. Then his spine straightened. It was sex between two consenting adults. He wasn't ashamed of what happened, and he sure as hell didn't need to justify himself to his little sister.

"So what's the plan?" His eyes roamed around the room.

"Find Sinclair, beat the crap out of him, and maybe help him dig his grave." Josh rubbed his hands together and slapped them on the top of his thighs as he started to stand up. "Now—"

"Sit down," Sarah demanded with a glare.

"I have a few leads I'm following up on," Caleb said. "Merrick's pulling some surveillance footage from around the mall in Billings. We'll start going through them this week. Even though it wasn't Sinclair in the car, we may be able to trace the guy back to him."

"Cora is off until Friday. When she's back on shift, it'll be easy to keep an eye on her at the bar," Logan said.

"And until then?" Sky asked.

Although he didn't look at his mother, he felt the weight of her expectant stare. He refused to be sucked in. Yes, Cora needed to be kept safe. But there was no way in hell he was going to be the one to do it. Not now. Getting close to her again would lead him down the same path he went Sunday night, and he didn't think he could handle that again.

"I'll drop by and see her tomorrow," Josh said with a

cocky smile.

Gavin came off his chair and was stepping toward Josh before he even realized he'd moved. When he did, he stopped short and sat back down, spinning his stool so his back was to everyone except Noah. He looked up at his oldest brother, his gaze glancing off the scar along Noah's cheek.

Facing the harsh reminder of what his defiance of Sinclair had done to Noah was even less appealing than the shaming gazes of his sister and mother, so he turned back around.

"I'll call her in for some management training," Noah offered. "Stuff she can do without exerting herself."

"All right, we have a plan." Sarah stood with a determined smile. "Caleb and Merrick will follow the surveillance leads while Logan and Noah keep an eye on Cora."

"I can help go through the video footage," Sky offered.

"Merrick doesn't need you underfoot." Noah scowled at her.

"She'll be fine." Caleb nudged her with his elbow. "Another set of eyes will get it done sooner."

"I want the files from the original accident," Gavin said. "There's gotta be something we're missing. Some link between the two accidents that we're not seeing."

There had to be a reason why after two years Sinclair came back for Cora, and Gavin wasn't going to let him slip away again.

TWELVE

TWO FULL DAYS OF mother-daughter time with no one else to play buffer was way too much, Cora decided. She rinsed off the plate she'd been scrubbing and placed it on the drying rack before draining the lukewarm water from the sink and dabbing her hands with a tea cloth. Her mother, Jill, scrutinized every move she made, probably searching for a missed spot to point out

Oh, she loved her mom, but their relationship was tense at the best of times. In the aftermath of the accident and her train wreck of a night with Gavin, Jill's presence had been a nice distraction, but the thought of another two days with her mother had driven Cora to drink. She took a sip from her second glass of wine, already looking forward to the third.

Of course, that would raise her mother's eyebrows and lead to a long lecture on alcoholism and the hereditary influence from her grandparents.

"Your apartment in Denver was so much nicer than this place. Of course, you were making better money so you could afford a nicer place," Jill said from her perch on the edge of the couch.

"I make good tips at the pub," Cora countered.

Jill gave an exaggerated shudder. "The bar should have been shut down years ago. There was a man murdered there, you know."

"Mom, that was like back in the nineties." Cora would have rolled her eyes if she hadn't known her mom would launch up onto her soapbox about manners and respect. "Noah and Logan bought the bar from their uncle a few years ago and worked hard to clean it up."

"This isn't just about it being a bar, Coraline. Your father and I worry about you. Darren is doing so well in Billings with his new position at the insurance firm. We just wish you would settle down in a stable job. We were so disappointed when you resigned from the museum. You'd been doing so well."

Cora forced a smile. A year and a half before, Jill had freaked when Cora mentioned moving to Denver. There'd been the massive guilt trip about not being able to visit on the weekends, and whether she'd remember to call each week. The conversation only encouraged her to move. As much as Cora had hated the idea of leaving Gavin behind, she'd relished the freedom from her parents constant nagging.

It was just like Jill to now be complaining about her coming back to Thompson Creek. Thank God her dad wasn't there with them in the apartment, because it would have been twice as bad.

The phone rang, cutting off any further comments from her mom, and Cora leaped for it. The number for Porter's Pub flashed across the screen.

"It's work, I need to take it," she told Jill and walked to her room as she answered the call. "Hello?"

"Hey, how're you holding up?" Noah asked.

"I'm good, all back to normal." She closed the door between her room and the prying ears of her mother. "Except for the stitches; they're starting to itch like crazy. Even the cream the doctor recommended isn't helping much."

"I thought we could step up the manager training. You up to coming in tomorrow?"

"God, yes, please."

Noah laughed at her overly-enthusiastic response. "I take it you're a little bored."

"Try going crazy. My mom's here." She flopped backward on the bed. "If I tell her I'm going back to work, I might get lucky, and she'll go home. Otherwise, well, at least, I'll have an eight-hour break, right?"

"That's one way to look at it. Come at ten thirty. That'll give us time to go through opening procedures."

She stared up at the ceiling, eyes narrowing as a thought occurred to her.

"You know, I see through this, right?" she said.

"Through what?"

"This attempt to maneuver me somewhere so one of you can babysit me."

"It's not babysitting," he denied. "And if you'd stayed at Gavin's place instead of going home—"

"Not gonna to happen."

"I'm not sure you understand how big a threat Sinclair is. Now that we know he's targeting you, we need to get ahead of him," Noah explained. "By keeping an eye on you, not only are we ensuring your safety, but it might also put him in our path."

She didn't want anyone looking after her, but as much as she disliked the thought of anyone keeping an eye on her, she grudgingly understood she was in danger. If sticking close to the Walkers helped them find the guy sooner, she'd suffer through it.

"I'll see you tomorrow." She hung up before he could try changing her mind about staying with Gavin, or worse, ask why she refused to stay with him.

It was a question she didn't want to face because she knew it would lead to a series of other whys she'd been avoiding since she left Gavin's bed.

Why had she given in to her desire?

Why had she believed it would make a difference?

Why was she so willing to accept crumbs from Gavin?

Why?

"Coraline?" Jill called through the door and followed it with a soft knock.

Cora squeezed her eyes shut and let out a deep sigh, but hopes that her mother would vanish were pointless. She sat up and ran her hands down her face. *Maybe she should skip that third glass of wine.*

Knowing Jill wouldn't give up, Cora opened the door, a tight smile on her face. She had a pretty good idea how her mom was going to react to the news she was going into work in the morning. It was a conversation she wanted over with quickly.

"What were they calling you about?" Jill asked.

"Noah needs me to go to work tomorrow."

"Phff," Jill snorted. "I hope you told him no."

"I said yes. He's training me for the assistant manager position," she explained, hoping the mention of a managerial role would soften her mother up. It was a vain attempt.

"Why bother? This is a temporary job. A few months from now, you'll realize you—"

"Mom, please stop," Cora begged. Frustrations built from years of hearing the same things and of disappointment and guilt being heaped upon her boiled over. "I don't need this right now."

"I'm sorry if you don't want to hear this, but it needs to be said. You're wasting your life, throwing away your education and good opportunities."

"Having you constantly tell me how much of a failure I've become is not helping me," Cora snapped. A flash of satisfaction passed through her as Jill's face paled.

"I have not called you a failure."

"Maybe you haven't said the word, but the implication is in everything you say."

"If you're reading that in my advice, perhaps it's something you're already looking for." Jill straightened to her full five-foot-four height. "I have only ever encouraged you to do what's best for you."

She didn't get it. From the affronted expression on her face, Jill clearly believed she was helping by continually deriding Cora's decisions. Arguing was a waste of time.

"I'm going to bed." Cora shut the door in her mother's face.

She stomped around her room, tugging her shirt over her head and yanking a tank top from the drawer to sleep in. The hurt look on her mom's face nagged at her, reminding her she should feel bad about upsetting Jill and for not wanting her there.

Halfway through pulling off her jeans, she froze. She shouldn't feel guilty for being hurt when Mom called her a failure. Why should Jill be the only one feeling hurt?

Darren was so right. Cora's whole martyr complex was all thanks to Mommy dearest. In complete honesty, her father also played a big part in it too.

She was so tired of it. How had it taken her twenty-four years to see how her mom manipulated her?

The question haunted her dreams, leaving her tossing and turning throughout the night until morning brought a welcome respite from thoughts of her parents as a vision pulled her from sleep.

Sinclair watched the door to Porter Pub open, his grasp on the steering wheel tightening as Gavin stepped outside and held open the door for the woman behind him. Trapped inside Sinclair, Cora saw her future-self walk alongside Gavin through the parking lot.

Sinclair reached for a stack of papers and she tried to make sense of the scrawling mess of notes, but Sinclair's gaze glanced off the paper and back to Gavin.

The darkness of night gave way to bright sunlight, and she saw the two of them in Gavin's Jeep pulling up to a large building in the middle of the country. Something caught Sinclair's attention, and he turned away, the vision fading as his focus moved away from Gavin.

Cora kept her eyes closed as the vision faded and left her in the dark again. The visions were making less sense. They'd started out innocent enough then turned menacing as Sinclair repeatedly caught Gavin in his line of fire.

Now, he merely observed. What was his game? And considering Gavin had no clue what Sinclair was doing, who was he playing it with?

It wasn't until her alarm went off and she rolled out of bed that she was conscious enough to consider regrets from the previous night's confrontation with her mother. And she had them. Especially when she walked into the living room to see Jill's packed bag resting by the door.

She rarely fought with her mother. Anytime Jill's poking and prodding caused a sting too painful to ignore, Cora gritted her teeth, smiled, and walked away. But as much as she regretted hurting her mother's feelings, she didn't regret her words.

"Morning," Cora said.

"Good morning." A chilly smile accompanied the greeting.

"Are you heading home today?" Cora asked and gestured to the bag.

"You're well enough to go back to work, so there's no need for me to stay."

"Mom—"

"It's fine, Coraline." Her tone suggested anything but fine. "You have your life; you don't want me to interfere."

Cora heard the slight tremor in Jill's voice, and there was the nagging guilt again. She hated how easily her mother could do that to her.

"I love you, Mom. And I am grateful you came down here to help me out, but I need to make decisions that are right for me," Cora said. "For now, that means being in Thompson Creek and working at Porter's."

Jill pursed her lips together and nodded.

Breakfast was a tense affair. Neither woman spoke, perhaps in fear that anything said would only make things worse.

Cora got ready for work then walked Jill down to her car where they exchanged a brief farewell hug. She pushed down the urge to apologize and somehow pacify her mother. She was done taking the blame.

She waited until her mother drove away before walking down the street to the bar. When she got there, she went through the side entrance and waved to Noah on her way to the change room.

Keeley stood at the mirror, a curler in hand as she finished creating the waves in her strawberry blond hair. She always bemoaned working before noon because she never had enough time to get ready. In reality, Keeley did her hair at work every day because she was always running late for some reason or another.

"What are you doing here?" Keeley asked, staring at Cora's reflection in the glass. "I thought you were off until tomorrow."

"Noah asked me to come in for some training."

"Training, huh?" Keeley wiggled her eyebrows and giggled. "Is that code for something?"

"Sorry to burst your bubble, but no. Manager training."

"Too bad. I really hoped you'd given up on Gavin and moved on to some equally hot muscle."

Cora turned her back to Keeley and shoved her purse in her locker.

"Noah's the boss," she said.

"So?"

She smiled at Keeley's response. Considering Keeley

had a serious case for Logan, Cora hadn't expected anything else.

Keeley unplugged the curler, pushed it to the side to cool down, and then moved to her locker beside Cora's. "You ever gonna tell me what's going on?"

"What do you mean?"

"You totally ditched me to spend Sunday night at his place. Which, by the way, pisses me off, because I was so going to hook up with Logan that night, and instead, I ended up sitting around at home waiting for you."

"Don't you mean you were going to *dream* about hooking up with him?"

"Whatever. So, what gives? What happened?"

"Nothing," Cora said, avoiding looking at her friend.

There was a second of complete silence before Keeley shrieked and grabbed Cora in a hug.

"Oh, my *God*. You slept with him!"

Cora tensed up in Keeley's arms, torn between embarrassment and the slightest feeling of glee that yes, she'd finally slept with Gavin. She wormed her way loose of Keeley.

"Spill! I want all the horny details," Keeley said, a massive grin lighting up her face. "I need to live vicariously through you."

"Uh, no."

"Oh, come on." Keeley pouted. "*Some* details?"

She thought of his hot body pressed against her, the delicious sensation of his hard flesh sliding within her, and a wave of tingles coursed through her.

"Not a chance," she said.

Shoulders sagging, Keeley gave her an over-the-top

look of sadness.

"All right, if you're not going to tell me how hot he was in bed, will you at least tell me why you didn't stay there? If Logan ever lets me into his bed, he'd have a hella hard time getting me out."

That small iota of joy Cora had felt vanished.

"It's complicated," she said. Keeley stared at her, and Cora squirmed under the gaze, slamming her locker shut. "I'll catch you later."

She had no intention of telling Keeley anything, particularly when she didn't even understand half of what was going on herself.

THIRTEEN

HE WAS GOING TO kill his brothers. He just needed to decide which one was gonna go first. He'd been contemplating it for the past week.

"Hey, sugar." Hailey sidled up to where Gavin sat in the back corner of the bar. "What's going on?"

"Not much," he replied and took a sip of his beer.

"Why are you way back here all by your lonesome?" She propped her hands on her hips and thrust her chest forward, stretching the pale blue t-shirt she wore across her breasts. He admired the view, but it didn't do anything for him.

"Just needed some quiet."

She laughed. "Most folks go home for that."

He shrugged and drained the beer from the bottle. No way in hell he was leaving. Shifting his chair to the right, he glanced around Hailey. His brothers hadn't moved. There, however, a man moving straight in his direction. Gavin went on alert, muscles tensing and eyes narrowing.

Hailey glanced over her shoulder to check out who had

captured his attention. She broke out a come-hither smile and reached a hand out to the man. The guy tugged her in close and gave her a kiss suited more for the bedroom than a bar. When he released her, she asked him to grab her a drink and then watched him walk to the bar before turning back to Gavin.

"New boyfriend?" he asked. She moved on fast, although, it wasn't like what they were ever more than fuck buddies.

"Maybe." She gave him a teasing smile. "You snooze, you lose, sugar."

"I never lose when I really want something."

"Neither do I."

She pulled out a chair and moved it so she sat beside him, able to see what he saw. He cranked his head to the side, despising the discomfort that festered inside him as she dissected his view.

"Interesting," she said, her eyebrows lifting. "You've got some pretty stiff competition. One girl, five hot guys fawning all over her. It's like some naughty sex fantasy come to life."

There were so many things wrong with her observation, the least of which was that four of those five guys were his brothers; the biggest issue being that Cora was the girl.

It had been like that every night since she started back to work. During the day, she worked her shift and then afterward, one or more of his brothers were eating dinner with her, laughing with her, taking her home. That day, Merrick had joined the pack.

He tried to justify their presence by saying they were

protecting her from Sinclair. She was in danger, and despite her protests and even her ability to shoot the small gun she carried in her purse, they needed to protect her as much as possible.

Yet, that didn't explain why they had to sit so close, or why she had to throw her head back to laugh, exposing the delicate line of her neck. Or why the *fuck* Merrick's fingers were stroking the back of her hand.

Gavin surged out of his chair and stormed toward them. When he got to the table, he ignored the surprised looks on his brothers' faces, yanked Cora's chair back, grasped her hand, and tugged her from her seat.

"What are you doing?" she asked.

Rather than answer, he kept a firm hold on her hand and forced her to follow him as he stomped the entire way to the manager's office. He closed the door and locked it as she snatched her hand from his.

"What's going on?" she demanded, crossing her arms over her chest.

Gavin paced the small space, struggling to figure out what the hell possessed him to bring her in there. He was actually surprised she hadn't put up a fight. Then again he'd caught her off-guard.

"You dragged me in here, and now you're not even going to tell me why?"

"I ..."

Damn, she was right. He acted like a complete ass, and once he had her alone, he didn't even know what he wanted to say. He just knew he couldn't sit there watching her anymore.

Stopping in front of her, he stared into her furious blue

eyes and nothing else mattered except losing himself in the feel of her. He cupped the back of her head and leaned down to close his mouth over hers. She tasted of the sweet Bahama Mama she'd been drinking. His tongue lapped along hers, wanting to consume her.

With an arm around her waist, he lifted her up and her legs wrapped around him. He set her on top of the desk, and his hands roamed over her back and down to her hips, holding them in place as he rocked against her.

A knock on the door pulled them apart, and breathing heavily, he pressed a kiss to her forehead. The knock came again, followed by a voice.

"*Gavin.* I know you're in there," Keeley called out. "Open this door right now or Logan will break it down."

He let go of Cora, stepping back to give himself space to think. While he tried to pull himself back together, Cora slipped off the desk and cracked open the door.

"Did you need something?" she asked Keeley as if everything that happened in the past five minutes was completely normal.

"Are you okay? Josh said Gavin went all caveman and carried you back here."

"He didn't carry me, and everything is fine," Cora said. "We're talking."

There was a pause then Keeley whispered, "Blink twice if you want me to stay, three times if I should call the cops."

Cora gave a soft laugh. "Keeley, I'm okay. Really."

"All right. I'll go, but only if you let me see Gavin first."

Cora's eyebrows drew down in confusion, but she opened the door wide so Keeley could get a good look at him.

"Damn it," Keeley said, a saucy pout wrinkling her face. "I was hoping he'd at least be partly naked."

"Oh my *God*, Keeley. Shut *up*." Cora slammed the door and then leaned her back against it.

Her face had gone such a bright shade of red, Gavin couldn't help but laugh. She scowled at him and reached out to smack his arm, but it did little to stem the flow of his deep chuckles.

He sat on the edge of the desk and rubbed a hand down his face.

"What the fuck are we doing?" he muttered.

"I don't know, but you can start by explaining why you practically carried me in here."

"Hell if I know." And he honestly couldn't explain the intense rage that had consumed him when Merrick touched her.

"That's not much of an explanation," she said. "And I think I deserve one."

Gavin tried to piece together a response, but nothing he came up with made any sense.

"I don't want you hanging around Merrick or my brothers."

She stood up straight, shock widening her eyes. "Excuse me?"

"That came out wrong. I mean ... Shit. I don't know what I meant," he said, then shook his head. "No, I did mean it. I don't want to watch my brothers slobbering all over you, and I definitely don't want Merrick touching you."

"You don't get to make those decisions." She jabbed a

finger into his chest.

A small part of him had been hoping she would give in and let him boss her around, but he'd known she wouldn't. She might not possess the assertive self-confidence Lela had, but when Cora stood her ground, she was impossible to move.

"I realize that. I just ... You don't have to sit with those guys. You could have sat with me." He almost flinched at how pathetic he sounded.

"Considering you've gone out of your way to not be anywhere near me for the last week, you didn't exactly give the impression that I'd be welcome."

His hands gripped the edge of the desk behind him, and a heavy sigh lifted then dropped his shoulders.

"Yeah, well, maybe I've been acting like an idiot."

"Or an ass," she suggested.

"Possibly."

"I'm not going to play games, Gavin. You made it clear you have no interest in a relationship, so what do you want from me?" she asked.

Six months before the answer would have been nothing; two weeks ago he would have said sex. That day ... sex was only part of it.

He pushed away from the desk and slipped his hand into hers, gazing down at the top of her head. He lifted their joined hands and tipped up her chin. Her features were so delicate, and her big eyes gave her a waifish look.

"Come with me," he said.

"I can't."

"We'll drive around and talk," he clarified at her doubtful look. "That's it."

"All right."

He led her out the side entrance and through the parking lot to his Jeep. As they climbed in, Cora paused and glanced around nervously, searching for something. Obviously not seeing what she expected, she shook her head and slid into the vehicle.

Despite his promise they'd talk, they rode in silence through the town. Although it was early evening, the sun had yet to settle, leaving the scattered street lamps flickering in the fading daylight. He drove without purpose, weaving around the town as he contemplated what to say. With anyone else, the quiet would have been awkward, but with Cora, it felt natural to just be with her.

"Pull in here," Cora said, pointing to a parking lot.

He followed her instructions and then parked the car in front of a set of wrought iron gates. The realization of where they were left him twisted inside.

"Why are we here?"

She didn't respond. Instead, she got out of the car and went around to the gate, slowly pulling it open. He opened his door and stepped out, resting an arm atop the frame of the Jeep.

"Cora," he called. "Why are we here?"

She walked along the dimly-lit path a few yards, before glancing over her shoulder at him. "Are you coming?"

She didn't wait for him to answer. Instead, she continued walking, disappearing behind a cluster of trees and down a slight hill. He slammed the car door shut. Of all the places in town to go to, she picked the one he'd successfully avoided for the past two years. He should have gotten back in the car and left, but that meant leaving her alone, and with Sinclair out there, he couldn't do that.

Shaking his head, he jogged down the path and caught up with her as she came to a stop. Standing beside her, he peered down at Lela's headstone. It was a simple arched stone, etched with her name and the dates spanning her life. Cora bent down to wipe away the naturally-gathered dirt from the face of the stone.

"It took me almost five months after she'd gone before I could come here," Cora said, straightening up. "Even then it was hard. I felt so guilty."

"It wasn't your fault."

After blaming her for so long, those words sounded strange. Yet, it was the truth. Sinclair hadn't forced them off the road because she gave him the finger; he did it because he was sick and determined to play his twisted games with the Walkers.

He cupped her face in his hands, tipping it up until she met his eyes.

"Cora, this is all because of Sinclair. You were as much a victim as Lela."

"She was my best friend. How can I not feel guilty about being alive while she's dead?" Tears filled her eyes and spilled over, sliding down her cheeks until they pooled against his fingers. His thumbs wiped them away. "When I woke from the coma and learned she was gone, my first thought was about you."

"That's because you always put other people first."

"No. I thought about you because I loved you and the one person standing between us was gone." She turned her face away, and his hands fell to his sides.

He didn't believe her because that wasn't who Cora was. The thought might have been there in some dark hidden place in her mind, a logical deduction in the midst of everything that happened, but her heart and soul weren't capable of wishing death on anyone.

"But she's still there, and I'm starting to think she always will be," she said.

"I loved her. I still love her. I wish I didn't, but I do."

"Her being between us has nothing to do with you still loving her. She's there because you won't let go." Her lips tilted up in a sad smile. "I don't want what you had with Lela. I want something that is only us that has nothing to do with the past."

He didn't understand what she meant, and he wasn't ready to hear it. All he wanted to do was focus on getting Sinclair and keeping Cora safe. She'd asked him what he wanted from her, but he didn't know the answer any more than he knew what she wanted from him.

"We should go before we end up locked in here," he said and extended a hand to her. She stared at it for so long he thought she'd refuse to take it. Finally, she slid her hand into his, and with darkness enveloping them, they returned to the Jeep.

Gavin started it up and reversed out of the parking spot. He headed toward Cora's apartment, and when he pulled up in front of the building, he turned the car off.

"You don't need to walk me up," Cora said and climbed out of the car. "I'll see you tomorrow."

She started to close the car door then stopped and stuck her head back in.

"There's something on the windshield."

He peered at the bottom of the window; sure enough, there was a dark envelope wedged under the wiper blade. He half got out of the Jeep, reaching around to snag the envelope, and then opened it. Trepidation filled him as he took out a single slip of paper.

How is our dear Coraline doing?

Fury ripped through him, crushing the note in his fist. Getting all the way out of the car, he swung the door shut and stomped around to the sidewalk.

"Let's go," he said, wrapping an arm around Cora's shoulder while he scanned the street for anything suspicious.

"What's wrong?"

He held up the crumpled note. "Sinclair. He, or one of his lackeys, was watching us. They were at the cemetery."

She led the way up to her place, and when she unlocked the door, he scooted in front of her and locked the door behind them.

"Wait here," he ordered, then did a quick walk-through of the apartment to make sure it was clear.

"What did it say?" she asked when he came back into the main room.

"It asked how you were doing," he answered, and he moved right up to her, lowering his face level with hers. "Have you been sick? Noticed anything different since the accident?"

"No, nothing. I swear."

"Are you sure?"

"Yes."

The thought of her going through some of the side effects he and his brothers went through during Sinclair's tests was sickening. He grasped her arm and pushed up the sleeve of her sweater until he found the spot where Sinclair had injected her. The area was clear, no angry rash or blisters.

"Gavin, I'm fine," she reassured him. "I'm not showing any kind of side effects, so whatever he did to me didn't work."

"Maybe, maybe not."

Sinclair's work was meant to be hidden. Gavin realized their options were limited. He couldn't dismiss Sinclair's taunting. Not when Cora's life was at stake.

"You need to have blood work done to find out what he did to you," he said.

"You told me not to worry."

"I was wrong."

"Okay, I'll call the doctor's office in the morning."

He shook his head. "Not for this."

"Then where?"

"SIEGE."

FOURTEEN

SHE SHOULD TELL HIM. *She should have told him when he told her about Sinclair and how the psycho might have injected her with something.*

Gavin was obviously familiar with strange, well-beyond normal crap. How else can you describe a childhood of forced confinement for a government conspiracy to perform genetic modification on children? Still, visions just seemed too fantastical. Any normal person would take her revelation as a cry for attention rather than seriously.

Cora stared out up at the massive brick building before her. It looked more like an elderly rich man's country estate. Flowers blooming in the wooden flower pots lining the window panes, and a rocking chair on the porch gave the illusion that someone inside liked to spend their days relaxing as they watched the bird feeder hanging from the eave.

It was the building from her vision. Somewhere out there, Sinclair watched them. In the vision, she hadn't realized what was hidden inside. It was a house of horrors.

From the outside, no one would suspect five innocent children had spent years trapped in the lower levels undergoing experiments that ravaged their bodies.

The night before, Gavin had told her more about what he'd been through, though she suspected he spared some of the more extreme details. Not once in his recounting did he mention how the marks on his back had been made.

She turned to Gavin and thought of how hard it all must be for him.

"You ready?" Gavin asked.

A lump lodged in her throat, making it impossible to speak. She was nowhere near ready. *How can anyone be ready for something like this?* She'd spent all afternoon thinking of excuses as to why she couldn't and shouldn't come. Yet, delaying only meant extending the constant fear of what she might learn.

She nodded and stepped up onto the porch then hesitated. *Knock? Ring the bell? Or just walk in?*

Gavin solved the dilemma by pressing a button on a security keypad to the right of the door. A moment later, a buzz sounded followed by the click of the door unlocking. He opened the door, holding it wide for her to walk through.

While the exterior had the appearance of a home, inside was as high-tech as any Silicone Valley corporation. Dark slate tiles offset the stark monotone walls and chrome railings. A few feet from the door stood a full body scanner with a security guard next to it.

"This way," the guard said and held out a bin for their

belongings. "All electronic equipment is to be left here. No recording devices are permitted on the premises. If you are found to be in possession of any audio, video, or still frame recorders, SIEGE Corporation will pursue prosecution to the fullest extent of the law."

Cora pulled her cell phone from her purse and handed it to the guard then placed her bag in the bin next to Gavin's wallet. She walked through the scanner and waited for Gavin on the other side. The guard pushed the container through a smaller scanner and then handed it to her once it came out.

"Dr. Nielson left instructions that you meet her in the Level I conference room after you've seen the technician," he said as he took the empty bin from her.

"This way," Gavin said.

She followed him to the reception desk where he signed in for both of them and then up a set of stairs to the second floor.

"How do you know where to go?"

"Some things you don't forget." He shoved his hands deep into his pockets. "After the Posthuman Project shut down, the government wasn't quite sure what to do with us. Both the Defense Department and SIEGE needed things to look good in the public eye. That's how Mark and Sarah were able to adopt us. But the board couldn't just let us walk away."

"What do you mean?"

"Up until we turned eighteen, we were required to come in for check-ups. It was one of the conditions Mark and Sarah agreed to for the adoption to go through."

They reached another doorway, and Gavin pushed the

button, waiting for the corresponding buzz. The room they entered could have been any other doctor's office in the country. Behind the reception desk was a middle-aged woman whose gaze followed them as they sat down on the bench pressed against the opposite wall.

"Should we check in with her?" Cora smiled at the receptionist.

Gavin shook his head, and she could tell he wasn't really listening to her. Instead, he glared at the woman as his thumb rubbed the back of his left hand.

"Do you know her?"

Gavin glanced down at her, and for a moment, she saw the scared little boy he must've been growing up there.

"Donna was a level one assistant." He held up his hand for Cora to see the small circular scar he'd been rubbing. "Lucky me, I got to be the first person she ever stuck a needle in. It only took her a dozen tries. Right, Donna?"

The older woman had the good sense to look away.

"I thought the Posthuman Project violated SIEGE's policies? How could they keep someone on who was part of it?"

"Well, Donna here had no clue the project was unauthorized. She was as much a victim of Dr. Sinclair as we were," he explained with biting sarcasm.

Cora suspected Donna overheard his remark because she abruptly rose from her seat and disappeared through a side door.

"I'm sorry you had to come with me," Cora said and slid her hand into his, linking their fingers.

When he first brought up coming to the SIEGE labs, she'd been hesitant, and if she were honest, she still was.

Even more so now that she understood the length the board went to in order to protect the company.

"I couldn't let you come alone." He scanned the waiting room. "We've suspected for a long time that SIEGE hasn't cut all ties to Sinclair."

"Then why are we here?"

"Because they know what Sinclair was working on. They'll understand what to look for."

"If they are still working with Sinclair then how can we be sure they'll tell us the truth?"

"We don't—" his hand squeezed hers briefly, "—but it's our only option."

A door opened across the room, and Donna appeared, a chart clutched to her chest.

"Through here," she ordered. She led them to an examination room and told Cora to sit on the exam table.

Cora hopped up, and the cold steel instantly had her wishing she'd skipped the mini-skirt and worn pants instead. She squirmed, trying to get the thin sheet of paper covering the table under her thighs. Then she caught Gavin watching her with a knowing smile. She wrinkled her nose, and he gave a soft chuckle.

Donna moved efficiently through the process, gathering a handful of vials of Cora's blood and then ushering them back out to the waiting room.

"How long until we get the results?" Cora asked her.

"Dr. Nielson will meet you in the Level 1 conference room."

Donna didn't wait around for any more questions. She went back behind her desk, twisting slightly so her back was almost entirely to them.

"Come on," Gavin said and took her hand, leading her down to the conference room.

With every step they took, the haunting sensation of needles pricking at the skin along his arms and his back assaulted Gavin. They got off the elevator, and nausea-inducing memories rolled through him.

Level I. Those halls defined his childhood with their sterile white walls and tiled floor that marked the few moments each day when he wasn't confined to his room or the class. They were the passageways that led him from his small sanctuary to the hell on Earth where Sinclair and his team nearly destroyed him.

When he turned eighteen, he swore he'd never come back, that he would never let SIEGE or Sinclair have control over him again. Yet, there he was, and he felt even more powerless.

"Gavin? Are you okay?" Cora asked.

"Yeah," he answered distractedly as he stared down the hall to the door marked with the number three.

He walked along the corridor and stopped in front of the door that had been his. The small window that once gave him a glimpse of the world around him was now a window into his past.

Peering through the glass, Gavin saw the room as it was ten years before. A small cot with a pile of books near the head was next to a table and chair bolted to the floor. The sink and toilet in the corner were hidden by a thin sheet suspended from the ceiling.

A suffocating weight fell on his chest. He took a slow, trembling breath and turned the knob. No longer locked to keep him in, the door swung open easily. The tiny space had been converted into a storage room with wire shelves lining the walls, loaded with medical supplies.

He walked into the room and knelt in front of the shelves facing the door. A sweep of his arm cleared the shelf and sent bottles tumbling to the floor. He ran his hand along the wall until he found what he was looking for—a series of grooves etched into the drywall made by digging his fingernails into it.

Twenty-six. Twenty-six trials he went through, and that was only after he'd been old enough to start keeping track like Noah told him to.

Taking his keys from his pocket, he reached back in and added one more line to his count.

"What are you doing?" Cora asked from the doorway.

He stood and turned to her, but she was busy checking to see if anyone was coming down the halls. She glanced back at him, her eyebrows raised.

"I kept track," he said. "We all did. One mark for every trial we went through. I needed to add one more."

"Why?"

"When the police and the feds showed up, I was strapped to a table in the lab. If they'd shown up ten minutes earlier, it would've been twenty-six." He looked at his keys and wiped away the powdered drywall. "From the time I was old enough to count until we were freed, I went through twenty-seven different trials."

Cora surged forward and wrapped her arms around his waist, burrowing her head into his chest. He encircled her in an embrace, and a feeling of peace settled over him.

"I'm sorry. I'm so sorry that happened to you," she whispered.

He smoothed her hand over her blond curls and then pressed a kiss to her forehead.

"Let's get this over with," he said.

He led her to the conference room, and they went inside. He hadn't expected Dr. Nielson to be there, so he was vaguely surprised to find her sitting at the head of a large oblong table.

"Gavin, it's a pleasure to see you again," Nielson said with a sickeningly false smile. The severe bun she'd pulled her dark-brown hair into only emphasized the harsh angles of her heavily botoxed face. "Please, Cora, have a seat. I'm Dr. Yolanda Nielson and Chief Science Officer of SIEGE Corporation."

Cora sat down on one side of the table, but instead of sitting beside her, Gavin stood behind her, his hands resting on her shoulders.

"Let's skip the fake pleasantries," he said. "What did he do to her?"

"I must say when I was informed about your request to test Miss. Evans, I was a little confused," She said. "You implied you thought Dr. Sinclair was still employed by SIEGE."

"Did I imply that? I'm pretty sure I flat out said it."

"It's public knowledge SIEGE Corporation terminated their professional relationship with Dr. Sinclair upon the revelation of unauthorized violations to the ethical standards of SIEGE."

Gavin sneered. "Unauthorized? I remember you being rather enthusiastic about the project."

Dr. Nielson sighed, and her left eye twitched.

"Prior to the discovery of Dr. Sinclair's work on the

Posthuman Project, I worked within the Agricultural Department of SIEGE," she stated. "Dr. Sinclair acknowledged that he acted in direct contradiction to the orders of the Board, independently and of his own volition."

Such a well-rehearsed answer. He could've recited it word for word from all the times he'd heard her say it or read her quote in the papers. He might've believed it, too, if she hadn't been the one to give him the final injection.

His hands tightened around the edge of Cora's chair until his knuckles turned white and his biceps quivered with barely-contained rage.

"You know damn well I'm not buying your crap story. What the fuck did he do to Cora?"

"We'll get to that." Dr. Nielson tapped her fingers on the table. She turned her icy gaze on Cora. "Have you noticed any changes? Fatigue? Blurry vision? Anything that seems even the slightest bit unusual?"

"No, nothing," Cora answered, her hand lifted, letting her fingers flutter over the small puckering of pink flesh along her hairline.

"That looks like you took a nasty hit," Dr. Nielson said and made a notation on the chart in front of her.

"Thanks to Sinclair running her off the road," Gavin bit off.

"When did this injury occur?"

"A week and a half ago."

"Really? It's healing nicely. Quickly." Another notation went on the chart. "So, physically you're doing well. What about emotionally? Psychologically?"

"You mean other than living in fear that I'm Sinclair's

guinea pig for his new science project?"

"A reasonable concern, I suppose. However, I'm more interested in the inexplicable. Extreme anxiety, night terrors—" Nielson's eyes flickered to Gavin and then back to Cora, "—hallucinations. Anything like those?"

"No."

He might not have been touching her, but Gavin sensed the tension that stiffened Cora's body.

"It's obvious you know exactly what Sinclair did," Gavin said. "So why don't you just give us the information we're here for and then we can leave, or I can respond to one of the requests for an interview I've received."

"That would be a violation of the gag order," she pointed out.

Rather than argue, he stared her down until she pressed her lips tightly together. Her fingernails clicked rapidly against the table then suddenly stopped. From under the clipboard, she pulled out a folder and slid it across to them. "This arrived five days ago."

"Yet you didn't contact anyone."

"The Board determined that since Sinclair was not acting on our behalf, it would be best to keep ourselves removed from the situation. When you contacted us, that was no longer an option."

Cora opened the file and found a photo of herself staring up at her. Subject 8 was scrawled along the bottom in red ink. With trembling fingers, she flipped it over, then the next page and the next.

Gavin caught enough glimpses of the pages to realize Sinclair had been monitoring Cora for a lot longer than a week. The sliver of control he'd been desperately holding onto snapped.

Tendons stretched, and his skin rippled as adrenaline pumped through his body, triggering the unnatural enzymes in his body to kick in. His heart rate accelerated, increasing the supply of oxygen to his bulging muscles and the sleeves of his shirt tore along the seams. He surged forward, stalking toward Nielson. Fear drained her face of all color as she watched the monster break free.

Nielson shoved her chair back, scrambling to raise the gun she'd hidden under the table. She pointed it, not at him, but at Cora. He suppressed the instinct to rush the doctor, knowing she wouldn't hesitate to kill Cora. Assessing the situation, he realized with Cora present the chances of successfully disarming Nielson wasn't worth the risk.

"Move back," she ordered, motioning with the gun and he craned his neck around to look at Cora.

The sight of him changing wasn't a pretty one. He'd seen his face in this state before. His brow and cheekbones protruded while the muscles along his jaw flexed then hardened, broadening his face.

Cora's eyes widened as she witnessed for the first time the monster SIEGE had turned him into. He saw the rapid fluttering of her pulse along the side of her neck, heard the slight catch in her breath. Her horrified expression pulled him back from the fury.

He drew in a deep breath through his nose and curled his fingers into fists, letting the bite of his nails into his palms relieve some of his tension. He took another few breaths until his muscles relaxed and the tight stretching of his skin faded.

"What did he do?" Gavin asked with enraged deliberation.

"He injected her with the PH-9E serum," Nielson replied.

"What's that?" Cora's fear was audible. "What will it do to me?"

"It's one of the Posthuman Project serums. As for what it will do to you?" The doctor shrugged. "The data he sent suggests this serum is a variation of the final one given to subjects one through six, however at this stage, the subject—"

"She's not a test subject. She has a name," Gavin snapped.

"At this stage, Miss. Evans should have been experiencing significant changes both physically and psychologically. Once the blood results are back, we'll have a better idea as to the extent of any genetic modifications that she's incurred."

Cora shoved back the chair, forcing Gavin to step to the side. She frantically closed the folder.

"I want to leave," she said. "Right now."

Gavin didn't hesitate. He grasped her hand and led her back to the elevator, ignoring the call from Nielson to wait. He thought he was doing the right thing bringing Cora there, trying to get answers, but it was a mistake. A massive, fucked up mistake.

SIEGE, Sinclair, Nielson: they were all the same. And now they all had samples of Cora's blood.

FIFTEEN

CORA HUDDLED IN THE passenger seat of the Jeep, hopelessly wanting to turn back the clock. But how far back to go? An hour and she'd never see what the experiments had done to Gavin. A week and no one would suspect Sinclair had done anything to her. Two years and Lela would still be alive. Six years and Cora would still believe it was only lust not love she felt when she looked at Gavin. Ten years and Cora could make the choice not to be friends with Lela, never giving herself the chance to interact with Gavin.

If she could do that, maybe her life would be something other than this mess. A heavy sigh escaped her, and she rested her head against the door frame.

"I didn't want you to see me like that," Gavin said.

She rolled her head to the side to look at him. He held himself stiff, his face unreadable, and she realized he was worried about her reaction. She didn't blame him. It had been scary to witness the transformation, yet underneath the unnaturally large muscles and the enraged focus, he was still Gavin.

She wanted to reassure him, yet what words could possibly take away years of pain and fear? Reaching over, she smoothed a finger down the side of his face.

"I love you," she said softly.

His lips twitched, and she liked to think he was smiling in return.

"You going to tell me now?" Gavin asked.

"About what?"

"I saw how you reacted when she asked you about side effects. I get why you didn't want to tell her, but I need to know."

Cora stared out the window, avoiding the sidelong glances he kept throwing her. She needed to tell him about the visions. The time for her excuses over. Besides, the more she learned about Sinclair and the Posthuman Project, the more she thought her visions weren't so strange after all.

Gavin started the Jeep and drove back to the side road leading to Thompson Creek. A road sign flew by, and panic surged through her. She knew that road. Not from her years of living in Thompson Creek but from the vision she had only days before.

She squeezed her eyes shut trying to remember what Sinclair's viewpoint had looked like. Yet, even as the images came back, she realized they were already passed the spot.

"Cora? You okay?"

Cora shook her head to clear it. "What? Yeah, I'm good."

"You look tired," he said.

"I am. I haven't been sleeping well," she admitted.

"Nightmares?"

"No, just ... Dr. Nielson asked about anxiety and night terrors. Have you ever had those?"

He gave a chuckle laced with sarcasm. "You don't get through the shit we went through and not have anxiety when you get out. I get night terrors sometimes. Sinclair's calling card. Anytime he's around, they start up."

"How is that even possible?"

"Who the fuck knows? A lot of the genetic modifications he made changed the way our bodies use and produce enzymes and hormones. I wouldn't be surprised if he implanted something in me."

It almost made sense. When Gavin first told her about Sinclair and the Posthuman Project, she did her research. Finding specifics, though, on the project or even Sinclair had been next to impossible unless you counted all the conspiracy theories that popped up. She read a couple of those but dismissed them when they veered into mind control and astral projection. Perhaps she shouldn't have been so quick to dismiss them.

"Is that what you've been having? Night terrors?" he asked.

"No. I almost wish it was." She took a deep breath and looked at him. "I've seen things. Things that aren't happening at that moment."

Gavin nodded, and she wondered if maybe she wasn't the only one having visions.

"I had hallucinations a few times," Gavin said. "Noah had a lot of them back in the lab."

"I thought they were hallucinations. I mean, I did when they first started, but then I found out that what I saw actually happened."

The car rolled to a stop on the shoulder of the road, and Gavin put it into park before turning to face her.

"Psychic premonitions?"

She'd expected doubt and a significant amount of skepticism. What she hadn't expected was how much it hurt to hear it in his voice.

"Visions, not psychic. It's … It's hard to explain. They don't just show just anything or everything, and it's not something I can control."

"Then what do you see?"

"You. At the bar, driving home, talking with your brothers."

"Those are all pretty normal things. Why would you think they're visions?"

"Because I saw you break your arm playing football with your brothers. Two weeks before it happened when I still lived in Denver."

The struggle to accept the idea of psychic visions flashed across his face. Finally, he nodded, though doubt continued to wrinkle his forehead.

"Okay. I need everything. Not just the bits and pieces you think are important. Everything."

"A few months after I moved to Denver, I started waking up in the middle of the night. I'd lie there completely awake, and then all of a sudden I'd start seeing images of you." Cora cleared her dry throat. "Like I said, I thought it was hallucinations. Some kind of post-traumatic stress."

"But it wasn't."

"No. Now, at least, I understand why they started.

Obviously, whatever Sinclair did to me after the accident was what caused this."

Gavin stared out the windshield, his eyes squinting in deep thought. He ran a hand through his blond hair and managed to give himself an impromptu pompadour.

"You said you only see me. Why?"

"I don't know. Maybe he wants me to know he's watching you."

"Watching me? Why would these visions tell you he's watching me?"

Cora swallowed around the thick lump in her throat.

"When I have a vision, I'm not there. I mean, I see what's going on but not through my own eyes."

"Whose? Sinclair?"

"I had no idea who he was. I caught glimpses of his reflection in a window or in a mirror, but it wasn't until I saw the photos from the security footage that I learned who he was."

"And you didn't tell me." Gavin slammed the palm of his hand along the edge of the steering wheel.

"I couldn't."

"That's bullshit."

"Really? You would've believed me if I told you that I was having visions of some guy following you and planning to kill you?"

He cranked his head to the side, and she heard the audible click of his neck popping. "The only reason you believe me now is because you have proof Sinclair did something to me. If I said something earlier, it would have come across as some sort of desperate cry for attention."

"Maybe, or maybe I would have at least been aware of

the danger."

She gave a soft chuckle. "Like you were after Caleb showed you the photos of Sinclair stalking you?"

"All right, I could've been a bit more careful," he conceded.

"You need to be." She thought of the guns Sinclair liked to brandish and the image of Gavin caught in their crosshairs. "Sinclair isn't just watching you. He's picking the perfect opportunity to kill you."

"What makes you so sure?"

"The gun he carries, and the fact that he's lined up his shot so many times I've lost count."

"Sinclair won't kill me. He'd view it as a loss of observational data. I don't know what he and Nielson are planning, but I'm not going to make it easy for them."

Cora stared at him incredulously. *How is he not taking this seriously?*

"This isn't some game, Gavin," she snapped. "Sinclair is going to try to kill you."

Gavin studied her for a long quiet moment until he must have come to some realization because his eyes narrowed on her. "Why did you move back to Thompson Creek? Why take a job at the bar?"

Her standard fib about not liking Denver was on the tip of her tongue, yet it refused to roll off. So many times she gave him lies or half-truths, and it never served either of them well.

"You came back to try and stop Sinclair," he guessed. "You had no clue who he was or why he would want me dead, but you thought you could stop him."

"I came back because I needed to," she said, "And

because I wanted to."

The silence that fell between them stretched an eternity. Cora tried to read his blank expression. Whatever he was feeling or thinking was so deeply hidden she wondered if he was even aware of it.

Eventually, he pulled back onto the road, driving until they came to a roadside diner. He parked the Jeep, and they went in and ordered dinner. Throughout the meal, Gavin questioned her about the visions, wanting specific details so he could determine which had already passed and which were still possible futures. With all of the visions she'd had, it was impossible to tell him everything, so she recounted what she remembered and then told him the rest was written in her journal at home.

It was dark by the time they got to town. He parked around the back of her building, and as they walked to the front, he placed a hand on the small of her back. Her steps slowed as she tried to delay the inevitable loss of contact once they were inside. Eventually, they made it upstairs, and he sat on the couch while she went to get the journal.

"This is most of it," she said. She handed him the book and then sat in front of him on the coffee table. "I didn't start keeping track until maybe a month or so before I moved back."

Gavin opened the book, his eyes skimming over her notes.

"What does the star mean?" He pointed to the small mark in the margin.

"It means it happened. Most of them I don't know if they did or not." She shrugged. "They're so generic in what happens you probably wouldn't even know."

"Gavin and a blond woman going into his apartment," he read. "Night. The man took off his gloves. Wrinkled hands, but not elderly."

"See? This is what it's like most of the time. Especially when I wasn't here. I had no idea what you were doing, where you were, who you were with." She gave a slight smile. "God, I sound like a stalker."

Gavin returned her smile but didn't say anything. Instead, he continued to flip pages, and as he neared the end of her notes, he slowed, taking the time to read each word.

"You're in these ones," he said.

Cora nodded. "I'm in them, but I'm still inside of him. I'm watching myself with you."

He gave a sexy smirk. "You realize how kinky that sounds, right?"

"You're just as bad as Keeley," she said, shaking her head, though she couldn't quite pull off a serious expression. "This is serious stuff."

"You're right, and we should definitely be serious about it. In the morning."

He tossed the journal on the coffee table beside her and then scooted to the edge of the couch. The movement caused her to spread her legs to make room for him. He hooked his hands high under her legs and pulled her forward and onto his lap.

"Gavin." His name came out on a sigh as she ground herself against him. Her skirt left her bare to the sensation of his jeans rubbing against the sensitive skin of her inner thighs. "We should stay focused on Sinclair."

"I'd rather focus on you." He leaned in, his mouth

hovering over hers.

"Is this a good idea?"

"Fuck, yes." His pelvis lifted and the hardening ridge of his cock pressed against her pussy.

She caught his lower lip between her teeth and gently tugged before closing her mouth over his. Her tongue darted in, enticing his into a sensual dance. The taste of him was heady. Rich and masculine and something that was uniquely Gavin.

A moan escaped her as his hands cupped her ass cheeks, his fingers curling in and slipping beneath the edges of her panties. She pulled her mouth from his and threw her head back as she rocked against him.

His lips skimmed across the exposed line of her neck, latching on at the point where neck and shoulder met. She shivered, and her nipples tightened in anticipation.

Cora gripped the bottom of her shirt and pulled it off over her head. Seated on Gavin's lap, her breasts were level with his face. He lapped his way down her collarbone, and through her black-lace bra, captured her beaded nipple with his teeth. He tugged on the puckered nub, then released it and did the same to the other nipple.

Gavin twisted them around until Cora's back pressed to the seat of the couch. He tugged at her thong, and she lifted her pelvis to help him get the delicate fabric out of the way. He slid his rough fingers through the soft curls and then between the folds of her pussy.

Her hips rose and fell as she desperately sought a deeper touch. He responded by slipping two fingers inside her, but the touch was too brief as he pulled out and circled her clit.

"Harder," she said, straining closer to his touch and groaned when he followed her order.

Then his fingers were gone, and he was tugging her up from the couch. He placed her in front of him and walked her to the bedroom.

He fiddled with the clasp of her bra then the loosened material sagged, and she let it fall to the floor. She started to reach for the zipper along the side of her skirt, but his hips bumped into her, and she moved toward the bed.

Reaching from behind, his hands massaged her breasts, and he plucked at her nipples. His teeth lightly scraped her shoulder, and grasping his forearm, she arched her back.

Pushing away from his hold, she climbed on the bed. Before she could turn over, he was behind her on his knees, his hands gripping her hips and pulling her back.

He gathered the back of her skirt and tossed it up across her back, leaving her ass bare and on display for him.

"God, you're so fucking beautiful," he said, fingers trailing over her skin, between her cheeks, down along her wet pussy to her clit. He tapped at the rigid bud he found, and she jerked in response.

"I want you inside me. Now," she panted.

He released her, and she heard the sound of his zipper going down and then the ripping of a condom packet. Moments later, his hard cock slid between her swollen folds, the head of his penis catching at her opening. She reached between her legs and grasped his penis, guiding him into her entrance.

His hips thrust forward, and only the hold he had on

her hips kept her from moving forward as well. She went down to her elbows, angling her body to deepen his driving thrusts.

"Widen your legs," he said, and as she did, his thumbs pulled apart the lower region of her folds. The stretching left her pussy aching, desperately trying to clench around his cock.

His balls tapped against her clit with each powerful thrust. Cora reached one hand down between her legs, finding her aching bud and rolling it beneath her fingers. Her heated flesh responded with a spasm.

"That's it. Come for me, baby," he groaned. He palmed the lush flesh of her ass and then gave it a gentle tap. The contact sent a sharp tingle through her, though it lacked enough force to even sting.

"Again," she said.

He answered with another tap. She arched, straining to reach the precipice of pleasure and rocked back, driving him deeper.

"Let go, baby. Just let go."

Her fingers clutched the comforter, and her toes curled in. A loud cry broke free as she convulsed around him, squeezing his cock as she gave into the shattering orgasm. Utterly spent, she sagged forward, the side of her face pressed to the bed.

Gavin gripped her hips, holding her in place as he kept moving, sliding through her slick passageway. Then he wedged himself completely within her and held still as he gave a throaty groan. His fingers tightened briefly, releasing her to prop himself above her.

Their gasping breaths filled the room with the sounds

of their sated pleasure. Inside her, she felt the slight pulse of his flesh, and she clenched her muscles around him. At the soft grip, his hips jerked, and her lips curved in satisfaction.

When their breathing slowed, and the last vestiges of their trembles faded, Gavin withdrew from her and fell onto the bed beside her. He took off the condom and tossed it in the bin next to the bed.

Cora rolled to the side and gazed at him, taking in the strong profile of his face. His closed eyes and the slow, steady rise and fall of his chest had her wondering if he'd fallen asleep.

She lifted a hand and brushed at a strand of damp hair from his forehead. His lashes fluttered open, and she stared into his warm, dark-brown eyes. In their depths, she found such confusion her heart ached for him.

"*Você não é nada para mim*," he whispered.

A wave of emptiness consumed the lingering sensations that only moments before warmed her with euphoria.

She had expected it. Gavin wasn't going to simply snap out of his grieving because she was a good lay, or even because he might actually feel something for her. So, it all cycled back to her and whether she was willing to accept the role of nothing in his life.

It was humbling to admit her answer to that was yes. Right then, at that moment, she would take anything she could get and to hell with the devastation she'd face when she'd finally had enough.

SIXTEEN

CORA BLINKED RAPIDLY UNTIL her eyes adjusted, and she was able to make out shapes in the darkness surrounding her. Beside her, Gavin twisted restlessly, tangling himself in the comforter. That explained what woke her.

She rolled onto her side to gaze at him. She could see the whites of his eyes as he stared up at the ceiling, but there was something about it that seemed off.

"Gavin? Are you all right?" she asked.

His head whipped around to look at her, but he didn't answer. He wasn't so much staring *at* her as he was staring *through* her, and she realized he wasn't really awake.

"Gavin, wake up." She placed a hand on his shoulder. The touch seemed to propel him deeper into his dream, and his arm lashed out, smacking his hand into her pillow, missing her by less than an inch.

Cora scrambled back and scooted off the bed. She flicked on the bedside lamp, and in the soft light, she was able to see him clearly. His face was contorted in a mix of fury and agony.

"Gavin," she called, but he didn't react so she reached over and grasped his bicep, giving it a firm shake. "*Gavin.*"

An agonized bellow exploded from him as he shot upright, his arms flailing around. Cora pulled away, giving him space to get his bearings. He continued to thrash around for a minute, seemingly unaware of her presence or even where he was.

His shoulders heaved with each gasping breath he drew in until they gradually slowed. He scanned the room until his eyes settled on her and he ran a hand through his damp hair.

"You okay?" Cora hesitantly climbed back into the bed.

"Yeah. I'm good."

He rubbed his hands over his face. She grabbed the half-empty water bottle from the nightstand and passed it to him. He tipped his head back and drained the water, his Adam's apple bobbing with each gulp. He handed the empty bottle back to her then flopped back on the bed.

"That must have been a pretty intense nightmare."

She placed the bottle on the nightstand and settled back next to him. He tugged her close, pulling her back against his chest to spoon her.

"Not a nightmare. It was a night terror."

"What's the difference?"

"A nightmare is basically a bad dream that happens during the REM phase of sleep," he explained. "With a night terror, it happens between sleep phases when a sudden fear interrupts the cycle, so essentially, I'm partly awake. Most people who have night terrors don't even remember having them."

"Most people, but not you?"

"No, I remember. Maybe because mine aren't random or natural. These are a result of Sinclair and the genetic modifications he made to me."

She was tempted to ask him what he saw, but it seemed like such an intimate question. A strange thought, perhaps, after what they had shared, but she suspected the answer would expose a part of him to her that no one else had ever seen before.

His fingers traced a swirling path down her arm before entwining with hers atop the comforter.

"Sinclair is always there," he said after a long pause.

"That's understandable. The things he did ... It can't be easy to simply put it in the past."

"I was Three."

"When you went into the lab?"

"Not when, who. I was Subject Three. I suppose I could have just as easily been Four, except they took me out a minute before Caleb. Three was the only name I had until Mark took over the job as the teacher at the lab and gave each of us names."

"Your dad worked there?" She was shocked that Mark Walker had been involved with anything that hadn't to those boys.

"Only for a few months. He took the job without any idea what was going on. He figured it out pretty fast and worked with the feds to get us out. Without him, we'd all probably be dead, or so fucked up we'd wish we were."

Cora stayed quiet, not wanting to interrupt him and risk him stop talking. She lifted their joined hands and

ANGELA FRISTOE

pressed a kiss to the back of his hand.

"That last day in the labs, when the feds raided the place, they found me strapped to an exam table. My heart had stopped, and Sinclair had already written me off."

Her chest tightened at the thought of how close he'd come to dying.

"Every time I have one of these night terrors, I relive another day in the lab," he said. "The needles, the cuts, those were nothing compared to what my body went through when his serums caused mutations."

"I'm sorry," she said, tears blurring her vision. "I'm so sorry you went through that."

She felt his head nod against her shoulder. Nothing she said would erase the horrors he lived through. Behind her, the thumping of Gavin's heart calmed, and the rise and fall of his chest slowed. She thought he'd fallen asleep but then he moved their hands to rest on her hip.

"What are we doing, Cora?" he asked as he slipped his fingers from between hers. They skimmed up along her ribs, stopping when they brushed the underside of her breast.

Cora thought of what Hailey had said to her about being willing to take what she could get. There'd been a part of her that had scorned Hailey for doing that. Yet, there she was, doing the exact same thing.

"I love you. That's all I can do," she answered.

Her words seemed to take him back. His fingers stilled, and there was a catch in his breath before he let out a deep sigh.

"Would you like to go to dinner?"

Cora twisted her head around to look at him. "You're

serious? Right now?"

"Yeah, I'm serious. Not now, maybe later this week."

She turned back around, trying to hide the smile that curled her lips up. He sounded so nervous and hesitant—so unlike Gavin.

"Like a date?" she clarified. She tried to tell herself that wasn't what she wanted, because to him a date meant something entirely different than her aching heart hoped.

His chest shook with a deep chuckle.

"Yeah, as a date."

Asking Cora out had not been in Gavin's plans. In fact, it was the opposite of what he'd intended to say. Yet, as her proclamation of love hung in the stillness of the silent room, all he could think of was that he wanted more than just sex from her.

She took her time answering and he wondered if he'd managed to fuck it up. Hell, he'd only ever asked out Lela, and that was when he was sixteen. In the time since Lela's death, he'd hooked up with Hailey and a few other chicks, but dating never entered into it.

"I'd like that," she finally said.

Gavin hadn't realized how tense he'd been until her answer triggered a rush of relief. His nose buried in her hair, he inhaled the sweet vanilla sense of her shampoo.

He reached down and lifted her leg, angling it to rest on top of his, leaving her open to his touch. He pressed his pelvis forward, and his hardening cock twitched in response to the feel of her moist desire gathering along the lips of her pussy.

"I wish I could love you. I don't know what I'll want from you in the future," he admitted. "For now, this is all I can offer you."

As much as he wanted to deny there were emotions involved, he couldn't. In her quiet little way, Cora had managed to wiggle her way under his skin. The thought of not being able to touch her, to taste her lips, or to hear her soft laugh left him feeling empty.

"I can accept that," she said. "For now."

He slid two fingers inside her then pulled them back out to circle her clit. Her body trembled, and he increased the pressure on her sensitive bud as she rocked her hips back and forth.

The sweet scent of her arousal surrounded him, and the urge to possess her took over him. He growled and ground his penis along the crease of her ass.

Watching as she reached up to play with her nipples, he learned that she loved to gently roll them and then give a firm tug. She tossed her head back, and he kissed his way up along the side of her neck. She gave a shuddering sigh as he lapped at her skin then gently blew on it.

"Do you want me to fuck you, Coraline?" he said as he flicked a finger over her clit. "Do you want my cock sliding in your pussy?"

"Yes," she gasped. "Oh, God. Fuck me."

He angled them so she lay partially back on him. Between her legs, he guided his penis to her entrance and sank in until he was completely enveloped in her warm pussy. She gripped him like a velvet fist milking his cock as he pulled almost all the way out. Gavin struggled to keep moving slowly, digging his fingers into the soft flesh of her thigh, but instinct took over, and his hips surged thrusting, driving into Cora's depths.

Tingles crept along the base of his spine, and his rhythm grew wild as he lost all sense of control. Tension seized him, and he slammed his cock into her one more time. His eyes squeezed shut, and he groaned as his climax tore through him and his seed spurted forth.

Around him, Cora's pussy milked his cock, and he pumped his hips. Letting go of her leg, he returned to her sensitive nub, rolling and tugging it in the same pattern she used on her nipples. Her hips ground back into him, and her back arched as she strained toward her climax. He rubbed in quick, hard circles until she gasped and spasmed around him.

He slowed his movements, dragging out their pleasure until he slipped free of her moist grasp, their combined juices coating his flesh.

"Shit," he said, and she tensed against him. "Please tell me you're on the pill."

She relaxed and gave him a slight smile over her shoulder. "I am."

A puff of air rushed out, and he swept a strand of her hair behind her neck. He'd never really considered whether he wanted kids. With Lela, they'd been too young to even start talking about it, though he knew she'd wanted children one day.

"That's good," he said. "I'm clean. I got tested a few weeks ago, and I haven't been with anyone else since."

"I haven't been with anyone since my last test, either."

He shifted uncomfortably at the thought of her with another guy. He refused to call it jealousy. No, it was more like ... *Fuck.* His arms tightened around her as he pulled in a deep breath.

Cora pulled out of his hold and turned around. She cupped his face in her small hands, rubbing her soft palms along his stubbled jaw, and gazed into his eyes.

The words were on the tip of his tongue. *Você não é nada para mim.* His entire body reverberated with the need to say them, to put her in her place, to remind him that no matter how mind-blowing sex with her was she was nothing to him. Nothing more than a body.

But as he stared into her beautiful blue eyes, he didn't want to say them. He didn't want to make her just another body. He might not have loved Cora, but the idea of her being nothing to him twisted his insides.

Her lips brushed along his with a fleeting touch then she whispered, "Sleep."

That one simple word was all he needed to keep the words unspoken.

SEVENTEEN

GAVIN SAT WITH CALEB and Logan at a table in the back corner of the bar. Caleb said something, and Gavin gave a one-shoulder shrug, hearing his brother's words but not processing. He was too busy watching Cora from across the bar. She filled her tray with drink orders and then sashayed across the floor, carefully balancing it with one hand.

She had on a pair of short shorts, and he swore he caught a glimpse of her ass cheeks when she bent over to clear the table. And he wasn't the only one who'd noticed. He saw the looks the guys around the bar gave her, but as tempted as he was to buy her a pair of shorts to hide her glorious ass from their perverted eyes, he refused to miss out on his chance to ogle her himself.

Something hit his forehead, and he jerked in response, looking down at the table to see a balled up beer bottle label. He glared at a smirking Caleb.

"You seem distracted," Caleb said then lifted his beer to take a swig.

Gavin grunted and shoved a cheese-and-sour-cream-loaded nacho in his mouth.

"What do you know about David McCarty?" he asked around a mouthful of food.

"The name sounds familiar." Caleb's brow wrinkled in thought. Gavin waited a moment as his brother pulled the name from his memory, which thanks to Sinclair's experiments, didn't take long. "He's a cop. He took Cora's statement after the first accident."

"Try *both* accidents." Gavin opened a file on his tablet and slid it across to the other man.

He'd spent the day looking into the police reports, something about it nagging at him. What were the chances that both times, Cora's account had been dismissed? When he first pulled the accident reports, they seemed pretty straight forward. McCarty signed the first statement while a different officer's name, Patrick Greene, was on the second.

It wasn't until Gavin moved on to the 911 transcripts that McCarty's name popped up again as the responding officer. He replayed every word Cora told him about what happened and realized she'd only spoken to McCarty. So, he pulled the reports again and that's when he discovered it.

"Look at the signatures." He used his fingers to expand the image they were looking at. "Different names, same handwriting."

"Son-of-a-bitch. How certain are you?" Logan leaned back in his chair.

"Hundred percent."

"You used the analysis software I sent you?" Caleb asked.

"Didn't need to. There were so many commonalities between these two, I figured it might be faster to check out this Patrick Greene's actual signature. So I pulled up his DMV file. This is a straight-up simulation forgery, and a crappy one, at that."

"You pulled his DMV file? Should I be worried about any trace coming back to one of my IPs?"

"Nope. Noah's girlfriend got it for me."

Logan raised an eyebrow. "And does Alicia know she helped you?"

"Well, technically she did Noah a favor by checking out Sky's new boyfriend. So I guess she thought she was helping Noah out." Gavin smirked. "Apparently, she had a lot of questions about why our twenty-year-old sister is dating a guy who's old enough to be her grandpa."

"All right, so McCarty is hiding something," Caleb said. "What?"

"No clue. All he did was take Cora's statement. I don't see anything different than what she told me. I can't see any reason why he wouldn't sign his own name."

Caleb pressed his lips together and tapped a finger on the edge of the tablet. "Let me do some digging. I've got a few connections on the force I might be able to hit up."

Gavin didn't like the idea of not being in control, but he wasn't in the same position as Caleb. His brother's work with TanTech opened a lot of doors Gavin wouldn't get through on his own. If they had time, he'd be able to figure a way to access the info, but time wasn't something they had. Sinclair had shown twice that he would risk Cora's life for whatever twisted reason motivated him. They needed to bring him down before he could try again.

"Has Merrick found anything on the guy who ran Cora off the road?"

Caleb shook his head. "He's accessed the local footage, but it's scarce. He's working on a different angle, looking into damaged rentals and repair shops."

"Fuck, this sucks." Gavin tipped his head back to gaze up at the ceiling and dug his fingers into his hair.

"At least you didn't have to work today," Cora said, staring down at him.

"Hey." He returned the smile she gave him. Her tongue peeked out to moisten her lips, and he was thrown back to that very morning when she'd used those lips for something other than speaking.

"I'm off in a couple minutes, you guys want anything else?"

"We're good," Logan answered for all of them. "Come sit with us after."

Her eyes flicked from Logan then back to Gavin. The hesitation was a glimpse into her uncertainty about how open they were going to be about being together. He gave a slight nod, and her smile grew.

"Yeah, I'll be back in a few minutes."

He watched her walk away, her ponytail swishing in time with her hips.

"How's she holding up?" Caleb asked.

Gavin glanced at his brother and found Caleb's eyes following Cora across the room. The inclination to punch his twin had his hands balled into fists, but he held back. Cora was a sexy woman, and men were going to stare at her. He couldn't beat up *every* guy who looked at her.

"She's fine."

"I don't think I've ever seen you be so civil toward Cora," Logan remarked. "For a while, I thought I'd have to fire one of you. Well, fire you."

"So much for family first."

"I thought we already settled this? Cora is family."

"How did things go at the lab?" Caleb twirled his empty beer bottle on its rim, a circle of condensation forming on the table.

"Nielson tried to deny working with Sinclair, but she had all of his notes on Cora. Whatever he did to us, he hasn't stopped."

"You really think that's what he's doing?"

"Absolutely. There was a photo of Cora with Subject 8 written across it." Gavin grabbed a bunch of nachos and dropped them on the small plate in front of him. "At first, I thought he was taunting me, letting me know what he could do. But Nielson's questions were too specific. She was looking for certain pieces of info from Cora."

"Did she get it?" Caleb tugged the nacho platter across the table, out of Gavin's reach.

"No."

"So all of this was bait? He didn't do anything to Cora?"

"He injected her with the PH-9E serum. Some kind of variation on the last test he did on us."

He was on the verge of telling them about the visions Cora had been having when he noticed his brothers looking past him. A glance over his shoulder revealed Cora walking toward them. She'd changed out of the snug black Porter's Pub shirt and into a wispy gypsy style top that barely clung to her shoulders.

His foot hooked around the leg of the empty chair beside him and pulled it out for her. The fact that it moved closer to him was pure coincidence. Placing her drink on the table, she slid onto the chair and gave a wide smile in greeting. He wasn't sure what he expected when she arrived, but the casual greeting, no different than what she gave his brothers, wasn't it.

"Gavin was just telling us that Nielson confirmed Sinclair injected you with some type of gene mutation serum." Caleb rested his elbows on the table and leaned toward Cora. "So, I have to conclude that you've been exhibiting symptoms."

She turned surprised eyes on to Gavin. "You didn't tell them?"

"I thought it would be easier if you explained."

While she told his brothers about the visions, he took the time to study her. Earlier, her hair had been pulled back into its normal high ponytail, keeping it out of her way during work. Now, though, her soft curls were loose covering her shoulders, and the sight brought a knowing smile to his face. Thanks to the scruff of his beard, she'd woken with a case of beard burn along her delicate skin.

Under the table, he slid his hand over her knee and up to her bare thigh. Her hand clamped down on his before he could go any further.

"We can use this," Logan said once Cora finished describing the visions.

"How?" Cora asked.

"We've been chasing Sinclair, always one step behind him. He's out there watching us, waiting to strike," he explained. "With your visions, we can figure out exactly when and where he'll be and grab him before he makes his move."

Caleb nodded, an eager look taking over his face. "You mentioned having a log of the visions. We need to use that data to find patterns with Sinclair's movements."

"There are no patterns," Cora said. "That's the problem. Everything is random, constantly changing."

Gavin and Caleb flashed each other identical smirks. Identifying patterns, whether binary, mathematical, or behavioral, was where they excelled. Nielson once told them their ability to find those patterns along with their eidetic memories were due to PH-02F, a genetic modifier that enhanced the brain's visual and information processing, strengthening synaptic efficiency.

"There's a pattern, and we'll find it," Gavin said.

"But Sinclair's movements are always dependent on you."

"That's exactly how we can manipulate them," Caleb interjected. "Once we understand how he's picking the moments, we can create a series of opportunities, pinpointing which one he'll follow through on."

Cora's shocked eyes flickered from brother to brother. "You're going to create opportunities for him? Are you *crazy*? The guy is planning to kill Gavin, and you want to give him more chances?"

Gavin understood her concerns, but Caleb's idea had the greatest probability of success. By controlling when Sinclair could strike, they'd be better able to catch him before he did anything. Yes, there were risks, but getting Sinclair was worth it. For what he did to them as kids, but more importantly for what he'd done to Lela. Gavin was determined to see him brought down.

"How would you even be able to do that?" Cora shook her head. "The situations are so normal. I wouldn't be able to tell them apart without there being something significant in each."

"That's why you'll be there," Caleb said.

A long pause ensued as each of them considered what that meant. It meant putting Cora in the line of fire, but he realized why Caleb suggested it. Cora's presence meant she'd easily be able to identify the events well before anything actually happened. It would keep Sinclair from suspecting they'd figured anything out. More important, was the fact Sinclair obviously kept tabs on Cora, and this would present him with more opportunity to do so.

"I'll bring Cora's journal by in the morning," Gavin said.

"Wait a second," Logan interrupted. "Can we go back to the question of involving Cora in this?"

"It makes sense for her to be there. It's the only way for us to pinpoint when Sinclair will hit," Gavin explained.

"What about asking whether it's worth risking her life?" Logan asked.

The incredulity in his voice caused Gavin to squirm in his seat, and he pulled his hand away from where it rested on Cora's leg. He resented the implication that he didn't care about Cora's life, but this was Sinclair.

"Think about what Sinclair's done to us, Logan. He almost destroyed us in the labs, he killed Lela, and now he's hunting us. We need to stop him. We need to make sure he pays for what he's done."

"And if Cora gets caught in the crossfire?" Logan's eyes

drilled into Gavin.

"I admit, it's not an ideal plan, but letting Sinclair go isn't an option anymore. We'll keep her safe," he assured Logan. Even to his own ears, his reasoning sounded weak. Beside him, Cora shifted in her seat, lifting a hand to rub the side of her neck.

"It's okay, Logan. We need to do this," she said. "If Gavin and Caleb think this is the best way, then I'm in. At this point, Sinclair being out there is just as dangerous for me as it is for you guys."

"Fine," Logan conceded, though his reluctance was evident. "Let's get started."

Gavin pulled up the notepad app on the tablet, and beside him Cora sank back into her seat, shoulders slumped. In his rush to start working on the plan, he'd almost forgotten about their date.

"Not tonight. We have plans." Gavin closed the tablet.

"We do?" Caleb asked.

"Cora and I have plans." Ignoring the curious looks on his brother's faces, he pushed his chair back and held his hand out to Cora. She slid her hand into his and stood along with him. "I'll catch up with you guys in the morning."

"I take it you didn't tell them about us," Cora said as they walked through the parking lot to his Jeep.

Gavin shrugged. "It never came up."

She made some kind of noise under her breath that left him wondering if he'd said something wrong. He shook his head dismissing the thought. Cora didn't play games like that. Not that it would have mattered anyway. He never willingly talked to his brothers about his hookups.

Okay, so Cora wasn't just a hookup, but he wasn't exactly planning on anything long-term with her, either. Hell, he still couldn't believe he'd even asked her out.

He unlocked the Jeep and held the door open as Cora slid into the passenger seat. Her shorts inched up her legs, and his palms itched with the desire to stroke her smooth skin. He quickly closed her door and went around to climb behind the wheel.

"So where are we going?" She tucked a strand of hair behind her ear.

"There's a new Mexican restaurant in Billings I thought we'd check out."

Going all the way to Billings was a bit risky with Sinclair out there, but he wasn't about to take her to the pub or one of the diners in town for their first date. Besides, Cora would know if Sinclair was going to make his move. Sticking close to her would be key to finding the son-of-a-bitch.

"Do you think it'll work?"

He glanced at her then focused back on the road. "I do. Sinclair's got a reason for what he's doing. I don't know what it is yet, but once Caleb and I go through your notes, we'll know how he's doing it."

"You said that whatever he injected into me was the same thing he did to you. So how come you don't have visions?"

"It was a variation, so he's adjusted it to obtain the results he wants. Which is probably why I have the night terrors while you're getting visions."

"I hate this," she said, the threat of tears in her voice.

He reached over to slide his hand behind her neck and

gently massaged it until she looked over at him.

"No more talk about Sinclair, Nielson, or SIEGE, okay?" he said. "Tonight, it's just you and me."

EIGHTEEN

JUST YOU AND ME.

It sounded so simple, so sweet. And totally unattainable. Wanting Gavin's words to be true didn't make them so. Whether it was Sinclair, Lela, or someone else, Cora didn't think it would ever be just the two of them.

It was nice to pretend, though, and it was almost too easy to. Sitting across from Gavin in the restaurant, she smiled and laughed at the stories he told her of his brothers and his sister. When he asked her questions, she answered as if he really cared about what she said.

"Do you miss Denver?" he asked as he laid his cutlery across his cleared plate. He somehow managed to devour his entire plate before she ate even halfway through her dinner.

She thought about Denver and what her life had been like there. Compared to Thompson Creek, it was a massive city. Downtown was packed with skyscrapers, and the freeways were always busy. She didn't miss the constant business, but there was no denying the beauty of the Rocky Mountains in the distance and the park outside the museum.

"Sometimes," she admitted. "There's a lot of convenience to living in the city, and Denver is beautiful. Although, I think Manitou Springs was my favorite place to go."

"I've been there a few times," he said in a hushed voice.

A far-off look took over his eyes, and Cora realized he'd probably gone with Lela when she toured the University of Colorado campuses. Cora had almost gone until she learned Gavin was going as well. The idea of spending time alone with the two of them, watching Gavin fawn over Lela, left her feigning illness. Lela hadn't been happy; she even accused Cora of not liking Gavin.

Gavin blinked rapidly and cleared his throat, and Lela's ghost vanished as quickly as it had come.

"Would you have stayed there if ..." his voice faded.

And there was Sinclair.

Cora shrugged, taking her time finishing her mouthful of food before answering. As delicious as the meal was, the thought of Sinclair turned her stomach. "Maybe. Working at the museum wasn't exactly what I wanted to do, but it was a good job, and I liked the staff. There was an opportunity to move up to a better position."

"I remember how much you loved art. The first time we met you had pencil smudges on your nose and chin and were carrying around a sketchbook."

"I did have a habit of doing that," she said. "It made a great look for senior portrait."

They laughed, though Cora was certain that wasn't the first time they'd met. The moment was seared into her memory, and she knew she hadn't started carting around that sketchbook until a few months after they met. What he recalled was most likely the moment he found out she and Lela were friends.

"Why did you stop?"

"Being an artist isn't a career; it's a hobby."

His eyebrows shot up. "That's not you talking. That's your mother."

She dropped her gaze to the plate in front of her, poking at the last few strips of fajita meat with her fork.

"I didn't think you'd ever met my mother," she said.

"I haven't, but from everything I've heard about her and the way you reacted at the thought of her coming to visit, it's pretty obvious she's more sensible than sensitive."

Cora chuckled. If only describing her mother were actually that simple.

"She loves me, and I know she wants the best for me, wants me to have a good life, but her ideas don't always match up with what I envision."

"Like giving up a career as an artist for a steady job?"

"Like that. Like moving to Denver and moving away from Denver." She snorted. "Like every other decision I make in my life."

She grabbed her drink glass and took a long sip of the tropical frozen margarita, wishing the sweet taste would cover the sharp bitterness of her words. Somehow, while striving to avoid the ghosts of the past, she left the door wide open for the bane of her existence.

"Let's not talk about my family," she said, placing her glass back on the table. She gave a grin that did little to relieve the tension caused by thinking about her mother. "What are your survival plans for the zombie apocalypse?"

"Zombie apocalypse?" he laughed. "Is this something I should be prepared for?"

As strange as her question was, it accomplished what Cora had hoped. There was no more discussing her mom, no opportunity for Gavin to think of Lela, and no way for Sinclair to slip into the topic.

The discussion spiraled from zombies to television and hobbies, and Cora realized how little she knew about the specifics of his daily life. And while he didn't hold the same love of the zombie genre as she did, they did both watch some of the same crime shows.

It wasn't until they were eating dessert that Cora let Sinclair weasel his way back in-between them. She dipped a sopaipilla into the small container of honey. The light, crispy pastry was one of her favorite desserts, yet it did little to distract her from Sinclair.

"Can I ask you something?" she asked.

"You just did," he said with a smirk. She rolled her eyes.

"Something about Sinclair," she clarified.

"Go for it."

"I get that the visions I have and your night terrors are both caused by whatever Sinclair injected into us. But you said the night terrors were like his calling card and they let you know when he's near. How can you be sure?"

"He told me. As part of the deal he cut, he was required to tell each of us about the anticipated effects of everything he'd done to us."

"Why would he want anyone to have that ability?"

"Apparently, the government wants their soldiers to be able to sense the presence of their enemy."

Psychic connection. He didn't say the words, but it's the only way Cora could think of to describe it. It was the same way she would describe her visions. She thought of how the variant of the serum Sinclair used on her allowed her to anticipate the enemy's moves. Gavin's night terrors and her visions were working together to find Sinclair.

"You look like you've figured something out," Gavin said.

"No, just thinking," she said, reluctant to force him into accepting another connection between them. Their conversation turned back to the mundane and thoughts of Sinclair slipped to the back of her mind.

Gavin watched Cora eat the last bite of the sopaipillas. A drop of honey landed on her lower lip, and her tongue peeked out to catch it. Damn, he wanted to taste that honey, to lick it off her lips. He could picture her lying on the bed naked as he drizzled honey down the middle of her chest and then back up around her nipples. He'd suck the sweet nectar from her rigid buds and—

"Gavin? Are you okay?"

"What? Yeah, I'm good." He shook his head, clearing away the image of her luscious, honey-coated lips. He coughed and under the table adjusted his jeans to ease the press of the zipper along his hardening cock.

"Are you ready?"

"Fuck, yes." He slid from the booth and held out a hand to help her out.

"Was having dinner with me that bad?"

"No, of course not." As they walked toward the exit, his

hand pressed to the base of her spine. "I was thinking we should pick up some honey on the way home."

"You said you didn't like honey."

He leaned down until his lips were next to her ear. "I didn't until I realized how much better it would taste if I licked it off your nipples."

Her eyes widened, and a lovely pink blush crept along her cheeks. "You are so bad."

A chuckle burst from him and he avoided the light swat she sent his way by taking a long step forward to open the door. When she'd passed through, he let the door swing shut behind them and draped an arm over her shoulder, tucking her against his side.

A few feet from the door, something changed. He wasn't sure what it was at first, but as the hair on the back of his neck stood up, realization dawned. Sinclair was there. Not somewhere in Billings or Montana. He was watching them right then, plotting his next move.

Cora stiffened beside him and he glanced down to see her searching the parking lot. That was all it took for him to know she'd seen the moment in a vision.

"Keep walking," he ordered, using his hold on her to keep her moving toward the Jeep. "Do you know where he is?"

"Somewhere across the street." Her eyes squinted as she tried to recall details. "He's behind a dark van or SUV."

Gavin pulled his keys from his pocket and shoved them into her hand. "Go to the Jeep."

"What are you gonna do?" She looked up at him, her face pale with fear.

"Find him. Go." He pulled his arm away from her shoulders and started to veer across the parking lot, heading toward the street.

"Gavin!" Cora screamed behind him.

He turned to find her running toward him. She threw herself at him just as a sharp crack of a gunshot echoed through the quiet street. He opened his arms and caught her as she fell against him. A flash of movement across the street drew his gaze, and a few moments later there was a squeal of tires as a dark sedan tore out onto the road and away from them.

He'd missed his chance. Sinclair was gone. He grabbed Cora's upper arm and tugged her along with him.

"What the hell are you doing? I told you to go to the Jeep."

"He was going to shoot you," she said as she climbed into the passenger seat and wrapped her arms around herself.

The tremor in her voice only fueled his fury toward Sinclair for daring to threaten them and at her for putting herself in danger. How could she have done that? He slammed her door shut and stomped around to the front of the vehicle before going back to yank open her door again. He paused to take a deep breath and some of his anger for her drained away as he took in the pale glow of her face.

"You knew what he was there, Cora. Why didn't you get in the Jeep?"

"He was going to shoot you," she repeated faintly.

"Well, he missed."

"I know." She loosened the hold she had on her left

arm and held her hand out in front of her. Blood covered her palm. "He hit me instead."

Shock cemented Gavin in place as he stared in horror at Cora's blood.

"I don't think it's too bad," she said and the shaky words propelled him into motion. He pulled her from the vehicle, turning her so he could see where she'd been hit.

The sleeve of her gauzy white shirt was ripped and through the blood-soaked hole, he saw where blood gushed from the side of her arm. He reached for the neckline of her shirt, gripping it in both hands. She leaned back.

"What are you doing?" She pressed a hand back over the wound.

"I need to see it and we need to stop the bleeding."

"So you're going to rip off my shirt? I don't think so."

"It's not like you'll be able to wear it again."

"No, but I don't fancy the idea of standing around half-naked for a bunch of gawkers to ogle." She inclined her head to the side, and sure enough, a small crowd had gathered outside the restaurant, drawn by the sound of gunfire.

How stupid could people be? Any intelligent person would be sheltered inside waiting for police to clear the area. Then again, he'd known what Sinclair had planned, yet he walked straight toward the coward.

"Fine. Sit down." He lifted her to sit her sideways on the seat, her legs hanging outside.

"Yo, man!" yelled their waiter from the side entrance of the building. He held up his cell phone and waved it in the air. "I called the cops."

"Thanks," Gavin called back. "We need an ambulance, too."

"No, we don't," Cora protested. "It's a scratch."

"Scratches don't bleed like this. You might need stitches."

"It doesn't even hurt."

"Because you're in shock. Give it a few minutes, and it's gonna hurt like a bitch."

He reached into the back seat and dug into his gym bag. Finding his hand towel, he pulled it out and nudged her hand away and replaced it with his towel-wrapped hand.

"What are we going to tell the cops?" she asked as the sound of approaching sirens reached them.

"Nothing."

"We're going to lie to the police?" She stared up at him in surprise.

"No. We tell them the truth. We didn't see who did it, and we can't describe the vehicle."

"But ..."

"It's the truth."

"So lie by omission."

"Sinclair has someone working for him in the County Sheriff's office, and he might have connections to the local police. Providing too much info could tip our hand and give Sinclair the edge again." He gave her a crooked smile. "Besides, what do you think would happen if we started going on about visions of the future and secret government experiments?"

A weak smile curled her lips. "Good point."

The police arrived, and while one of them spoke to

Gavin about what happened, the other gave first-aid to Cora until the ambulance arrived. Gavin watched with eagle eyes as the EMT took over, cutting away Cora's shirt sleeve and checking the wound. At the EMT's urging, Cora agreed to let Gavin take her to an emergency center. Two hours and ten stitches later, they were headed back to Thompson Creek.

The pain meds the doctor gave her kicked in and she was fast asleep, her head resting precariously on the seatbelt. She looked so tiny wearing his old Seahawks hoodie, her face framed with random curls that had escaped her ponytail. He reached over to smooth some of the loose strands back and noticed a few droplets of dried blood on her cheek.

His fingers tightened on the steering wheel as he thought of how close she came to getting seriously injured or killed. Goddamn Sinclair. The man had already taken so much from their family, Gavin refused to let him keep getting away with it.

Beside him, Cora stirred. She gave a yawn as she sat up and rubbed her eyes with her palms. "Are we home yet?"

"Almost. How are you feeling?" When she didn't answer, he glanced over to find her staring straight ahead, unblinking. "Cora?"

He nudged her thigh and then gave it a shake. Still no response. Telling himself not to panic, he slowed the Jeep and veered to the side of the road. He was in the process of unbuckling his seat belt so he could move and get a better look at her when she blinked and looked at him.

"Sorry, I must have fallen asleep." She glanced out the window. "Why are we stopped?"

"Are you okay?"

"Yeah, I just ... I had a vision."

"Want to talk about it?"

She shrugged, and as he pulled back onto the road, she described what she'd seen. Most of it was Sinclair focusing solely on him. Other than knowing the location and approximate time of day, there was nothing to distinguish it from any other day.

They arrived at her apartment, and he walked her up, following her in to make sure it was safe. She laughed at what she considered over-protectiveness, but he wasn't willing to put anything past Sinclair. After he checked that the place was safe, she went to her room and collapsed on the bed.

"You want me to stay?" he asked.

"No, that's okay. I'm going to crash, and that wouldn't be much fun for you."

He leaned over her, resting his hands on either side of her head.

"Sex isn't the only reason I'd stick around," he said and was rewarded with a sweet smile.

"Take the journal. It's on the coffee table."

"Okay." He gave her a gentle kiss, lingering for a moment at the taste of honey that still clung to her lips. He lingered a moment, then slowly pulled back. "Sleep. We'll talk in the morning."

NINETEEN

GAVIN PULLED THE DOOR to Cora's apartment closed behind him. That's when it hit him. He should stay with her. Leaving her alone didn't sit quite right. Even if she slept the entire time, he should have stayed so she didn't wake alone in the morning. But it was too late. The door was locked, and despite his ability to hack any computer system known to man, picking locks was another matter.

Downstairs, a quick scan of the street assured him the area was clear of Sinclair. Yet the stillness of the night and the lack of people anywhere nearby made him hesitant to walk away. He stared up at the window to her living room and shook his head. *She'll be fine*, he told himself. Sinclair wasn't after her. The safest place for her right then was far away from Gavin.

Ten minutes of aimless driving later, he pulled up to the back of Porter's. The pub had been closed for nearly an hour, but he knew Noah would be there. The guy lived and breathed that place. Gavin used his key to enter the side door, and sure enough, found his brother holed up in the office running sales reports.

"What the hell are you doing here?" Noah asked when Gavin appeared in the doorway to the office.

"Came for a beer." Gavin shoved his hands in his pockets and leaned against the door frame. "You're losing your edge. I thought you'd take me out before I got a foot in the door."

"You breathe so heavy I heard you before you even made it to the door." Noah shut his laptop and rose from his seat. He brushed past Gavin, who turned to follow the older man out to the main room.

"You really need to get a life," Gavin said as he sat on a stool. He watched Noah pull a couple beers from the fridge behind the bar and caught the bottle Noah sent sliding across the surface of the counter.

"I have a life," Noah replied. "That's what a career, house, and a girlfriend are—a life."

"Great, thanks for the reminder of everything I don't have." Gavin twisted off the bottle cap.

"You've got a job and Cora."

Gavin snorted. "I work in a bar."

"So do I."

"You own the place. I bartend. I'm pretty sure that's not the career Mom and Dad would choose for me." Hell, bartending didn't even qualify as a career by *his* standards.

Noah gave a one-shoulder shrug and nodded his head. "And Cora?"

"She's ..." *How the fuck to describe what was going on with them?* "Not my girlfriend."

Noah folded his arms and rested them on the top of the bar as he stared at Gavin. "You go on dates with her? Call her? Fuck her?"

"Jesus, can you give it a rest?" His nerves prickled at that phrase. *Fuck her.* Yeah, they'd fucked to the point that everyone and everything else ceased to exist, but it wasn't just *fucking*.

"You know what you're doing?" Noah asked.

That question and the accompanying doubtful look was exactly why Gavin had planned to go home after leaving Cora nestled in her bed. He knew this is what Noah would do, yet he went there anyway.

"No," Gavin answered honestly.

Cora was messing with his mind, and the shit going down with Sinclair only made things more complicated. Maybe if Sinclair weren't in the midst of fucking up their lives, Gavin would have a moment to think clearly and figure out what was between Cora and him.

"She loves you," Noah said.

Gavin nodded and took a swig of his beer, avoiding his brother's eyes. Cora's feelings for him weren't a secret, but he didn't relish the idea of talking about them with his brothers.

Not that Noah was a big talker. Of the six brothers, he was the quietest, partly because of his personality, but it was also due to habit.

When they were freed from the labs, Noah's hearing had been so acute, the sound of his own breathing threatened to drive him crazy. He'd been sedated for weeks before he could handle normal volumes. His heightened senses were the reason he'd been spared having to attend high school. It wasn't until a few years ago that he stopped reacting to loud noises and bright lights. Gavin wasn't sure if the effects of that particular serum faded or if Noah simply gained control over his ability. Regardless, it left Noah being labeled the strong and silent one of the bunch.

"Something feels off about this," Noah remarked. "Sinclair's making this all too easy."

"Maybe he's not as smart as we give them credit for." Even as he spoke, he dismissed the thought. Noah was right; it was too easy.

"Bullshit."

Noah rubbed one hand over his short beard. The motion drew Gavin's eyes to the scar that started under the hair and snaked up to Noah's left eye, a reminder of what a mistake it was to underestimate Sinclair. It was a lesson he learned when he was seven.

None of them ever went to the testing room willingly, though they never fought back. Until Gavin decided he wasn't going to make it easy for Sinclair. Normally, they were alone in the lab during testing, but that day, Sinclair brought both Gavin and Noah in. Looking back on it, Gavin figured that's probably what made him feel so brave.

When Sinclair went to strap him in, Gavin exploded. Fists swinging, he connected with the doctor's face. Then Aiden was there, wrapping his arms around Gavin, trying to restrain him. That's when Noah flew into the mix. He jumped on Aiden's back, scrambling to get some kind of hold on the man.

At the ages of seven and nine, the boys' had little control of the monsters Sinclair created, and Aiden and the doctor had even less. Even the team of security guards who ran in at Sinclair's calls struggled to contain Noah and Gavin. It wasn't until Aiden took a scalpel to Noah's face that Gavin stopped fighting and learned fighting back only hurt those you cared about.

He suspected Sinclair was depending on him to remember that lesson.

"Sinclair took a shot at me tonight. Before it happened, I could feel him watching us, but I couldn't spot him." He picked at the label encircling his bottle, ripping it into small pieces.

"You're safe, though."

"Only because of Cora."

"How so?"

"She had a vision of it. She didn't realize until it was happening, but it was enough to give us a bit of warning."

"But he still got off a shot?"

Gavin shifted on the stool as the gut-clenching fear he felt in those few moments after the shot resurfaced.

"He hit her instead of me."

Noah stiffened, then relaxed. "I'm going to assume since you didn't lead with that info she's okay."

"It grazed her. I took her to an emergency clinic. She got a few stitches then I took her home."

He didn't tell Noah it was a minor wound. It didn't matter how minor or how close it had been. She'd been shot. The stain of blood on her shirt, the warmth of it pooling against his hand as he tried to stop the bleeding; those things were what mattered. She could have died.

Reaching into his back pocket, he pulled out the spiral notebook Cora used to record her notes. He opened the book, combing through the pages. Her delicate scrawl filled each page with details that would help bring Sinclair down.

"He's been watching me for months, possibly years." He closed the book and slid it across to Noah, but his brother didn't take it.

"Logan told me about the plan to use Cora's visions. To use Cora," Noah said. The long pause he left before speaking again told Gavin exactly what Noah thought of the idea. "You sure that's still the best plan?"

Cora had been in Sinclair's line of fire. If Gavin followed through with his plan, she'd constantly be in danger. Yet, what was the alternative? Sinclair escaped punishment under the law before. He had the connections and resources to do it again. Could he simply let Sinclair walk away?

He didn't even need to think about it. *No.* Sinclair destroyed Gavin's life. He killed Lela, robbing her of a life with Gavin. Even if Sinclair willingly walked away from Gavin, the Walker family, and Cora, he didn't deserve to. Sinclair needed to be brought to justice. He needed to suffer like Lela had as she drowned in the river, agony ripping through her as her lungs filled with water—like Gavin had as his life collapsed around him until he was nothing more than a hollow shell.

"It's the only plan," Gavin said with a raspy voice.

He brought the beer bottle to his lips and met Noah's eyes, seeing the disappointment and concern his brother didn't speak of. He met the gaze defiantly. This wasn't a decision he made lightly. He understood the risk to Cora and himself, but he had a chance to avenge Lela and end the man who haunted him. He couldn't pass it up.

"I'll keep her safe."

"You sure you can?" Noah asked.

God, he hated his brother sometimes. Of his five brothers, Noah was the one always willing to call bullshit on him. Half the time, he didn't even have to say anything to get Gavin to admit the truth. Honestly, Gavin didn't know if he could keep Cora safe, but he didn't want to think about that. Admitting it out loud would make his doubts real, and if they were real, then he'd have to confront them.

Was he actually willing to sacrifice Cora in the name of revenge?

It scared him to think he might have to.

TWENTY

PURGATORY WASN'T REALLY A concept Cora was familiar with, but what little she did know explained what she was experiencing. How else could she describe being caught between heaven and hell? And that's where she was.

Each night, she came home with Gavin to her apartment. They talked, laughed, made love. They did everything that a couple would do. Then morning would come, and that little piece of heaven vanished as she saw the empty look in his eyes as he said the words: *Você não é nada para mim.*

After weeks of it, she shouldn't hurt so much every time he said it. If anything, it hurt more because while she fell deeper in love with him, he continued to view her as a means to an end.

She wanted to be angry. She wanted to scream and rail at him. She didn't. Sinclair had done so much damage she couldn't blame Gavin for wanting to stop him.

"That good, huh?" Keeley said as she dug her elbow into the Cora's side.

"What?" Cora blinked, pulling herself out of her thoughts.

"Oh, please. Ever since you and Gavin started this whole dating-but-not-dating-but-looks-like-dating thing, you've been floating around all starry-eyed." Keeley twirled a strand of her hair and fluttered her eyelashes as she gave an over-the-top dreamy smile.

Cora laughed at her friend's silliness. "I have not."

"Okay, maybe not every minute, but you've been doing it enough that I can tell when the two of you have been getting it on, and I have to say I'm a bit leery of going into the locker room after walking in on the two of you last week."

A gasp exploded from Cora, and her eyes darted over to see if any of the kitchen staff overheard, but the two men were too intent on their work.

"We were not doing anything in there," she denied in a hushed tone.

"Only because I interrupted." Keeley giggled and flicked the cloth she held at Cora.

Cora snatched up a plastic water jug and, slamming the lid of the ice machine open, scooped up some ice. The lid dropped back down, punctuating Cora's lack of denial.

"So? You ever going to give me details?" Keeley asked.

"Unlike some people—" Cora raised her eyebrows and looked pointedly at Keeley, "—I keep my private life private."

"Get your mind out of the gutter. I'm not asking for sex deets. I was talking about all the other crap."

"Mmhmm." Cora rolled her eyes doubtfully.

She passed Keeley the ice-filled container and grabbed

another two from the shelf, filling them up as well. Ice water wasn't exactly in demand at the pub, but that day Merrick had reserved a table for a group of TanTech clients during lunch.

"Seriously, though," Keeley said. "What's going on between you guys? One week he can barely look at you without going into full-on rage, and now he's sleeping at your place every night."

"It's complicated."

"What isn't?"

"This is different." Cora wanted to talk to Keeley about all of the barriers that were in her relationship with Gavin, but they all cycled back to Sinclair, and she couldn't break Gavin's confidence.

"Why? Because of his dead fiancée? Because he has commitment issues? Or because of Sinclair?"

Cora's head snapped around to stare up at Keeley.

"How do you know about Sinclair?"

"Sky tells me pretty much everything."

Sudden tension stiffened Cora's back. The thought of other people talking about her visions and what caused them left her fuming. "Such as?"

"That Sinclair is the doctor who tortured her brothers, he's stalking Gavin, and he seems to also be targeting you. Oh, and she might have mentioned that the reason you and Gavin are dating is to try and lure Sinclair out into the open."

Cora sighed in relief. Sky hadn't told Keeley everything. Though, she suspected her brothers wouldn't be too happy knowing she was blabbing all their secrets.

Avoiding answering Keeley's question, Cora carried the

water jugs out to the reserved table. Escaping a curious Keeley, though, was like getting rid of a tic—nearly impossible.

"So? Is it all for show like Sky says?" Keeley followed on her heels, carrying a basket with cutlery and condiments.

"No. Maybe ... I'm not sure how to explain it. I mean, yes, part of it has to do with Sinclair, but not all of it." She pulled a stack of napkins from her waist apron and placed them onto the table. "Can we not talk about this anymore?"

Keeley threw up her hands in defeat. "All right, I won't bug you anymore. I want you to promise me two things."

"What?"

"First, I want you to think about whether this thing you two have going on is real, because as hot as Gavin is he can be a major asshole, and I don't want you getting hurt."

Cora nodded, unable to speak around the lump forming in her throat.

"Second, you've got to get me some pictures of his ass." She laughed at Cora's gasp. "Come on, this might be my one chance to see the backside of a Walker."

"You are so horrible."

"That's what makes me so good," Keeley tossed back as she went to unlock the front entrance. It was only a few minutes past opening, but two of their regulars were already waiting.

The afternoon flew by. The extra business they'd had after Dixon's closed was still going strong. There were only a handful of eateries in town, so one closing usually meant an influx at the others, though with their over twenty-one policy, Porter's Pub didn't benefit as much.

The constant stream of customers kept Cora occupied, enough that she could almost put Keeley's requests out of her mind. Occasionally, though, one of them slipped in. The request for nude photos of Gavin was easy to dismiss. No way was she going share that image. For whatever length of time she had him, he was hers and hers alone.

It was the other request that lingered, nagging at her as she took orders, delivered drinks, and tried to maintain conversations with customers.

Was this thing between her and Gavin real? It was sad how quickly she came to the conclusion that no, it wasn't real. Things between them had moved so fast, yet they'd reached an impasse. As much as Cora wanted a future with Gavin and the chance to build something with him, he was just as determined to keep himself separate.

Once they brought down Sinclair, where would they be? Cora suspected they'd be right back to where they were two months before; tip-toeing around each other.

That wasn't what she wanted, and despite Darren calling her a martyr, she wasn't willing to spend her life waiting for Gavin to decide if he wanted her fully and completely.

After her shift, she stopped by the back office and found Noah parked behind the desk, sorting receipts.

"Hey, need something?" he asked.

"No, I was just wondering if you had a minute to talk."

"That sounds serious. Come on in." He put down the receipts he held and pushed them slightly to the side as she closed the door behind her and sat across from him.

"What's up?"

"I'm moving back to Denver."

The words erupted from her before she'd even had an opportunity to think them through. Yet, once said, it was as if a weight had been lifted. Noah didn't say anything, just stared at her until her nerves took over.

"I don't know when I'm leaving. I don't even have a job or a place to stay yet, and I'll be here until we stop Sinclair, but ... that's my plan. To move to Denver. Soon."

Her legs jiggled, and she pressed her hands to her knees to stop them. Noah continued watching her, his dark, heavy brows pulled low over his eyes.

"I just wanted to give you a heads up so you could start looking to hire a replacement."

"Okay," he said finally, and her shoulders sagged in relief. "Thanks for telling me."

She stood and turned to open the door, pausing with her hand on the door knob. She glanced back at Noah.

"I'd appreciate it if you didn't tell anyone. At least not until I know when I'm going."

Noah nodded, and not for the first time, she wished she could read his expressions.

"I'll see you tomorrow," he said and turned back to his receipts.

She hesitated before turning and leaving for home. Despite her inability to figure out what Noah thought of her not telling Gavin about her decision, she trusted he wouldn't say anything.

Back in her apartment, she tugged off her work shoes and tossed them in the small closet near the door. Gavin was picking her up in just over three hours, and she wanted to get a few things done before he got there.

She showered, then, twisting her hair up in a towel to dry, went back to the living room. On her laptop, she pulled up her resume to update her job history. The line about the museum drew her eye, and she grabbed the phone to call her old boss.

He sounded vaguely surprised to hear from her, so she asked about the recent exhibit they'd hosted and then worked her way into asking about job openings. When he mentioned a position opening up after Christmas, she practically begged him for it. That gave her just over three months to deal with Sinclair and pack up what little life she had in Thompson Creek.

After she hung up, she realized she was running out of time before Gavin arrived. She rushed about, getting dressed, and fixing her hair. When he knocked on the door, she was busy applying a coating of mascara.

With one hand holding the mascara wand, she used the other to open the door.

"You look great," he said and leaned in to give her a peck on the cheek. The tepid greeting only served to remind Cora at how not real things were between them.

"Come on in," she said and walked back to her room. Applying the mascara took longer than it should have, yet she couldn't stop trembling as the reality of what she was hiding from him hit her.

She came out a few minutes later and found him flipping through the notebook, reading over the latest details she'd added. She didn't need the book to know what the night held. Gavin was wearing a black vintage rock band t-shirt and jeans.

"Chinese food again?" she said.

"How'd you guess?"

She took the book from him and flipped back a few pages.

"Smashing Pumpkins shirt, my new blue tunic dress, Peking Gardens," she recited then handed him the book to see for himself. "He'll be in a car a block down the road. No gun this time. He's just watching."

Gavin read over the page before tossing it onto the coffee table. "I'll call Caleb and have him back up."

Yet another reminder that their dating was for a purpose other than love or even lust.

"Sounds good," she said with a tight smile.

Throughout dinner, she pushed back thoughts of the dead-end their relationship was trying to enjoy the time with him. He talked about a computer program he was helping Caleb design. He didn't call it a job, though it sounded like one. She told him about a new book she was reading that she thought he might like, and when they left the restaurant, she pretended he was looking at the stars, not scanning the street for Sinclair.

Safely in the Jeep, though, pretending got hard. Gavin pulled out his cell and called Caleb. She listened to Gavin's side of the conversation, and it was enough to know Caleb spotted Sinclair, but there'd been no opportunity to get to him.

If he had ... then ... She didn't know. Gavin had ruled out taking Sinclair to the police, the mole created too big of a risk of Sinclair walking away.

"What's the plan?" she asked as Gavin drove.

"Same thing. Nothing's changed. We wait until we can grab him. Making a move when he's got a chance to escape doesn't make sense."

"No, I mean, after. After you catch him, what's the plan? Do we call the police? Can they even do anything?"

"No police."

"So, what happens?"

His expression hardened. "We stop him."

Gavin didn't say it, and if she was honest with herself, she didn't want to hear him say it. Sinclair had faced imprisonment before and walked away. He'd evaded the feds for years. There was only one way to stop him.

Silence settled between them for the rest of the ride and followed them up to her place, neither of them willing to give voice to what exactly stopping him meant.

Enclosed in her tiny apartment, Gavin gathered her in his arms, and she lost herself in the feel of his hard muscles. She reached up and tangled her fingers in his shaggy hair then down to his nape where it was shaved close.

"Stay a while?" she asked as she gazed up at him.

He answered by lifting her up so she could wrap her legs around him and then carried her to the bedroom.

For a while, she forgot about Sinclair and about Denver and everything other than the passion consuming her as she gave herself over to Gavin and the pleasure he offered.

And when he spoke those heartbreaking words, she smiled and rolled from the bed as if the life she was leading was normal and amazing. When she came back from the bathroom, he was dressing, so she pulled on a tank top and pair of yoga pants.

"Do you want a beer?" she asked as she walked from

the bedroom, Gavin following behind.

"Nah, I gotta drive home," he said as he sank onto the couch. "I'll take a water, though."

The suggestion that he spend the night was on the tip of her tongue, but she knew better than to offer. If he'd wanted to stay, he wouldn't have left the bed. She went to the small kitchen and grabbed two water bottles. Setting them down, she picked up her cell phone. There was a missed call from her mom and a bunch of text messages from Keeley encouraging Cora to join her and Sky at a country bar two towns over.

Cora texted Keeley that she was in for the night and placed the cell back down. She'd call her parents in the morning. Grabbing the waters, she turned around, only to find Gavin standing on the other side of the breakfast bar, watching her with narrowed eyes. She jerked, upright, fumbling with the bottles.

"Holy shit, you scared the crap out of me." She took a deep breath and held out one of the bottles.

He took the water. "Anything you need to tell me?"

"No," she said, her forehead wrinkled in confusion.

"Really? You're not looking for a new job?"

Over his shoulder, she saw her open laptop, the bright white of her resume lighting up the screen.

"Were you spying on me?" Offense seemed like the best idea.

"Your computer was open and on. If you want to hide things, you should set up your screen saver and require a password when it restarts."

"Good idea. I'll do that before I go to bed." She walked around to the couch and gently closed the laptop as she sat down. She'd gotten rid of the screensaver and password protection because she had a bad habit of getting frequently distracted, and it was a pain in the butt to continually enter it in.

"So?" He crossed his arms over his chest as he leaned back on the counter.

"Okay, yes I was planning on getting a new job."

"I figured that already. Why hide it?" His head tipped to the side. "You can't think I'd be upset about you not working at the bar, or that I'd tell my brothers before you had a chance."

"No, I talked to Noah earlier today."

"So?"

"I've got something lined up for after Christmas."

"You're a master at stalling," he said cracking a smile. "What's the job?"

"At the museum. In Denver."

"Denver."

How could one little word have so much power? Yet, there it was, ripping at the delicate threads that held them together.

She rubbed her hands along the top of her thighs then stood and paced to the window. She nudged the pale blue curtains to the side and stared down at the street below.

"Lela's always here, isn't she?" she asked, not sure if the question was directed at him or herself.

"She was a big part of my life and yours."

Cora glanced over her shoulder at Gavin and realized that as much she wanted him to heal and move on, that might never happen.

"No. She is part of yours. You won't let her go. I want a

future with you, but not if it means always come in second. You keep clutching at her memory, dragging her back from the grave."

Anger reddened his face, and he shoved away from the counter, taking a menacing step toward her. The muscles along his jaw ticked.

"You don't know shit. Fuck you," he said.

She tried to hear something in his words other than the raging fury that flashed in his eyes, but there was nothing. How quickly the last remaining pillars of her fragile hope crumbled around her.

"Fuck me," she said, nodding. "Because that all this ever was. Fucking. *Não sou nada para você.* I am nothing."

TWENTY-ONE

REGRET WAS A SICKENING feeling, or maybe it was shame. Hearing those words thrown at him, knowing she'd understood him each and every time left Gavin speechless.

What could he say to fix things between them? For three days, he'd been trying to figure out what to say, but anything he came up with only seemed like it would make things worse. If he was honest, he didn't know if he wanted to fix them.

He hadn't asked Cora to love him. He didn't want her to, and he sure as fuck never promised her anything other than sex.

From across the room, he watched as she unloaded a tray of drinks at a table, chatting and laughing at whatever the group of guys was saying. His eye twitched, and he turned his attention back to the keg he was supposed to be hooking up.

"Dude, I got this," Josh said, hovering behind Gavin. "Aren't you off?"

"Yeah, I just wanted to get this hooked up."

Gavin stood and wiped his hands on the top of his thighs. He couldn't have cared less about the beer. He only stuck around after his shift because of Cora.

"You need to spend less time here," Josh said. "Go to the gym, go shopping with Mom."

A snort burst forth from Gavin. "Did you actually just suggest that?"

"Okay, so skip the shopping. You get the point." Josh pulled a rack of glasses toward him. "Now piss off."

Gavin walked out from behind the bar and went into the staff area. Normally, he'd have sat at a table and had a beer, but that meant sitting in either Cora or Keeley's sections, and neither appealed to him. He and Cora had resorted to communicating through his brothers, and every time Keeley looked his way she gave him the stink eye.

Rather than have guilt heaped on him, he strolled back to the manager office. Noah and Logan were both off for the day so the room was empty. He sat behind the desk and turned on the computer, listening to the muffled sounds of the bar drift around him. When it finished loading, he opened a secured file that contained scanned images of Cora's journal along with all of the other pictures, footage, and data they'd been collecting on Sinclair.

Despite his and Caleb's confidence in their ability to find a pattern in the glimpses Cora had of Sinclair's actions, they had yet to find anything. When she'd described them as sporadic and general, she hadn't been downplaying the visions. There really was no pattern he could find.

Splitting the screen, he created a spreadsheet and began diagramming each of her visions, working backward from the most recent. After an hour, he had a colorful data mine that would be absolutely useless in terms of finding Sinclair.

What was Sinclair doing? It frustrated Gavin to hell and back that he couldn't get ahead of Sinclair. Craning his head to the side, he squeezed his shoulder blades together, arching his back, and let out a deep sigh at the satisfying pops it made as his spine realigned.

From the kitchen, he heard his brother's voice and resigned himself to the loss of solitude. Caleb would want an update on Sinclair and the plan.

"You figure it out yet?" Caleb asked when he appeared in the doorway.

"Other than the fact that Cora and I are together in all of the recent ones, there's nothing." Gavin pushed the laptop across the desk, turning for his brother to see the color-coded spreadsheet. "I've been over these so many times and still haven't found anything. Different dates, different times. Sometimes he has a gun, sometimes he's taking pictures or making notes. I don't get it."

Caleb sat down and rested his elbows on the desk, linking his fingers together. Leaning forward, he took a moment to study the data Gavin had organized.

"It's there," Caleb said as he shut the computer down.

"The fuck it is."

"Sinclair's a scientist. Everything he's doing has been thought out, planned for the purpose of gathering data. There's a pattern. The problem is all we have is what Cora sees, and they're only pieces."

As much as Gavin hated it, Caleb was right. They didn't have everything, and that meant their plan might not be the wisest choice.

Gavin leaned back in his chair, tipping his head to stare at the ceiling. They needed to think like Sinclair. Objective, plan, implement, observe. He'd obviously moved to the observation part of his process. Sinclair was methodical in every piece of data he collected. There was no way he would be as random as the visions suggested.

"What's the pattern? What's the pattern?" Gavin murmured as he rubbed a hand over his mouth. Abruptly he sat up and looked at Caleb with a smile. "What we need is a pattern."

"Ya think?" Caleb gave him a curious look. "That's what we've been looking for."

"No. We need to *make* one. We've been so busy filling in these details Sinclair is letting us see that we missed the opportunity to fill them in with what we want." Gavin grabbed a pencil and a piece of paper from the printer, then started drawing boxes in a circular arrangement. "What are the details Cora's visions provide that would help us figure out when Sinclair will strike?"

"Location, people, time, clothing," Caleb listed. "And what Sinclair does."

Gavin wrote each item in a separate box, separating the location into one for him and one for Sinclair.

"We can't control everything, but if we manipulate the pieces we want, Sinclair won't have any choice but to follow along."

Nodding in understanding, Caleb slid the paper toward himself, looking at the six boxes.

"So what do we do? And how?"

"He shifted from watching just me to it being Cora and me so we give him that." Gavin jotted down his and Cora's names in the box marked people.

"The time is always different," Caleb noted. "So we control that. Same goes with location."

"Exactly, but where?"

"The old Cattlemen's club," Caleb suggested. "It's on the edge of town, no street lights, so it's dark by nine. It'll be harder for him to hide in a vehicle and for him to spot us."

Gavin nodded and wrote their chosen location in the box and then added ten as for the time. The club was the logical choice and not just because of the reasons Caleb gave. The abandoned building was the furthest away from any houses. It would give them a place to do what needed doing, and the time would give them the cover of darkness.

"What about clothes?" Caleb asked.

"If we make the time and setting the same then clothing becomes the marker of time. We would create a schedule of clothing choices so we would know which day it was."

The two of them spent the next half hour going over minute details, working out a plan. From the get-go, including Cora had been a risky plan, and it still was. The difference now was that Gavin felt there was something he could do to shift the odds to their side.

"So, do I get the pleasure of sharing this with Cora?" Caleb pushed his chair back from the desk. "Or are you going to eat crow and do it?"

"I'll do it," Gavin agreed reluctantly. "She's off in twenty minutes."

"You want to talk about what's going on with you two?"

"Fuck no." He picked up the papers, folding them before shoving them in his pocket. "Shit. I didn't make any promises. She knew what this was before it even started."

"All right," Caleb said, holding up his hands. "Just keep in mind if the two of you aren't on the same page with this plan, it's beyond worthless. It'll put both of you right out in the open for Sinclair."

"I know. It's all good."

Caleb's hard stare had Gavin squirming in his seat. He didn't blame his brother for the obvious doubt. Hell, things between him and Cora were about as far from good as possible.

"I'll fill the others in, and we can start setting up some sort of schedule rotation." Caleb stood to leave and paused in the door to look back at Gavin. "That cheap ass laptop is enough for Noah and Logan, but if you're going to be working on the Sinclair case, at least have the decency to pick up one of your old computers from the storage unit."

Gavin grunted as Caleb left. It was a tempting idea, though, after almost a year of sitting in a dusty storage locker, they'd be in need of some updates.

Staring up at the clock suspended above the filing cabinet, he watched as the seconds, then minutes, ticked by. His mind swirled with thoughts of Cora, Sinclair, Lela, and how much he was willing to sacrifice.

A few weeks ago, it had been almost easy to admit

ending Sinclair was more important to him than keeping Cora safe. It hadn't been a pretty thought, but it had been honest. Now, the idea of putting Cora in Sinclair's line of fire made him sick to his stomach. Yet, he couldn't walk away. He couldn't let Lela's killer go free.

The clock hit the hour, and Gavin let out a long sigh. He needed to talk with Cora before she left for home, but he wasn't going to try to talk in the locker room. Confining himself in that small space with her, with only the folding screen separating them, was far from a good idea. Noah and Logan seriously needed to get their asses in gear and create separate changing areas.

Ten minutes after her shift, Cora walked past the office door, her purse slung over her shoulder and wearing her leather jacket. Gavin quickly rose from the desk and went after her.

"Cora," he called as she pushed open the side exit.

She turned back around, but there was a hesitation as if she had to consider her options before talking to him.

"Do you have a minute?"

"Not really," she answered, and the tone of her voice told him he was pushing his luck. "I'm meeting up with Eve."

"Where?"

She closed her eyes and tipped her head back until it thumped against the door. "What do you want, Gavin?"

"To talk. We figured out what to do about Sinclair."

"Fine, you can talk while we walk."

"I can drive," he offered, then held up a hand as she scowled. "Or we can walk. That's fine."

He followed her outside, and they walked through the

parking lot in silence. When they reached the sidewalk, he launched into a description of the plan. She didn't say much, simply nodding and making the occasional humming noise. It was unnerving to not have any clue as to what she was thinking.

"We can go over the details tonight," he said as they arrived at her building.

She moved to the side so a couple could pass by. "I told you, I'm busy."

He gritted his teeth, pushing back the familiar searing in his muscles. *How could this not be more important than going out with Eve?*

"Sinclair is out there. We need to do everything we can to stop him."

"I understand that, Gavin, but I'm not doing it now. We can talk about ..." Her words trailed off as she gazed past him, staring at someone walking along the other side of the street.

Gavin twisted to see who she was looking at, but despite the bright street lights overhead, he didn't recognize the guy.

"That's him," she said, her hand lifting to point at the man.

"Who?"

"The guy who ran me off the road."

The tension within him exploded and a furious roar burst from him, echoing along the quiet street. The man turned at the sound, and across the street, Gavin saw his eyes widen right before he took off running.

Gavin ached to give chase, but his body was beyond his control as he underwent the shifting from man to monster. Adrenaline pumped through him, and he heard the sound of his shirt tears at the seams. A fierce growl erupted from him as his muscles settled and with a last twitch gave way to fury.

He surged forward, running after the man and rapidly closing the distance. Feet pounding the concrete, he ignored the curious looks from the few people he raced by. He was dimly aware of Cora calling his name, but it did nothing to quench the hunger inside him. The only thing that mattered was catching Sinclair's henchman.

The sidewalk ended, and the man stumbled over the uneven ground. Gavin reached out and gripped the back of his shirt, pulling him back up. The man spun around, his arm swinging toward Gavin.

Gavin let the feeble punch fall, and it glanced off his jaw, little more than the pawing of a puppy. It was enough, though, to prod what little humanity Gavin had left to step back and give the monster full rein.

His fist smashed into the soft belly of the man, causing him to double over and placing his face in the path of Gavin's other fist. He flew backward, landing on the ground and then attempted to scurry back. Gavin pounced, falling to his knees, and punched the man's face.

"Where's Sinclair?"

"I don't know who you're talking about!" the man cried out.

Gavin hammered his face once, twice.

"Where is he?"

"I don't know." The words were garbled as blood trickled from his mouth.

With a hand wrapped around the guy's neck, close to

the jaw, Gavin lifted until only an inch separated them.

"You work for Sinclair. So where the fuck is he?"

He hit the man again and was rewarded with a satisfying crunch of a broken nose. His arm drew back, intent on delivering another blow, but hands grabbed his biceps, yanking at him. He refused to be stopped so easily and tried to yank away from the hold.

"Gavin!" Josh said from behind him. "You need to calm down."

Hunching his back, Gavin strained his head to the side, fighting the urge to turn on Josh. Another set of hands joined Josh's, dragging him away from Sinclair's man.

"Let me go," he growled.

Blood covered the man's rapidly-swelling face, and the sight spurned his monster on, feeding his hunger to end the man in front of him.

"You need to get control. Now," Caleb ordered him. "This is not the time or place for this."

He gripped Gavin's jaw, forcing him to make eye contact. Then with a sharp push, Caleb turned Gavin's face so he could look at Cora.

She stood a few feet away, and the look on her face was all it took to harness his animal. He stood and stepped toward her, but she retreated, fear and horror masking her pale face. His heightened senses picked up the slight tremble in her hands, the quivering of her lower lip, and the sound of her thumping heart.

It was at that moment he realized that while he had long ago accepted what his body could do, the monster was more a part of him than he'd ever wanted to accept.

TWENTY-TWO

AS SOON AS GAVIN took off running in the direction of the pub, she'd pulled out her cell and dialed Caleb. The man had already been bloody by the time she got there, but Gavin hadn't stopped. He kept up the assault until Josh and Caleb pulled him away.

When he moved toward her, she hadn't seen the Gavin she'd loved for so long. In his place was a monster that looked ready to destroy anything and anyone capturing his wrath. And his eyes were on her.

Fear is such an ugly word, almost as ugly as it felt. Yet there was no other way for Cora to describe what her emotions as she watched Gavin beating that man in the middle of the street.

Instinctively, she took a step back, and he froze, the creature he'd become began to retreat. The heavily muscled frame faded back to Gavin's familiar form, and the pronounced angles of his face softened.

He was Gavin again, and she could almost believe she imagined the whole thing. Except the blood smeared along his hands and splattered across his face and raggedly torn shirt refused to let her forget he'd been moments away from killing someone.

"Cora, are you okay?" Caleb asked.

She swallowed around the lump in her throat and nodded, not trusting her ability to form a coherent response.

"Holy shit," Josh said, ramming his fingers into his shaggy hair. "What the hell were you thinking, Gavin?"

Gavin didn't respond, simply continuing to stare Cora. She flinched under the constant weight of his eyes, and he turned to his brother.

"This is the fucker who ran Cora off the road." His hands clenched into fists and took a few steps away, distancing himself from the unconscious man.

"How sure are you?" Josh asked.

"It's him," Cora said, hating the tremble in her voice. "I'm positive."

"Soon as he realized we'd seen him, he took off running," Gavin said. "Piece of shit wouldn't tell me where Sinclair is."

"What the fuck are we gonna do with him?" Josh nudged the guy's leg with his foot.

The four of them stood there, gazing down at the man. There was a part of Cora that looked at him objectively and wanted to offer aid. Yet at the same time, she couldn't dismiss the fact he easily could've killed her. *Who knows, whatever he injected her with may be doing just that.*

"All right," Caleb said, rubbing a hand over his mouth. "Josh, you need to go back inside before Keeley and Janet start panicking about not having a bartender. Gavin, you need to go home, get yourself cleaned up."

"What are you going to do?" Josh glanced at him.

"Call for an ambulance. I'll tell them I found him on the way to my car."

Cora released a breath she hadn't even realized she'd been holding. Somewhere in the back of her mind, there'd been the thought that they intended to kill him. She had no sympathy for the guy, but killing him seemed far from reasonable.

"The cops are going to question him," Gavin pointed out.

"True, but do you really think he'll want them digging into why you beat the shit out of him?" Caleb shook his head. "There's no way for him to report you without giving himself and Sinclair up."

"Good point." Gavin nodded. "Cora can come with—"

"I'm going home," she interrupted. The thought of going anywhere with Gavin alone right then was terrifying. All she wanted to do was forget last thirty minutes had ever happened.

She tried to read his expression, but her own emotions kept getting in the way. They had her believing what she saw there was more than regret.

He reached a hand toward her, and she took another step back, unwilling to fall under the spell his touch would inevitably cast over her.

"Cora—"

"No," she said, cutting him off again. "It's not up for debate."

The brothers started to protest, but she didn't stick around to listen. She turned on her heel and walked down the street to her apartment. With every step she took, images of Gavin enraged and covered with blood flashed through her mind.

At the SIEGE lab, she caught a glimpse of what he could physically become, yet nothing had prepared her for what that truly meant. The absolute fury marring his face, the way he so viciously attacked that man—none of it resembled the Gavin she knew, and when he looked at her afterward ... she hadn't seen him anymore. Those few seconds when he moved toward her, all she'd seen was the monster.

She was almost at her building door when she realized Gavin followed her in his Jeep. Not wanting him to stop and try talking to her, she picked up her pace, almost jogging the last few feet to her door. She entered the foyer and turned to close the door behind her, spotting Gavin as he drove by.

Up in her apartment, she collapsed on her bed and curled into the fetal position with a pillow clutched to her chest. She tried to reconcile what she knew of Gavin with this new side of him that was beyond his control. It terrified her how quickly it all happened. She wanted to believe he wouldn't have hurt her, but she couldn't be sure.

How much of Gavin was left when the monster came out?

What scared her even more was if Sinclair did this to Gavin as a child, what might he have done to *her*?

The ringing of her cell phone dragged her from her thoughts, and she rolled over to grab her phone from the nightstand. Eve's name flashed across the screen.

She'd completely forgotten about their plans to go see

a movie. She hesitated a moment, trying to think of an excuse to get out of going, before accepting the call.

"Hey, how's it going?" she asked.

"Good as can be expected when you have a six-year-old projectile vomiting all over your bathroom," Eve answered.

"Oh, God, that sounds disgusting." Cora nearly gagged at even the thought of the mess Eve was dealing with.

"Yeah. Needless to say, movies are out. I'm so sorry. There's no way I can leave him with his dad."

"I totally understand," Cora said, a little relieved she didn't need to lie. "We can go another night."

"I'm just hoping this round of the flu bug is the last for the year," Eve said with a heavy sigh.

"Has he been getting sick a lot?"

"No, that's what's so weird," Eve said. "Up until maybe May, I don't think he'd ever been sick before. Now, every other day he's either vomiting, got a fever, coughing, or something else. Every time I take him to the doctor, though, they say the blood work comes back perfectly fine."

"That sucks. I hope he feels better tomorrow."

"Thanks. If he's not, I'm going to try taking him to a different clinic. Are you okay? You sound a little strange."

"I'm good." As good as could be expected after seeing the man you love change into some hulked up monster and nearly kill someone.

"Are you—Crap! I gotta go." Eve hung up as Cora heard the sound of retching in the background.

Cora placed her phone back on the nightstand and lay back down, throwing an arm up to cover her eyes. She didn't want to think about Gavin. She wanted to go back to when the most complicated part of her life was accepting he didn't love her.

She rose and went to the bathroom in search of her sleeping pills. When the visions first started, she bought the pills, hoping they'd keep her asleep through them. They hadn't helped with the visions, and in the end, she gave up on them when she found getting to sleep without them was harder.

Dreams, though, provided no escape for Cora as her subconscious only delved further into the horrors of what Sinclair did to Gavin and what might happen to her. Gavin became the beast, stalking her as she ran through the cemetery. She fell across Lela's grave, and her body began its own transformation, shifting her bones and muscles until she took a form so grotesque and terrifying even Gavin's beast ran from her.

Cora's eyes flew open at the sound of knocking on her front door. In the dark, she scrambled to get out of bed and turn on the light. She stumbled down the hall to the door and lifted up on her tiptoes to peek out the peephole. Gavin stood there, leaning against the opposite wall. She sank back onto her heels and took a deep breath.

Gavin noticed the peephole darken as Cora pressed her eye to the other side and then lightened again when she pulled away. Coming to her place might not have been the greatest idea, but the fear he'd seen in her eyes and the way she retreated as if expecting him to attack her haunted him. He couldn't let her go on thinking that.

He jiggled his keys in his pocket. The door didn't open, and he thought she planned to ignore him. He couldn't blame her if she didn't. They'd already been on shaky ground before, and now she'd witnessed what he was capable of, the violence that the monster he was thrived on and hungered for, he wouldn't have been surprised if she wanted nothing to do with him again.

The door opened and revealed a slightly mussed Cora. "What are you doing here, Gavin?"

"I wanted to talk."

"It's the middle of the night."

"I would've come earlier, but I knew you were going out with Eve." He gestured toward the apartment. "Can I come in?"

She pressed her lips together before nodding with a sigh and stepping back to let him in. His shoulders sagged as the tension they'd been holding faded. He sat on the couch and rubbed his hands along his thighs. Cora went to the window and peeked out the curtains before turning around to face him. Crossing her arms, she leaned back against the window sill.

"Why did you come here?" she asked.

"I ..."

Why the fuck had he come here? His knees bounced with nerves, and he pushed off from the couch to pace the small room. It shouldn't matter if she was scared of him. She was just another lay, a body to pass the time with and relieve the natural urges of his body. It shouldn't matter.

But it did. Because as much as he wanted to put what they had neatly into a little box labeled "Sex", that's not where she was. Somehow, she'd snuck through his defenses and the further in she got, the harder it was to justify keeping her out.

"I never would have hurt you," he said, coming to a stop in front of her. "You know that, right?"

She didn't say anything, and his chest tightened.

"Even when I'm ... like that, I would never hurt you. Please tell me you know that."

"How can I? I'm nothing to you," she said, turning her face to the side.

"That's not true. And I'm a complete asshole for ever saying it."

He gazed down at the top of her head. Short frizzy strands poked out in all directions. He cupped her chin, tipping her head back to look at him. When her eyes met his, he melted into the blue depths.

Earlier, he'd wondered if he wanted to fix things between them, and to be honest, he'd still been wondering it five minutes before, but staring into those sorrow-filled baby blues, he realized fixing things with her was all he wanted.

"You were right about me holding onto Lela. There were days after her death that keeping her memory alive was the only thing that kept *me* alive," he admitted. "The pain I felt knowing she's gone was a reminder that I was still alive. I didn't want to lose that."

"Pain isn't the only way to feel alive," she said.

He let go of her chin and threaded his fingers into her wild curls. "I don't know if I can give you what you want. I can't predict what will happen in the future, but I know right now, I want to be with you. Only you."

"I can't stay here waiting for you to decide on a future, Gavin. I have to do what's best for me, and that means moving on with my life. In Denver."

Frustration twisted in Gavin's gut. He wanted to rail at her for not giving him time. Except that's exactly what she'd given him—space and time to heal—but instead of using it to let go of Lela, he'd used it to drive a deeper wedge between Cora and himself.

"You don't leave until after Christmas, so give me until then," he pleaded. "Two months."

She wavered, and that second's pause was enough for him to press his advantage.

His lips captured hers in a fierce kiss, and the gentle surrender of her lips was all the answer he needed. His teeth nipped at her lower lip, and she opened her mouth to his tongue. He slipped his hands under her cropped top. She shivered at the soft brush of his fingers along her ribs. With his hands under her bra, he enveloped the lush curves of her breast, flicking his thumbs over her nipples.

He pressed his thigh between hers. Her knees bent, pressing her to his leg. She let out a soft moan as she rocked against him. He gripped her hips, stilling her motions and holding her tight to him.

Gathering her in his arms, he carried her to the bedroom, kicking the door shut. He laid her in the center of the bed. Her shirt and pants came off, and he stood to admire the sight of her withering on the sheets in only her pink lace panties and bra. She raised her arms above her head and gave him a come-hither look that went straight to his cock.

Instinct urged Gavin to tear the last remaining pieces of clothing from her and pounce, fucking her until they were consumed by physical sensations and neither of them could think. But he wanted it to be more.

Whatever it was between them had started with nothing more than the desire to slake his lust, yet he was in so deep he couldn't tell where the lines in the sand were. So fucking deep he wanted to lose himself so completely within her that every excuse he'd used to keep them apart faded away.

He watched as her fingers slid under her the delicate material of her panties, and his mouth watered at the memory of her sweet taste. A soft sigh escaped her as she stroked herself.

"Are you just going to watch?" Cora asked.

"Fuck no." He yanked his shirt off and pulled off his pants, lowering the zipper carefully over his hardened flesh.

While he undressed, she got to her knees, crawling across the bed until she was at the edge, only inches from him. He kicked away his pants and briefs, and his cock stood out, seeking the object of his desire. Cora answered its silent plea by grasping him and stroking him firmly. She made a soft humming sound and guided him toward her mouth.

The first touch of her moist tongue sent sharp pulses of ecstasy through him. She swirled her tongue around the head of his penis before drawing him into her mouth.

Her eyes gazed up at him, and she started humming again. His last coherent thought was that he'd never seen such a beautiful sight.

TWENTY-THREE

THE OLD CATTLEMAN'S CLUB wasn't Cora's idea of a date, nor was it a place she wanted to be going at night. Yet, that's exactly what she'd done every evening for the past three weeks. She spent the days working or at home then Gavin would pick her up, and they'd drive to the abandoned building at the edge of town.

The club had once been as high-class as you can get in a place like Thompson Creek, modeled from the locals' idea of what ranching should be like thanks to shows like *Dallas* and *Dynasty*. But just like those shows faded away, so had the Cattleman's Club. Inside, the over-the-top luxury was still evident in the chandeliers and the plush chairs now torn and soiled with dust.

The plan Gavin and his brothers created made perfect sense. Forcing Sinclair to go where they wanted, when they wanted. At first, their strategy hadn't seemed to work as days passed with no visions. Then, in the last week, they started again, only this time the random nature was gone. She could watch Sinclair and know precisely when it was happening.

All they'd been waiting for was the date, and now they had it. Soon, all of it would be over.

"If Sinclair isn't going to be here tonight, why are we?" Cora spread out a checkered blanket on the floor in the middle of the room.

"Because even though we trust your visions, we can't trust that they show us everything." Gavin placed the picnic basket at one end of the blanket then helped her smooth out the wrinkles. "We need to establish our presence here every day regardless of if we think he's out here."

"I suppose."

His argument made sense in a way, but there were still so many factors they couldn't control that they seemed to be ignoring. Not knowing what Sinclair did outside of the visions was just one.

"Besides—" Gavin grasped her hand and tugged her close to him, "—I thought this place was romantic?"

Cora laughed and wound her hands around the back of his neck. "Maybe if this were nineteen-eighty and I had a thing for guys with feathered hair. Now, it's filthy, and I'm pretty sure I saw a rat the other night."

"So it's not the greatest place for a date," he admitted, nuzzling her neck. "But Caleb and Noah wanted to do a walkthrough of what'll go down tomorrow. Which is why, as tempting as I am to lay you down and have my way with you, we're going to have to wait until we get home."

Home. She loved how that sounded, as if what they had went beyond just sex. She'd promised him nine weeks, and a third of that was gone already. With each day, it got harder to imagine leaving. She couldn't keep going on the way she was with him, but she knew she didn't want to be anywhere else, either.

"Do I need to come back later?" Noah's voice came from the other side of the partially-opened door. The two of them broke apart and turned to stare at their unwelcome guest.

"Come on in," Gavin said, stepping back from her. "I was telling Cora we were to go over the plans for tomorrow."

"Was that what you were doing?" Noah arched a brow "Good thing you didn't ask me to do it."

Cora rolled her eyes and sat down on the picnic blanket, reaching for the basket.

"Can we get this over with?" She pulled out a glass and a bottle of wine. She held the bottle out to Gavin, and he pulled his pocket knife to cut the foil covering the cork.

"Okay, so let's run through the plan," Noah said, leaning against a small square table. It wobbled under his weight, and he quickly stood up.

"I thought Caleb was coming too," Gavin said as he sat on the blanket beside Cora.

Noah shook his head. "There was some kind of security breach at the SIEGE lab, and Merrick wanted him to do a system analysis. It'll also give him a chance to poke around a bit more without raising any red flags."

"Isn't that a conflict of interest?" Cora asked Noah. She poured herself a glass of wine then pushed the cork back in and placed the bottle in the basket. "Wouldn't they be worried about having one of you working on their security systems?"

"That would imply they have something sinister to

cover up. Which, according to Nielson, is the furthest from the truth."

"All right, let's do this then," Gavin said and pulled out the chocolate chip cookies. He removed the top of the container and looked at the cookies with a scowl before sealing them back up. Despite his willingness to devour anything Cora cooked, his stomach had been rolling with a strange sensation the past hour.

"Caleb and I are going to arrive around eight," Noah said.

He held out his hand and took the container from Gavin. He had snagged three cookies before Cora snatched it away, placing it safely in her lap. She didn't spend an hour baking for them to be gone before she had even one.

"Caleb found a spot near the church with a good view of the entire back of the building," Noah continued. "I'm going to be up front, across the street in the field."

"At ten, Cora and I will walk over after work and head inside."

"Sinclair will follow us from the pub in a white car." Cora searched her memory for the details. "He'll park halfway down the block at the end of the parking lot and watch."

"We don't know how long he'll be there, but as soon as he rolls up, Logan will grab him," Gavin said.

"Then Caleb and I will move in." Noah rubbed his hands together, brushing away the cookie crumbs. "I want to check out the vantage points, make sure I can see the two of you through the window, and that there's a clear path to where Sinclair will be."

Noah left, and silence settled between Cora and Gavin. They'd skipped over the whole part about what they did once they caught Sinclair, and she was glad. She didn't want to hear the details.

She took a long sip of her chardonnay, letting the smooth fruity flavor linger on her tongue. Moving her glass in a circular motion, she swirled the last of her wine until it touched the rim.

"It will work," Gavin reassured her. "We have to do this. He won't stop. He'll keep coming after us until he gets what he wants."

"I know. It's just..."

Gavin rose to his knees in front of her, cupping her cheeks in his hands. She gazed up at him, loving how the seriousness of his expression deepened the intensity of his brown eyes.

"Sinclair has stolen so much from me. I won't let him take you too."

A loud clang like a pot falling on the floor came from the staff area, and both of them froze, straining to hear. Gavin surged to his feet, grasping Cora's hand to help her up.

"Noah?" he called.

When there was no response from his brother, Gavin motioned for Cora to stay quiet and pointed to the front entrance. She moved toward the door then hesitated when she realized Gavin wasn't with her. A glance back revealed that he was moving in the opposite direction, toward the kitchen. He peeked over his shoulder and inclined his head to the door. She nodded and carefully continued, making sure to avoid the floorboards she knew would creak under her weight.

At the sound of a gun cocking, she spun around. Sinclair stood at the entrance to the kitchen, a gun pointed directly at her. With everything she'd learned about him, she thought the nondescript man she saw in her visions would be more imposing in person. Yet, if anything, he was less. He stood slightly less than average height with a round face made distinctive only by his gold-rimmed glasses.

"Miss. Evans, leaving so soon?" The smile he gave made her skin crawl. "I'd rather you stick around for a few minutes. Come on over, it's been a while since I've seen you up close."

Instinct urged her to run, but that meant leaving Gavin behind. She took a few steps into the room then patted the side of her leg, feeling for her bag. It wasn't there. Spotting it beside the picnic basket, she cursed under her breath. *What was the point in carrying a gun in her purse for protection if she didn't carry her purse?*

Gavin shifted so he stood partially between her and the doctor. He could see the gun wavering as Sinclair debated who to train the weapon on.

"I must say," Sinclair said. "I'm impressed with the show the two of you have been putting on. I almost fell for it."

"Almost? You're here, aren't you?" Gavin straightened his shoulders. Any sign of weakness would only empower Sinclair and make him less likely to make a mistake.

"I am, but I suspect you were perhaps expecting me tomorrow."

His face impassive, Gavin refused to give Sinclair even

a hint of the frustration and anger bubbling inside him.

How the fuck had Sinclair gotten so close without any of them noticing? Now that Gavin was aware of his presence everything clicked into place. The night terrors he had the night before, the way the hairs on the back of his neck had stood up all day, and the queasiness that had him turn away chocolate chip cookies. All were signals that the enemy was near.

"What do you want?" Gavin asked, unwilling to let Sinclair drag out this game he was playing.

"I want what I've always wanted. To finish my research. It was almost done. You were supposed to be the final one. Then Nielson stepped in and altered the dosage." The gun shook before Sinclair steadied his hand. "You can't even begin to comprehend the amount of time and research that goes into each trial. I spent years attempting to reproduce the exact variables."

The picture of Cora from Nielson's folder flashed through Gavin's mind. Subject 8. Dean was Six.

"Who's Subject Seven?" he asked.

"He's irrelevant." Sinclair gestured dismissively, waving his weapon through the air. "He didn't even make it through the third round of modifications. The only useful thing about him was that I finally realized I didn't need to recreate the experiment when I could simply observe you. It was more challenging than being in a lab, but it was sufficient."

Gavin kept his eyes on Sinclair, but in his peripheral vision, he searched for something he could use to distract Sinclair. There was little within his reach, and moving would expose Cora.

"And Cora?"

"Ah yes. A happy mistake, I guess you could say."

Gavin's jaw flexed as he gritted his teeth, struggling to retain his control.

Sinclair gave a strange grunting noise and immediately, Gavin sensed the monster within him retreating.

"My assistant didn't follow protocol as closely as instructed. His instructions that evening had been to temporarily detain your girlfriend while I advanced my study." He gave a mocking sad sigh. "Unfortunately, you weren't even in the vehicle, and Miss. Tavares expired unexpectedly."

Hearing him dismiss Lela so callously as if she were no more than a cup of spoiled milk was too much. Gavin snarled, his back muscles bunching beneath his shirt, stretching the material. Sinclair made the noise again, and while Gavin's monster sat back, it hovered under the surface, bristling at Sinclair's command. His stomach clenched in fear. If Sinclair could calm the beast, then what else could he make it do?

"It was fortunate, however, that Miss. Evans survived and allowed me to take the project in a completely different direction."

"What did you do to me?" she asked, and Gavin felt her move closer.

"PH-9E was intended to further develop Gavin's sensory capabilities. He'd already demonstrated an unnerving ability to detect my presence." The gun jabbed in their direction. "In you, however, it caused the development of extrasensory perception I never even considered. Precognition, if you will, though it really has less to do with parapsychology and more to do with a heightened ability to evaluate and determine the probability of future events."

Sinclair sat in one of the velvet-covered chairs, placing the weapon on top of the table, though he kept his hand resting atop it.

"It was kind of you to keep a record of your experiences," he said. "Your notebook was quite informative. It inspired me to move on to the next phase of the Posthuman Project."

"What's going to happen to me?"

Gavin heard the tremor in her voice and hated knowing that despite all his assertions that their plan would work, and she'd be safe, she wasn't.

Sinclair tossed his head back and laughed.

An enraged roar erupted from Gavin, and he lunged forward. The gun whipped up, and Gavin staggered to a stop as he noticed it pointed past him to Cora. The beast within him clawed at his insides, its craving for vengeance locked in a battle with Gavin's goal of keeping Cora safe.

"Move again, and I'll shoot her," Sinclair said. "See, Miss. Evans is expendable. Finding a substitute subject is as easy as walking down the street. As for you, well, I just don't have the length of time needed to invest in such an undertaking again."

It seemed strange to feel relieved, but Gavin did. Whatever Sinclair did to Cora wasn't on the same scale as what happened to him and his brothers. There was a possibility she'd never have to experience the dark presence of a monster taking control of her.

The sound of someone breathing from the other side of the wall in the kitchen drew Gavin's attention. It was so faint, he knew Cora and Sinclair hadn't picked up on it. At first, he thought it was Noah, but the pitch was too high. It was a woman, but who? Yolanda Nielson would have no reason to hide from Sinclair, yet who else could it be? And how the hell did she get in here without Noah noticing?

"What do you want from us?" Gavin asked.

"With Miss. Evans? Nothing. With you, though, an opportunity to complete my work with you," Sinclair explained. "Finalizing your results will allow me to focus on the next generation of Posthuman subjects. I've been gradually implementing the preliminary stages since the spring. I expect the subjects to be ready for stage two by the time I'm done with you."

"You sick bastard," Gavin spat at him. "How many lives have you destroyed this time?"

"Six seemed to be my lucky number."

The monster tore its way free, and Gavin doubled over as his body transformed from man to beast. His groans of pain swiftly turned to growls of fury. This time, unlike the others, when Sinclair made the grunting sound, the beast refused to retreat completely, and Gavin found himself trapped in a motionless body.

His vision focused on Sinclair, pinpointing the vein in his neck that pulsed furiously. That's where he'd strike. He'd lock his hands around Sinclair's neck and squeeze to build the pressure, then when he released his hold, his fingers would dig in and shred the flesh from him. It would be a slow and painful death, befitting the man who let Lela suffer in agony as she died at the bottom of the river.

A figure ran through the open door of the kitchen, swinging a baseball bat. Gavin recognized Eve as the lightweight aluminum bat she swung connected with Sinclair's shoulder.

"Where is my brother? *Where is he?*"

Sinclair stumbled, lifting an arm to shield his head and giving Gavin the opportunity he'd been waiting for.

In three long steps, he reached Sinclair. Grabbing the older man by the arm, Gavin turned him so he could see Sinclair's face as the life was ripped from him. He wrapped his fingers around the wrinkled flesh of Sinclair's throat and squeezed.

Behind him, he heard the screams of Cora and Eve, felt the tug of hands on his arms. The sharp report of a gunshot echoed through the room just as something slammed into Gavin's chest. His hands loosened their grip, and he lurched to the side, knocking over a small round table and going down on one knee.

He stared at the gun Sinclair held, and the scent of sulfur drifted from its barrel. The crack of another gunshot resonated and Sinclair flew backward into the wall. Blood slid down his face for the hole now marking the center of his forehead. Sinclair's body slumped to the side and fell over.

"*No,*" Gavin yelled.

This wasn't how it was supposed to end. This wasn't the punishment Sinclair deserved. The beast howled. He was the one who should have done it.

"Gavin?" Cora's voice called to him, and he turned to her. Her small pistol was clutched in her shaking hand.

She killed Sinclair. The fact reverberated through him, leaving him weak at the loss of purpose.

"You killed him," he whispered. He pushed to his feet taking a lurching step toward her.

TWENTY-FOUR

CORA'S FINGER TIGHTENED ON the trigger, and the kickback of the gun jerked her arm up. Time slowed in that moment as she stared at Sinclair, riveted by the hole that appeared on Sinclair's forehead. Behind him, red droplets sprayed out, spattering the wall just before he hit it. He slid down, leaving smears of blood along the paisley wallpaper.

Numbness took over, and she gazed down at the gun in her hand, saw the slight sway of it, yet she couldn't feel anything.

A horrific yell jarred her from her trance and Cora turned to Gavin. Even in its distorted state, Cora could see the anguish lining his face.

"Gavin?"

"You killed him." The harsh despair in Gavin's voice tore at Cora's heart. Those three words were more painful than anything else he ever said to her as he turned his fury from Sinclair to her, decimating the fragile hope she'd had that he might feel something other than lust for her.

He stood and stumbled forward, and she could do

nothing more than watch as his features wavered between his and the beast's. His hand reached for her, and she flinched, but the blow she expected never came. Gavin collapsed before her, and her fears that the monster he'd become would kill her vanished.

Rolling him over, she found a blossom of blood forming on the front of his shirt. Sinclair's shot had missed her, hitting Gavin instead.

"Oh, God. Oh, God," she muttered, grabbing at the worn material, trying to rip it apart. She gave up after a second attempt and shoved it up. Blood pumped from a wound near his shoulder. She placed her shaking hands over it, and the warm fluid coated her hands.

She looked around frantically for something to use to stop the flow and saw Eve a few feet away, sobbing into her hands.

"Eve!" she screamed, and her friend lifted her head. "Help me! Pass me the blanket."

Eve dragged it over, and Cora bunched up the corner and pressed it to the wound. She took a deep breath, telling herself to calm down. Beneath the pressure of her hands, the rise and fall of Gavin's chest reassured her he was alive.

Noah burst through the front entrance and scanned the room, taking in the scene. He ran over and crouched next to Cora, pressing his fingers to Gavin's neck. "What the hell happened?"

"Sinclair was here. He shot Gavin," Cora explained in a halting voice. "We need an ambulance."

"Let me take a look," he said. She reluctantly removed her hands, and he peeled back the blood-soaked cloth.

"It's pretty high on his shoulder. That's good."

"We should call the police."

"No!" Eve said, scurrying over to them. "We can't."

"Eve—"

"Please! They have Jamie," she begged.

"Who?" Noah asked.

"Dr. Barker said they took him to the hospital, but he lied." Tears trickled down her cheeks. "

"Who the hell is Dr. Barker?"

Eve gestured toward Sinclair. Noah looked from Eve to Sinclair then to Gavin, his face that familiar unreadable mask. He pulled out his cell phone and pressed a button.

"Cattleman's Club. Come clean up your mess," he said gruffly then shoved the phone back in his pocket. He slid his arms under Gavin and lifted. "Let's get him out to my truck. It'll be faster if we take him."

"What about Sinclair?" Cora trailed behind him.

"SIEGE can deal with him."

She followed him from the building and climbed into the back of the cab. Noah maneuvered Gavin in so his head rested on Cora's lap and she could continue applying pressure. She glanced out the window and spotted Eve standing dejectedly in the doorway to the building.

"Noah, what about Eve? Will Dr. Nielson help her?"

"Shit." Noah closed the door to the cab and stomped across the street. He gripped Eve's arm and practically dragged her to the truck.

Eve and Noah got in the truck, and he sped off, spinning his tires on the loose gravel road. On the drive to the hospital, Cora called Gavin's parents. She tried to stay calm, but from the scowl Noah gave her in the rear-view mirror, she suspected her hysteria shone through.

When they pulled up to the emergency drop off, chaos erupted around them. Noah jumped out shouting for help and then Gavin was being removed, placed on a gurney, and wheeled away before she could even get out of the truck.

She ran after them, but a set of locked doors swung shut behind them. There was little she could do but stare through the rectangular window until they disappeared into a room. Her hand smacked the door, leaving a bloody hand print behind.

"There's a restroom over there. Why don't you go wash your hands?" Noah suggested. "I'll go to talk to one of the nurses and see if we can find out what's happening."

"Where were you, Noah?" Accusation gave her words a sharp edge. If he'd been there sooner, Gavin might not have been shot.

"A few of Sinclair's lackeys blitzed me" He gestured to a gash along his temple that she hadn't even noticed. "They got in enough whacks to knock me out."

"He's going to be okay, right?"

Noah's lip twitched then curled into a half smile. "Gavin's a tough son-of-a-bitch. He'll be back to normal in a couple days."

She wanted to believe him, but she didn't.

***

Seven hours later, four of which Gavin spent in surgery, she started to believe Noah.

The constant beep of the machines hooked to Gavin might have been annoying at any other time, but as Cora sat there staring at his still form, she felt nothing other than relief. He was alive.

"Has he woken up yet?" Sarah asked as she came into the room.

"Not yet, but he was getting restless a few minutes ago. The doctor doesn't think he'll wake for a few hours."

Sarah smiled sadly. "He doesn't know Gavin."

Sarah and Mark had been so calm about the whole thing. Cora wasn't a parent, but she knew how her mom and dad would have reacted to hearing she'd been shot. Hysterics would have been a mild way to describe their response.

From the few times she'd meet Sarah, she'd been surprised how calm and strong Sarah was in the face of everything SIEGE and Sinclair had done.

"He'll be all right," Sarah reassured her.

"How can you be so sure?"

"Sinclair did a lot to hurt the boys, but rapid recovery was one of the few I don't complain about anymore. Although, when they were younger, I think suffering a little longer from broken bones and such would have made them a bit more cautious."

Cora stared at Gavin's hand resting in hers. Only minutes before, it had been limp in her grasp, now there was a tension in it as if he were attempting to hold on to her. It gave her a small ray of hope that maybe they'd be able to find a way through this together.

"Gavin mentioned you planned to move back to Denver."

Cora nodded. "I was going to go after we stopped Sinclair. But now ..."

"When I first met my husband, I knew immediately

that he was the one. I was lucky that Mark felt the same way. Our biggest struggles didn't come until he took the job with SIEGE. I'd heard the conspiracy theories involving them and couldn't figure out why they'd need a teacher in a science lab. But Mark needed a job and thought it was the perfect opportunity to try something different. He came home that first day absolutely devastated."

Cora couldn't even begin to image what he'd seen or felt when he discovered what SIEGE was doing.

"Taking those six boys in was the hardest thing we ever did. The best, but the hardest. There was no guarantee that they would be able to function outside of the lab, or that they'd ever be able to have normal lives. Gavin wasn't one I worried about. From the moment he entered my life, he's been rolling with the punches. Oh, he lets you know when he's not happy, but he just keeps on keeping on. Or, he did until Lela died."

Sarah walked around Gavin's hospital bed and lifted his other hand. The tenderness in her touch left little doubt that she loved Gavin as if she'd given birth to him herself.

"I like you, Cora," Sarah said. "I know you would make Gavin whole again, and I want that for him more than anything. But if you make it to Denver, I think you'll have made the right choice to go."

Sarah didn't wait around for Cora to come up with a response. She pressed a kiss to Gavin's forehead and gave his hand a squeeze before leaving the two of them alone again.

Cora sat back in her chair, absently rubbing her thumb

over the circular scar on the back of Gavin's hand.

She wanted to stay. Eight hours before, if Gavin had asked her, she would. But now, it wasn't an option. She'd seen the look on Gavin's face when he realized she'd killed Sinclair. It was an expression she'd never forget.

Gavin's fingers tightened around her hand, and he shifted restlessly and muttered something. She then laid his hand on the bed and rose.

Outside of his room, she found Sky sitting in a chair and gave her a weak smile.

"I'm going to go grab a coffee," she said.

"I'll go with you," Sky offered.

"Actually, I just need a few minutes to myself."

"Oh, okay. I'll go in and sit with Gavin then."

Cora took the elevator down to the lobby, but instead of going to the cafeteria, she went out the exit and sat on a bench, watching the constant flow of people coming and going.

It only took her a few minutes to make up her mind. She pulled out her cell to call her brother and beg him to give her a ride home.

TWENTY-FIVE

GAVIN REACHED FOR HIS beer, wincing as the motion pulled at the still healing wound. He rubbed the sore spot with a grimace before chugging the last few sips of his drink.

It had been a week since he'd been shot, and while his doctor was surprised by his rapid recovery, he knew he wasn't back to a hundred percent yet.

Cora's soft laugh caught his attention, and he quickly found her at the end of the bar, talking with Josh. It was the first time he'd seen her since the Cattleman's Club, though Sky told him Cora had been by his side right up until he woke.

She'd been avoiding him since, and he wanted to know why. Initially, he reasoned that with Noah taking off with only a vague phone call mentioning SIEGE, she'd had to step up to help Logan. But that hadn't explained why she wouldn't take his calls.

She slung her purse over her shoulder and headed for the door. Gavin pressed his lips together tightly as it swung shut behind her.

"You can a take a shot or not?" Logan asked, poking the tip of his pool cue into Gavin's arm, leaving behind a dusty blue smudge.

Gavin rolled his shoulders then lined up his shot and gently tapped the cue ball, sending it across the table with just enough force to bounce off the side and nudge the eight ball into the corner pocket.

"If you're going to cheat, you should at least try to be subtle." His brother dug out two balls from a pocket and rolled them to the opposite end of the table.

"It's not cheating," Gavin protested and started racking the balls. He let his gaze drift back to the door. "It's natural talent."

"Natural, my ass." Logan lifted his beer glass in the air and waved it at Josh, who nodded in acknowledgment. "Have you heard from Noah?"

"Not since he decided to go on his little hunting trip."

Noah had been pretty tight-lipped, only mentioning it had something to do with Cora's friend Eve and her brother. Gavin still wasn't sure what the hell that was about. He remembered Eve showing up, but he couldn't figure out why.

There was a lot about that night he didn't remember, and the one person who could give them the answers he needed, refused to talk to him. Somehow, in the time between Eve bursting in, swinging her bat, and when he woke in the hospital, he lost everything again.

Lela was dead. Sinclair was dead. There were no answers from him, no revenge, and now Cora might leave.

"Fuck this," Gavin muttered and tossed his pool cue on the table.

Grabbing his coat from the hook on the wall, he ignored Logan's confused look and stomped through the bar and outside.

He jogged down the street, turning the corner onto Main Street just as Cora disappeared into her building. A quick glance showed the road was clear, and he ran across and to her building door. At the top of the stairs, he found her searching in her purse for her keys.

"Cora," he said.

Startled, she jerked her head around looking like a doe caught in headlights.

"What are you doing her, Gavin?" she asked.

"We need to talk." He stepped forward when she started to protest. "Don't give me some shit about this not being a good time. You've been avoiding me all week. I think I deserve some answers."

She studied him in silence before answering, "All right."

He followed her inside, watching as she nervously moved about the room, hanging her bag in the closet and shifting half-filled boxes out of the way.

He'd known she was still thinking about going back to Denver, but seeing her packing, it finally hit him. *She was leaving.*

"Sorry it's such a mess. I've been busy at the pub the past couple days," she explained.

"Two months," he said.

"What?"

"You told me you'd stay until after Christmas. This looks like you're leaving sooner."

She licked her lower lip and briefly caught it between

her teeth.

"I am."

"So, that's it then? You decide you want out, and you go?"

She crossed her arms and leaned against the edge of the breakfast bar, staring up at him. The defeat he saw reflected in her eyes stabbed at his chest.

"I can't do this anymore, Gavin. Waiting for you is like waiting for the apocalypse. It's never going to happen. Especially after Sinclair."

"What does that mean?"

"I killed him."

"He needed to die, Cora. You heard what he said about continuing his experiments. Who knows how many people he hurt, or even killed."

"But I was the one to do it." She shook her head, causing her ponytail to swish along her back. "Before it happened, I knew you wanted to be the one to kill him for what he did to Lela."

"Not just for Lela. For my brothers, for me, for you." The residue of anger shuddered through him. "To him, we were all lab rats, and even though he said he was done with you, he wasn't. He never would have stopped. I couldn't let him do that to you."

"The way you looked at me when you realized I'd done it ..." Her words trailed off, but he could fill in the blanks.

"I wasn't angry you shot him. I was angry you had to. I put you in danger, and then I couldn't even protect you."

He closed the distance between them and tugged her into his arms. While she didn't return the embrace, she didn't push him away, either. Instead, her hands curled into the front of his shirt, and she pressed her forehand against his chest.

He stared down at the top of her head inside and sighed. The soft push of air stirred the short curly strands that had escaped her ponytail.

"Stay," he said.

"I can't."

"Why?"

"I can't be second. Not anymore."

With a finger under her chin, he tipped her face up so he could look into her eyes.

"You're not second, Cora," he said. "I can't change the fact that I loved Lela, and I wouldn't want to. For a long time, I didn't want to accept that she was gone. I didn't want to move on with my life without her, but it didn't matter what I wanted. Life moved on, dragging me along with it.

"Then you were there, and suddenly I wanted something more than to wallow in my memories. It scared the shit out of me." He rubbed his thumb over her cheek, wiping away the stray tear that trickled down.

Cora's heart ached, torn between wanting to stay and knowing she couldn't accept anything less than what she was willing to give. Everything. She would give him everything, and it's what she needed in return.

"I want to stay," she admitted in a voice softened by sadness. "But I need more than lust or gratitude. I need you to love me."

Gavin closed his eyes, and Cora's stomach sank. This is why she left the hospital before he woke, why she hadn't taken his calls.

Você não é nada para mim.

She might have hoped for more, she might have even deluded herself into believing that he must have felt something for her, but deep down she'd known. She was nothing to him.

"I can't love you like I loved her because I loved her for entirely different reasons." He opened his eyes and cupped her face in his hands. "Just like I would never have loved her like I love you."

Cora's breath hitched, and she wondered if she'd misheard him.

"I love you, Cora," he repeated and then proceeded to cover her mouth with his in a tender kiss.

Elation blossomed within her, and she slid her hands around his back, clutching at the hard muscles. Propelled by an urgent passion, she arched her body into his. Her lips opened to the press of his tongue.

Gavin's hands slipped dawn and gripped the back of her thighs, lifting until she could wrap her legs around his waist. She held on as he walked them to the bedroom and then fell backward on the bed.

Loosening her legs, she sat up, straddling him and tugged her shirt over her head.

"You're so fucking beautiful." Gavin's fingers delved into the cups of her lace bra to find her nipples.

Rocking against him, she threw her head back and moaned.

"Tell me what you want," he said.

"I want you to fuck me."

"No." He rolled her over, propping himself up on his elbows, and her eyes flew to his. "No fucking, no sex. Tell me what you want."

"I want you to love me."

"I do. I will. *Você é minha vida*," he said, kissing a path from her neck down to her navel then looked up at her through hooded eyes. "You are my life."

He nipped at the quivering flesh of her belly before tracing a swirling pattern with his tongue back up to the sensitive spot below her.

"Stay," he said.

"Yes."

* * *

The End

The SIEGE Series continues with TAKEN

coming early 2017.

* * *

Thank you so much for reading DARKEN! I hope you enjoyed it. I hope you'll consider leaving an honest review on Amazon, Goodreads, and/or your blog. If you'd like to learn more or connect with the author, please visit www.angelafristoe.com. You can also sign up for my newsletter to keep informed on deals and new releases.

Books by Angela Fristoe

Romance Books

SIEGE Series
DARKEN
TAKEN
Coming Winter of 2016

Winter Souls (**The Othala Witch Collection**)
Coming November 3, 2016

Hunted (**The Isa Fae Collection**)
Coming May 2017

Young Adult Books

Songbird

The Woods of Everod Series
Waken
Rising

A Touched Trilogy
Lie to Me
Heal Me
Watch Me

ABOUT THE AUTHOR

ANGELA FRISTOE grew up in Alberta, Canada. She dreamed of becoming the next Dian Fossey or Jane Goodall, until she realized she wasn't all that keen on the outdoors or animals. Instead, she went into education and focused on elementary education and helping struggling readers. Her passion for writing grew after being ignited by The Hunger Game and Twilight crazes. Angela lives on Vancouver Island with her family, where she is pursuing her writing career while continuing her work in the education field.

For EXCLUSIVE content and deals sign up for Angela's newsletter on her website angelafristoe.com

www.ingramcontent.com/pod-product-compliance
Lightning Source LLC
Chambersburg PA
CBHW020240180626
46810CB00006B/2293